Tobias S. Buckell is a Caribbean-born US author who spent much of his younger life growing up aboard boats in Grenada, then on boats with various family in the British Virgin Islands, and again in the US Virgin Islands.

Since 2006 he's been a full time author and free-lancer and also works for the independent publisher Subterranean Press where he looks after their ebooks.

Praise for *Arctic Rising*

'an intimate techno-thriller about an ecological showdown in an ice-free Arctic… moves swiftly'
Publisher's Weekly

'Buckell shifts his narrative into overdrive, almost providing his readers with whiplash as they must keep up with his change of pace. This change occurs at the right time and Buckell successfully provides the reader with a book which not only offers action, but also explores the positives and negatives of global warming without too evidently landing on one side of the argument or the other' *SF Site*

'Buckell sails into near future Earth science fiction with gusto'
SF Signal

'Only time will tell where Mr. Buckell will next ply his novel writing trade, but with *Arctic Rising*, he's penned an entertaining, thought provoking thriller that co[illegible]me of M[illegible]vels'

Also by Tobias S. Buckell:

Arctic Rising

HURRICANE FEVER

TOBIAS S. BUCKELL

1 3 5 7 9 10 8 6 4 2

First published in the US in 2014 by Tor at Tom Doherty Associates, LLC
Published in the UK in 2014 by Del Rey, an imprint of Ebury Publishing
A Random House Group Company

The Random House Group Limited Reg. No. 954009

Addresses for companies within the Random House Group can be found at:
www.randomhouse.co.uk

A CIP catalogue record for this book is
available from the British Library

The Random House Group Limited supports The Forest Stewardship Council® (FSC®), the leading international forest-certification organisation. Our books carrying the FSC label are printed on FSC® -certified paper. FSC is the only forest-certification scheme supported by the leading environmental organisations, including Greenpeace.
Our paper procurement policy can be found at:
www.randomhouse.co.uk/environment

Printed and bound in Great Britain by Clays Ltd, St Ives PLC

ISBN 9780091953539

To buy books by your favourite authors and register for offers visit:
www.randomhouse.co.uk
www.delreyuk.com

For Karen Lord

1

s the sun dipped low over Miami's canals and waterways, it glittered off the skyscrapers and the pools of ocean between them. Puddleboats meandered from lobby to lobby to pick up passengers. Traffic along the bridges and secondary roads arching over the Miami waters bunched up with anticipatory evening rush hour traffic.

Four security guards surrounded Zee in the lobby of the Beauchamp Industries offices, including one of the sketchy guards who always wore thick black turtleneck sweaters with long sleeves to hide his neo-Nazi tattoos. They'd been waiting for him as he walked out of the elevator, into the black-marble-walled lobby with back-lit mirrors and large bamboo plants.

They patted him down quickly, then turned him back toward a table near the elevators.

"You can't leave," the guard with the long sleeves muttered in his thick, Eastern European-accented English. "We need to look inside your briefcase."

Zee wore a dark blue suit and purple-rimmed designer glasses, a look that vaguely suggested middle management. That is, if someone didn't notice the extra-athletic build and dancer-like posture hidden underneath the clothes.

He sighed. It had been such a close thing. Three months infiltrating the building. And many more prior to that figuring out that this was the location in which a secret secondary biotech lab had been concealed. Something Beauchamp Industries didn't want anyone to know about.

"Your briefcase, please," the guard repeated.

"What's wrong?" Zee asked.

"Just open the briefcase."

Zee looked at him. Thickly built, a bullish neck and squashed face; there were signs the man's nose had been broken multiple times. A bruiser. Twice Zee's size and able to throw his weight well.

"Okay," Zee said. He set the black briefcase on the table, pushing aside a potted fern, and flicked the two latches. The briefcase opened up. Nestled gently in between papers, a screen, and some oatmeal cookies, was a stainless steel injector. "I think this is what you're looking for."

The four guards took a step back. They might not be sure of what exactly was going on upstairs, but they had some idea that it was a bio-technology lab. And as general security contractors, they had a feeling there shouldn't have been a floor up near the top with a dedicated lab in the company's general offices.

"You will need to come with us," the guard with the uncomfortably hot long sleeves said solemnly.

"I understand," Zee said, and picked up the injector.

All four men stared at him as he jammed the point into his forearm and triggered the device. It hissed, spitting whatever it had contained down past Zee's skin.

"Catch!" Zee said, and tossed the injector at them. They flinched back from it, which gave Zee the second he needed to close with the big guy. He flipped him into the table and pulled the gun out from his belt in one smooth sequence.

With gun in hand, Zee spun and ran for the doors with a head start. The dangerous one, still shaking his head, pushed away the help of the other guards. He patted his belt and swore. "Call Dmitri!" he shouted, and ran after Zee.

Outside on the docks around the skyscraper, Zee circled around for a second until he found a fast-looking powerboat. It took a second to smash the console open and jump-start it. He cast the ropes off and powered away, but not before the large guard jumped from the dock into the back of the boat.

"You must stop," he told Zee.

Zee jammed the throttle up, surging the boat away from the dock at full speed, its wake splattering up against the sides of nearby downtown buildings as they ripped through the Miami canals. There'd been a time when these had been side streets that the Army Corps of Engineers fought to keep dry with dikes and walls, but ten years ago they'd finally accepted defeat. The ground under Miami was porous; they couldn't stop the ocean from bubbling up even if they built dikes around the entire city. This wasn't Denmark, this was Miami, all former swamp. So the lower floors of buildings had been waterproofed, barricaded, and the streets lined to divert and control the waterways. If he was quick about it, Zee could get this powerboat right back to his safe house and call in help, and never step foot on a dry road.

But he was going to have to hurry, because he was going to need all the help he could call in from his safe house very, very soon once that injection took hold.

A more immediate problem was the very determined guard behind him.

Zee spun the wheel and unbalanced the man. He elbowed the guard in the gut, but it seemed to have little effect. The guard's pupils were wide as he bear-hugged Zee and then head-butted him. The powerboat careened off a wall and smacked off another boat. People shouted at them as they zagged past.

The world faded for a second, and then Zee sputtered back to consciousness with a face full of blood.

"You're coming back to meet Dmitri, and then Dmitri will take you all the way up," the man said, his voice slurred. "Stop fighting. You're dead man already. We know you are with Caribbean Intelligence. And that injection will kill you."

The bear hug was breaking his ribs, Zee realized. The man had ingested a fighter's cocktail at some point: a dose of some slow release Adrenalin, as well as some other mixture of drugs to enable a spurt of speed and immunity to pain. None of the kicks or jabs Zee threw affected him at all.

The guard let go of Zee to grab the wheel. The powerboat, out of control, had turned for one of the docks.

Zee hit him in the head with the gun. As the guard shrugged that off, Zee flipped him out of the boat. Behind him, another powerboat appeared in the canal. Zee glanced behind and saw three shaved heads.

Friends of the guard he'd just thrown overboard.

There was a large park five miles away. Acres of natural preserve. A safer place to continue this battle where people wouldn't get hurt in the crossfire. More open water to lose his pursuers in. Zee gunned the powerboat to full speed.

With a virus injected into his skin, the longer he waited to get help the more danger he'd be in. But first he was going to have to take care of his determined pursuers.

Well, all he had to do was get back to his safe house and make a call. After that . . . Bullets stitched the back of the powerboat, making him wince.

Just focus on getting to the safe house, he told himself. From there he could call for backup.

2

Destruction brewed in the far-off trade winds. A storm sucking up moisture and heat, a dervish with a damaging appetite that ponderously barreled its way across the Atlantic toward the curve of the Caribbean islands scattered in an arc from Florida to South America.

The spinning mass had been tagged by algorithms and scientists days ago as Tropical Storm Makila. Makila's winds topped out at around sixty miles an hour. The same sort of wind speed you got if you stuck your face out of the window of a car on a highway.

Curious satellites watched it form off the coast of Africa and bear its way across Hurricane Alley toward the center of the Caribbean.

And then, slowly curve.

The question always was: where would it hit? Weather sites showed animations and projections based on the best guesses of supercomputing networks. From the island of Dominica, halfway up the Caribbean chain, all the way up to Florida, people warily paid attention.

"Roo!" someone in a boxy yellow Suzuki honked a horn and shouted. "Stocking up good for Makila?"

Prudence Jones, or Roo as everyone called him, looked away from the eerily cheerful clouds in the sunny sky. He flicked dreadlocks out from his eyes and waved back. The car pulled away before Roo could tell who it was, and he looked back up at the sky.

The real hint of the storm to come out there was that lack of wind. The trade winds always swept through the Virgin Islands on their way to the larger island of Puerto Rico, keeping the air crisp and salty here on the east side of the island. But now the stillness let the sun bake the exposed asphalt and concrete of the town of Red Hook, let it glitter off the water, and let it choke the air with humidity. The winds were being sucked up by the distant storm.

Soon the humidity would be blown clean away. The sky would turn ominous. Winds and waves would scour any boats still bobbing in Muller Harbor here in Red Hook.

And that included Roo and his catamaran, the *Spitfire II*, if he didn't get out of the harbor today.

Roo carefully checked that the groceries wouldn't fall off the folding dolly, then paused. Something twitched in the back of his mind: the young man leaning against a corner of the wall on the far side of the parking lot. The one pretending not to be eyeing Roo.

How long, Roo wondered, had that been happening? He'd missed it. Caught the calculating look only by chance when he'd turned his head to see who'd honked, his eyes not making it to the windshield of whoever had hailed him but stopping at the wall for a second, then snapping back.

And then he'd continued checking his boxes of canned and frozen meals, thinking back to what had briefly flicked across his retinas: a somewhat overly muscled boy with a determined clench to his jaw.

Ratty sneakers. Old jeans. Scars on his fingers. Recently healed?

Shifting feet. He was getting prepared. Like a boxer before a match.

Shit.

Roo stood up and left the cart on the ground. He had cut between the store and an apartment building nearby, headed for the street to cross to the marina. But this was a good spot to get held up. Thirty feet of shadow, just out of sight of the road, right on the edge of the parking lot. Roo walked quickly back toward the store. The young man moved to intercept.

Roo sighed and backed up, reaching for his back pocket.

"Easy rasta." The young man had a gun in his hand now. "Don't be reaching for no trouble."

"It's my wallet," Roo said. "You want me to continue?"

The young man's mouth twitched. Over-challenged, a little

too hyped up and nervous. He hadn't done this too often. Roo wondered what the story was. Recently out, struggling to get a job? Moving in the wrong circles? "Gimme it," the man demanded.

Roo tossed the wallet at his feet. And nodded at the groceries. "All yours."

His mugger shook his head. "I saw you reading a phone on the way in."

Roo blinked. Now *there* was a dilemma. He figured he'd lose the groceries and cash and some cards.

But the phone.

He thought about it for a second, and then shook his head. The young man moved from nervous anticipation to careful anger.

Roo'd spent over a week getting the new phone set up. A lot of tweaks and software to make sure he remained as invisible in a networked world as he could possibly imagine.

Most people who lost a phone, they could just redownload their settings when they logged in.

But Roo wasn't most people. The exotic software that he preferred to use kept him safe, and it ran locally. And even then, every month he purchased a new phone. Started from scratch.

He'd just gotten it set up.

It was a pain in the ass to do it every month. He wasn't going to do it again this week. Particularly not with a storm bearing down on him.

No. He shook his head again. "No. You can have everything but the phone."

The mugger glanced left, then right, judged that shooting

Roo would not be the smartest thing to do right away, then raised the gun to smack him with it.

He probably thought he would knock the phone out of him.

Instead, Roo walked forward.

There was no sweet ballet of moves, but a split second's worth of damage. A knee to the groin, elbow to the nose, and a quick flip that put the youth on the ground, groaning.

Roo examined the gun he'd taken at the same time.

It was too light. No ammo.

He checked it to confirm his suspicion. Then bent over the young man. Roo tugged at the graphene paracord bracelet on his left hand. A few seconds and he could tie the kid up, leave the gun next to him, and send him right back to the place he'd probably just gotten out of. Toughen him up. Give him more chances to meet the real dangerous criminals there.

So Roo just picked up his wallet. The young man, hardly more than a kid, would come out of jail more of a menace than he'd go in. Roo knew that well enough.

He retrieved his groceries and wheeled them past the mugger, who now groaned and snorted blood over the concrete parking lot.

Roo grimaced and then stopped. Squatted next to him again.

"Hey, rudeboy?" Bloodshot eyes flickered open, scared. "Take a vacation," Roo told him softly, and held all the bills in his wallet up in front of his face.

The eyes widened. Big bills. Roo liked having escape money on him. Always.

Roo pressed ten thousand in cash against the boy's chest. "I have a price, though. You willing to hear me?"

His mugger nodded.

Roo let go of the cash. "I see you doing this again, I won't be gentle. You'll be an old man with a limp, understand?"

A few minutes later, with a lighter wallet and a faint frown on his face, Roo threw the empty gun into the ocean while standing at a marina dock just down the road. He shoved his hands in a tattered old jacket with an MV *Tellus* patch on it and stood silently for a moment.

A single, foreboding streak of dark clouds had crept onto the horizon over the green and gray hills of St. John, the next island east of St. Thomas and just a few miles across the sea. The glimmering white sand beaches were visible from here. But if Roo turned around and looked back, this side of St. Thomas would bristle with high rises and commercial activity. People weren't on vacation here, they were living.

Time to get back to the boat, he thought, eyeing the clumpy slash of dark in the sky. Time to batten down.

At the Sand Dollar, an obnoxiously nautically themed bar attached to a waterfront hotel just by a set of docks, Roo eased his way down into a leathery Islay whiskey. He'd spent half the day storing stuff and checking over the catamaran one last time. From the corner of the polished wooden bar he squinted out over the muddy water of the harbor.

"You staying here for Makila?" Seneca asked, checking his glass as she moved past with a couple beers in hand. The short blond bartender was a bit of a feature attraction for half the regulars growing roots on the creaky wooden stools here. She had a touch of sunburn on her cheeks today. Probably spent the weekend on a beach in St. John with her roommates. She was halfway through college somewhere up in the U.S. and working here in the summer, still in the honeymoon period of living here when she spent every spare moment she could on a beach.

"Just waiting for Delroy to get out of school. Then we head down to Flamingo Bay." She didn't know where that was, he saw, and added, "It's on the western tip of Water Island. Lots of mangroves in the inside part. We can tie up. It's not a full hurricane, we should be okay."

Seneca shook her head. "I can't imagine living on a boat. Let alone staying on board for a storm."

Roo shrugged, and she moved on.

"She likes you," Tinker growled. A large Viking of a man in grease-resistant overalls and a giant black beard, he nudged Roo hard in the shoulder with an elbow.

"She likes everyone," Roo muttered. "It's her job. You get your engine fixed? We gonna see you down at Honeymoon?" Tinker was, in theory, a mechanic. He did odd jobs around the harbor for trade. Food, parts, whatever. He owned an ancient diesel-powered Grand Banks motor yacht. It was a behemoth; seventy feet long and powered by two fuel-hungry, notoriously grumpy motors, it would have been a palatial ship to a prior generation.

Nowadays, who the hell could afford the fuel to run the damn thing?

Not Tinker. He'd gotten a deal on the motorboat and gotten it to Red Hook. Limping in on faulty machinery and fumes from the Bahamas. He'd anchored the damn thing, and it'd been sitting in the harbor through two hurricane seasons. And Tinker had become a fixture at the bar. Another piece of human driftwood tossed up here in St. Thomas.

Tinker was working on converting the engines to take leftover oil from fryers. He had tanks of the shit fastened to his decks, collected from restaurants all around Red Hook. Every once in a while the engines would chug and belch out the smell of grease and fried food all over the harbor. And then they'd fall silent.

"No," Tinker looked down. "Not this storm." He'd have to shelter on land at a friend's, wondering yet again if his home would be there in the morning. Or whether he'd find it dashed up against the shore somewhere.

"Sorry to hear it," Roo said, genuinely. He nodded at Seneca. "Tinker's next; on my tab, yeah?"

She nodded.

"Thanks, Roo. Another beer, Seneca." Tinker tapped the counter. "Storm shouldn't be too bad, right? Sixty-five miles an hour, they're saying. Was thinking I might ride it out."

Roo looked at the harbor, open to the ocean. St. John's hills in the distance. A green ferry cut through the rolling waves, chugging its way over to the other island with a load of cars and people. "You don't want to do that, Tinker."

Tinker shrugged. "Got a lot of chain laid down for my anchor."

"Let the ship ride by herself," Roo counseled.

"Maybe," Tinker said. "And afterwards, I'm going to try and get south for the season. Maybe I'll see you in the Grenadines for once."

Roo smiled at Tinker's perennial optimism. "I'll buy you drinks for a full week if I see you in Bequia," he said with a smile, knowing full well he was never going to have to pay out on that bet.

Tinker raised his beer happily, Roo raised his glass, and they tinked them together.

"How's Delroy?" Tinker asked. "He putting you in the bar today?"

Roo shook his head. "Just a long day prepping my boat. Delroy's okay." He glanced at the wooden-rimmed clock over the multicolored bottles in the back of the bar. Okay, but late again.

It would be tempting to go walk toward school to find him. But Roo killed that impulse. Delroy was almost ready to graduate. Nothing much he could do if the boy was ready for trouble.

And he'd kept out of trouble the last couple years well enough.

Roo had drifted away from the islands. Been recruited away from them and into to a different life. He'd had nothing to hold him down back then. No one but a brother who, understandably to Roo now, didn't want to have anything to do with him.

When Roo came back to the Virgin Islands, he found not only the buildings changed, the people he'd known gone or moved on to other things, but found his brother had died. His wife as well.

Roo found his nephew Delroy stuck with a foster family doing their best. But Delroy was twisted up with anger and loneliness that they couldn't handle. He'd been throwing in with a crowd as angry as he was, looking to define himself with trouble.

So Roo picked him up.

There wasn't much trouble Delroy could imagine or cause that Roo hadn't seen. And Roo needed a hobby in his new retirement.

He had made Delroy his hobby.

New school, new life. New family.

Delroy didn't turn into a scholar. But he calmed down.

Roo set his empty glass on the bar. "Tinker, you give Delroy a ride out when he gets here? He let his cell phone go dead again. Or left it in his room again."

"Yeah, man."

Roo soaked up the sun as he hopped into a fifteen-foot-long semirigid inflatable dinghy. He untied from a cleat with a quick half flip of a wrist and tossed the painter down into the fiberglass bottom, then flicked the electric engine on.

Most of the boats with people living aboard them here in the harbor had already fled. Either south for the summer, to hide from hurricanes, or to hurricane holes—places naturally still and fetid, which meant very little storm surge. Tie your boat up in a spiderweb of ropes to mangroves and with anchors out on all points, and you would ride the storm just fine.

There were usually maybe fifty boats that had people living on board them anchored here. The other fifty or so were hobbyists. People who used boats like most people used boats: for fun, on weekends.

Halfway out to the *Spitfire II* Roo's phone buzzed.

He ignored it for a second. Focused on weaving the dinghy around boats at anchor. The electric motor wasn't as fast as the old gas-powered fifteen-horsepower motor that he used to roar around with. But he could get this one charged up via the ship's solar power. Slow for cheap was good.

The phone buzzed again.

If that was Delroy, he was going to have to figure out how to hitch that ride with Tinker, as he had many times already. Or swim.

Roo had made Delroy do that once.

But they needed to get moving soon. Roo slowed the dinghy down and pulled out the phone. It was an incoming call. But with a blocked number.

That . . . was next to impossible. Not with the setup Roo had.

He licked his lips, suddenly nervous. Flicked at the screen to answer and put the phone up to his ear, trying to shield it from the occasional spray of saltwater.

"Hey old friend, it's Zee," said an utterly familiar voice. Roo smiled for a second at the blast from the past. He started to reply, but the voice continued quickly. "And if you're getting this message from me, it means I'm dead."

Roo killed the throttle. The dinghy stopped surging forward and just pointed into the waves, bobbing slowly.

"Listen, I'm sorry to lay some heavy shit on you, but I kinda need a favor," the voice on the phone continued.

3

When Delroy clambered onto the back steps of the *Spitfire*'s left hull, backpack slung artfully under one arm, he looked suitably abashed. Tinker waved from his creaky wooden dinghy, kicked the motor into reverse, and headed back for shore to root back down at the Sand Dollar. His beard kicked about in the wind.

"I was . . ." Delroy started to excuse himself.

"Don't matter," Roo said. "Toss your bag in your cabin. We leaving."

The *Spitfire II* had a traditional European catamaran look: a large organic cabin straddled the space between the two thin and rakish hulls. Large oval windows, tinted black, gave it its not-from-Earth look. It also created sunny open spaces in the main cabin, which had a dining table and comfortable settee. The galley, up against the side of the main cabin, featured granite-topped counters and a two-burner stove.

Roo walked from the rear cockpit's semi-open area where he had greeted Delroy back into the main cabin. He crossed the galley and through a sliding door forward into a tiny second cockpit in the front of the catamaran.

The forward decks of the two hulls were accessible from here, as was the netting spread between them. Roo bounced across the netting with a practiced moon-walking step to the motorized windlass on the right hull.

He leaned against the stainless steel railing with a hand and kicked the manual brake on the motor off. He checked the anchor chain running through it, making sure the windlass's wheels could catch the links and engage the chain.

Then he walked back through the main cabin to the rear cockpit. Delroy looked up from pulling his shoes off.

"I know, I know, you in a hurry to get to Honeymoon Bay," Delroy said, still trying to apologize. "I promised I'd be back in time. But . . ."

It might have been that girl he was seeing. Or a friend. Or trouble. Roo didn't care. He moved to climb up into a slightly raised area on the right of the cockpit where the wheel was mounted. He tapped one of the clear windows looking out over the top of the main cabin.

This was the nerve center of the thirty-seven-foot-long catamaran. The sheets from the sails all led into the tiny, raised control center. The sails were all roller furlinged; a press of a button unrolled the sails out. From here Roo could adjust the sails, steer, and power the catamaran.

The clear window booted up. Navigation equipment, weather reports, GPS, speed indicators, autopilot, and sail controls all flickered on.

Roo glanced at weather predictions, thinking, and then noticed Delroy staring at him. His nephew knew, by now, that something was up.

"Ain't Honeymoon Bay we going for just yet," Roo told Delroy.

The teenager frowned. "Where we going?"

"Tortola."

Roo tapped the screen and the motorized anchor winch whined as it began to pull the anchor chain up.

"Tortola?" Delroy was confused. Three days of tracking Makila, planning for Makila, getting ready. Now Roo had changed it all up. Roo knew his nephew was wondering if his uncle had gone mad.

"Something I have to do," Roo said.

"Right now?" Delroy's face twisted with incomprehension. "Makila coming for us . . . and we heading for Tortola?"

"It'll take four hours," Roo said. *Spitfire II* made good time. It was four already. "We get there at seven or eight, depending. Makila won't hit until late tomorrow."

Delroy stared at Roo. Normally Roo lectured him about being calm, not taking risks. Roo knew he was having trouble processing this sudden tack in behavior.

"Look," Roo said. "You can stay on land in Tortola at a hotel, if you want. But I need to get there quick."

"Take the damn ferry," Delroy said.

"No. No, not a good idea." There'd be more sophisticated

ople-scanning equipment taking a close look at everyone assing through customs, even in little old Tortola. Iris scanners, gait recognition cameras feeding patterns into central databases.

It was safer to get in after hours. Go into town with the dinghy without passing by anywhere official. Give him the time he needed. Then Roo could slip out in predawn. Clear customs at Jost Van Dyke, where it was all real old-fashioned paperwork and he would be in a better position if people were looking for him.

It was a touch of paranoid thinking. But it had never hurt him before.

Not with a call like that.

"It's just a PO box," Zee's voice had told him. It was a recording that had been triggered. Maybe a piece of software on a site sitting somewhere, scanning the news for a death notice. Or that hadn't been reset by a called-in password check, thus triggering out a message. "There's something waiting for you in there. I need you to keep it safe. It'll help you, or whoever you think it's safe to give it to, find my killers. Revenge from beyond the grave . . . you know? You'll know what to do."

Roo rubbed his forehead. "Just get up on deck, Delroy, and start hosing off the chain." He didn't want the nasty mud that would be coming up on the chain getting sucked into the anchor locker stinking up the starboard hull of the catamaran.

It had been a sunny week and the solar panels on the top of the main cabin had filled up the ship's batteries to capacity. Roo gunned the two electric engines to swing them out past Cabrita Point, crammed with its multicolored hotels and upscale condos that looked out from their perches over the sea toward St. John, squared architecture's corners clashing with rolling hills.

Pretty real estate, but Roo could always move to *anchor* his home off any of the sparkling white beaches they saw in the distance. Hell, he could even anchor right in front of those expensive condos.

The farther away from Red Hook and into the ocean, the taller the swells grew. And the wind kicked up nicely.

Roo let the mainsail out from the cockpit, motors whining slightly as winches spun to pull the sail out from inside the mast where it was neatly rolled up. The *Spitfire* leaned only just slightly as she caught the wind. Unlike a monohulled ship, there would be no dramatic pitch as the sails filled out.

They were moving along nicely now. Roo cut the engines off and unfurled the jib. The great triangle was yanked smoothly all the way back down just past the mast and the mainsail. He trimmed it all with a few more corrections of the electric winches.

"Watch the wheel," Roo said to Delroy when he got back in from scrubbing the muck off the decks the chains had dragged up. He set the autopilot and checked the blips and projected paths of other ships in the area on his windscreen. The autopilot would handle most situations, steering around other ships and avoiding reefs. If Roo really wanted to, he could probably ignore sailing the little catamaran until they reached Road Harbour. It would maximize speed, trim the sails, all while guiding them along the edge of St. John and then tacking out for Tortola.

Hell, he'd even once fallen asleep with the autopilot on and been woken by its "destination reached" bleat of an alarm on a trip to Virgin Gorda. Roo'd opened his eyes, blearily, staring at a beach just a hundred yards away from the bow of the ship as the autopilot kept the catamaran paused, pointed into the wind.

It was a long way from the old days, where you'd sit at the wheel and adjust the sails, aiming the ship yourself for hours on end with nothing but your thoughts and the wind in your face.

Roo ducked down into the galley and made turkey melt sandwiches. Fresh French bread, organic turkey, crisp lettuce, all of it grown at the new fifteen-story vertical farm in the unlikely location of Bolongo Bay.

Outside the large oval windows located just over the galley's stone countertops, the crisp, white sandy St. John beaches passed by on the port side of the catamaran. Solomon Bay and Caneel. Tourists splashed around in the clear water or beached themselves on colorful towels like contented seals. They'd jet out before Makila hit and leave the cleaning up after the storm to everyone who actually lived here. The tourists would come back once the beaches were sparkling again.

Maybe he was no different. Living on the boat, never fully engaging with everyone on land. Separate somehow.

"Uncle Roo!"

Roo realized he'd been standing at the galley, staring out the window. Just letting the boat rock under his heels, swaying with it as it moved over and through the swells.

"Roo, man, I'm hungry," his nephew complained.

The sandwiches had been finished a long time ago. Cut into pairs of neat triangles with cheese dripping over the sides.

What the fuck was he thinking, actually going to a dead drop when he'd been out of the system for so long? A dead man's dead drop.

That was spy shit.

Roo had left that spy shit behind.

He wasn't hitting the gym every day. Wasn't training hand to hand. Wasn't running any cells or playing any networks. No, he spent his time reading books and keeping the old catamaran in good shape.

And making sure Delroy made it through high school.

But he'd taken that kid out at the grocery store easily enough, right?

But that was just a kid, Roo, he told himself. He lifted the lid of the fridge built into the counter and pulled out two sodas. *A kid not much older than Delroy.*

Delroy looked him right in the eye. "What got you all moody, Uncle? What's all this about?"

"I . . ." Roo squinted. "I have to do a favor for a very old friend."

"Right now. Before the storm? On Tortola?"

"Yeah." Saying it made it real for Roo. He put the can

down and looked out over the side of the rear cockpit toward St. John as the catamaran's autopilot skirted the lighter-colored water of the reefs. "Fifteen years ago the Caribbean Intelligence Group formed up. All the islands pooling resources. We tried to create a network to stop the big countries pushing us around. But there wasn't money for all of us to create some super spy agency. In the beginning we had to go and ask for help. Seventeen of us analysts went to train in London with the SIS, what everyone usually calls MI6. Known Zee ever since I met him at Gatwick Airport, waiting to get picked up. Ended up figuring out how to use the bus together because they forgot we were coming."

They'd both been wet, cold and shivering, pulling their luggage around annoyed commuters.

Roo looked over and saw Delroy smirk. He didn't really buy much of the "uncle as ex-spy" stories Roo occasionally let slip. Roo knew the boy figured him for a desk jockey trying to puff his chest and talk things up.

"He was the closest thing I had to family for five years," Roo said. "Before I went north."

"North to the U.S.?" Delroy asked. He'd taken a few massively open online courses from star professors and was curious about living on a campus in a new country. Roo had been, carefully, encouraging the notion. No one in their family had ever even gotten to college. Not Roo, not his brother.

"No, not America," Roo said. "The North Pole."

Roo's family had lived on Anegada, the only island in the Virgin Islands that sat on a flat bed of coral. The rising ocean had swallowed it, leaving it as what it had been hundreds of thousands of years ago: little more than a submerged reef north of Virgin Gorda.

The family had scattered. Roo, rootless and wandering. His brother, Vincent, to try and build a house on a bad piece of land in Virgin Gorda, looking for just the opposite. Vincent hunkered down for hurricane after hurricane as the summer seasons grew more intense.

Rescue workers found Roo's brother in the remains of the house along with his wife, both their backs broken by the debris of cement and roof beams, with baby Delroy sheltered between them.

Delroy sighed. "So why can't your friend from Intelligence just go do his own damn favor? Why he causing trouble for us now?"

"He said he was dead," Roo said.

"He said he was dead?" Delroy's face screwed up, squinting as he absorbed that.

"He left me a message," Roo said. "So I'm going to Tortola."

4

The sun had long since slunk over the ocean's horizon. The sloping hills around Road Town glittered with light and activity that Roo paid little attention to. Instead he stared at the mailbox center across the road from the restaurant and absentmindedly picked apart a chicken roti with a fork. He could see through the glass front to a large desk, with hundreds of keyed mailbox slots on the wall behind. Displays of packing material dotted metal grids in the lobby area. A trickle of people on electric mopeds coasted down the street, engines adding a random background whine to the air.

"You want more coffee?" The young woman who had served up the quick meal from the counter was outside, washing down the plastic tables with a rag. "We almost closed, and I'll go toss it out soon."

Roo shook his head. "Thanks."

"All right. After we lock up you can sit out on the chair, we don't bring them in."

She left a trail of lemon-scented cheerful weariness in her wake.

The mailbox store would also shut down any moment now. Open late for an average mailbox center here, but they seemed to have a large business going. Lots of shorts-wearing live-aboard yacht types from Road Town harbor were meandering in and out.

And at least one sharp-looking man in a suit. No doubt fresh off a private jet.

That was the real moneymaker for these mailbox centers here: offshore companies. There were probably a hundred corporations living inside the small office across the street. Western companies claiming headquarters here using just a PO box.

Westerners, oil rich sheiks. Criminals.

Money moved around between PO boxes to different tax regimes. And ended up wherever a CEO needed it, so that companies could choose the tax rate they paid at, if at all.

If there was an address at the bottom of a piece of Viagra spam to legally detail the company that had sent it, it was probably really just an address shared with hundreds, or thousands, of other companies: an address just like the one Roo was staring at right now.

To be fair, there were people who didn't have postal addresses just because they were on the move. Like Roo. Living aboard a boat, coming into shore to get mail. Or even neotribal homeless moving across the world with their antimicrobial tents and flat-pack composting toilets. They had their physical mail sent here, scanned and e-mailed to them. They had boxes held until they knew they'd be holding a position for more than a few days and then triggered forwarding.

But mailboxes for people like Roo were probably more incidental than the core business of offshoring business.

Roo sipped badly burnt coffee and grimaced as he continued watching the street. Looking for rhythms out of place. People like him. Trouble.

Of course, the real trouble could be a tiny camera somewhere he'd never see. He could use a sniffer to look for telltales: wireless, heavily encrypted video feeds. But encrypted Wi-Fi was getting better and better at blending in with background radiation, or piggybacking other data to burrow inside and hide. It would take days to certify the area as clean.

Roo didn't have days.

He sighed. Twenty minutes before closing time now. A sparrowish woman with her hair pulled back in a wavy bunch was tidying up and looking at a wall clock.

The doors behind Roo locked shut. The cook, a thick-armed man, with his hair tied back into a hairnet when Roo'd only briefly glimpsed him in the back kitchen, squeezed past him.

"Evening, man," he said, nodding at Roo. Then behind, in a flirting tone, "'Night, Mary. You going out? Going wok-up on anyone special now?"

"Man, I'm too tired for that. I'm going home."

"Let me come home and relax you good," the cook said with a smile.

"Quit vexing me and go home to you wife," Mary shouted back at him.

"Hurricane coming. You want someone good to keep you warm at night," the cook tried.

Mary laughed. "You don't have what kind of heat I need," she said in a rising tone.

The cook mock-staggered back and spread his arms to Roo as if to say 'see, I tried,' and then turn to walk up the road. "One day, Mary."

Mary ignored both Roo and the cook to walk in the other direction back toward town. Roo watched them go, then turned back to the mailbox company front.

Was he going to risk going in?

Two questions gnawed at the back of his brain. One was: who killed Zee? And the other was: how much trouble was Roo inviting by coming here?

He and Zee had joined the Caribbean Intelligence Group when it was just starting to roll. The CIG had initially bloomed down south, with Barbados cozying up with Trinidad and Guyana to deal with the increasing Venezuelan naval hostility. And then the CIG had become necessary when news broke about the big oil finds in the Caribbean basin.

There were large nations out playing for blood when it came to easy natural resources. CIG formed up to give the South Caribbean information about who was up to what. At the very least they all needed protection against the last gasps of petro-corporations struggling to keep the old high-profit days going.

Barbados, one of the few islands with a standing professional army in the southern Caribbean, albeit a small one, fielded the equipment and muscle to get CIG agents where they needed to be.

And in a flattened world, small didn't have to be ineffective. CIG could hire the same crack Eastern European freelance hackers the CIA constantly tried to buy off to quit breaking into sensitive high-level networks. They didn't need to sneak an expensive military jet into hostile airspace to move around. A private jet could get someone from Grantley Adams Airport in Barbados to mainland China easily enough.

CIG styled itself as a group of patriotic ex-bad-boys at first. Toughs working with anarchic hackers like Anonymous to release information to change the political atmosphere in the basin, or embarrassing foreign diplomats trying to buy off the Caribbean. In the past the former colonial empires divided up negotiating with each island to use their power imbalance for leverage. Suddenly those nations faced more united fronts. And even bands of islands trying to negotiate with major cities instead of larger countries. With thirteen sovereign nations serving on the UN, and with some of those island nations having populaces in the hundreds of thousands, a single Caribbean nation's vote was cheap. CIG helped the South Caribbean work as a bloc.

Since 1823, U.S. agents claimed the Caribbean as the backyard of America thanks to the Monroe Doctrine. CIG headquarters in Bridgetown set off a firestorm of Caribbean chatter when a picture "leaked" online of the brass plaque on the inside door of their headquarters that said FUCK MONROE.

Most Americans hadn't picked up on the reference, but Caribbean politicians had, and suddenly diplomats were knocking on doors and asking what the hell CIG was.

And after that little stunt, CIG got folded within CARICOM, the larger political entity that had been creating a common Caribbean economic zone and tighter integration of the islands. Suddenly CIG members weren't tricksters and men like Roo given a second chance to reform their lives, but clean-cut kids getting recruited from the University of the West Indies. And just as suddenly, Roo had found, he was sent off to the Arctic to keep an eye on larger world politics. Shivering his ass off between icebergs so that CARICOM had eyes on the ground.

He hadn't seen Zee in a long, long time. Last he'd known, Zee was head of an ad-hoc team monitoring Middle East money trying to run away from the worst of the post-oil situations to settle in Trinidad, as well as Indonesian and Chinese influence buying.

Last he'd heard.

Before Roo'd gotten out of it all.

There were so many foreigners playing around in the Caribbean. All of them convinced they were part of some "exotic" game, dragging their shiny mega-yachts down into the islands to host clandestine events while anchored off pretty sandy shores.

Any of them could have gotten Zee into a shitload of

trouble that blew back on him. The upper echelons, the bankers and corporations and rulers of the world, they didn't like pushback in what they regarded as neutral vacationland.

Fuck.

Fuck them all. Roo snorted and crossed the street.

"Watch you-self!" a man in a blue suit shouted, swerving his moped to dodge Roo.

"Sorry, sorry." Roo hopped to the sidewalk.

"Hi." The woman at the desk smiled brightly. And in a precise and careful, half-imitated British BBC broadcast, half-Tortolan accent, said, "I'm sorry, if you're here to get a box we are just about to close. . . ."

"Box ninety-five three four," Roo said, wincing as the repetition of the box number made him recall the sound of Zee's voice.

The desk lady froze.

"Nine five three four?" she asked.

"Yes." Roo glanced around. What had he missed? Something was wrong.

"On box nine five three four, there is an extra security feature. It is a verbal password; we do this for our executive plans." She had a phone in her hand. "If you don't get it right, I promise I will call the police. Someone came in this morning and tried to get me to open the box. They tried to *bribe* me."

She sounded outraged by the thought, and she eyed Roo suspiciously.

Someone else had been here already. Which probably meant the mailboxes were being watched. Roo had missed it.

But never mind. He was here. No turning back.

"The password is: 'I'm one sad motherfucker,'" Roo said with a sad smile. Because that was a very Zee sort of password, the one he'd left on his post-death message.

Roo glanced around, jumpy, waiting for something bad to happen. But she nodded primly and walked behind the wall of mail slots and boxes. The mailboxes hadn't been attacked. A simple gunman would have worked, disguised as a robbery. Maybe whoever wanted in was waiting to break in. Or just waiting for the hurricane to pass.

Roo had his back to a wall of glass. He couldn't help trying to keep his eyes both on the windows and door while also trying to watch the desk lady.

He slunk his back up against the wall and tried to rest casually on an elbow against the counter.

She came back a second later, though, and handed Roo a small rubber tree frog the size of a fingernail. She set it carefully on counter, and Roo picked it up.

It was very green.

On the stomach it said PRESS ME. Roo had to squint to read the text.

When he did, the frog stuck a silvery, square tab of a tongue out at him.

"Damn, Zee," Roo said, wiping the corner of his eye with the palm of his hand. Even from beyond the grave Zee was treating this whole thing as a joke. But it wasn't. Whatever was on this scuffed, old tree frog drive had killed his friend. And Roo hadn't made many of those.

"Damn," he said again, as the lady watched him blankly, waiting for him to leave.

She held up a large roll of tape. "I have to get the windows ready for the storm," she said. "I have to close up now."

Roo nodded. He pocketed the tree frog. "Is there a back door?"

"No," she said politely, even though Roo figured it was a lie. Box 9534 had been enough trouble for her today.

Roo left, rushing out the door and abandoning all pretense of casualness. A white man with carefully gelled hair in khaki pants and a floral shirt turned the corner and started walking down the street after Roo.

This was what happened when you didn't use a tasking service to go do the pickup. Send some anonymous stranger with the password and watch him from a distance. Have them drop the package at the side of the road, get a series of other strangers to hand it randomly around town and back to you.

But Roo'd been impatient, and setting that up took time. Time the oncoming hurricane had taken away.

This is what you got when you exposed yourself. When you got impatient.

Or when it got personal, Roo thought.

He moved quickly, zigging through Road Town's roads to make sure he was really being followed.

He was.

Roo couldn't shake the tail. It wasn't so much that the man was good, but just determined and not worried about being spotted. So Roo led him down to the dinghy dock and through the empty, almost graveyard-like marina. Then back out again. Roo had his phone out, flipping through events lists.

He found what he was looking for. Smiled.

He led his tail back out of the marina and onto the roads, sidewalks, and shops again. A fast powerwalk around the concrete curve of the harbor to a pier where tourists onboard a large pontoon boat sang along, out of tune and not caring, to a local band.

Roo held up his phone and the two crewmen at the gang-plank looked at it and nodded.

At the top Roo turned and looked back as the crewmen held up their hands. "Sorry man, we full."

Roo's tail stopped, confused for a second. "I have cash," he muttered.

"Nah, all the tickets sold," they told him.

The white man glanced up and Roo, his mouth parting slightly in surprise. Roo could see the hint of a holster under his shoulders, now that he stood still in the light. Roo tensed, wondering which way this would go. They were very much in a public place. Neutral territory.

Usually.

"*All* the tickets?" the man asked. "Because the boat only looks half full."

"All the tickets sold out."

For a moment, the man in the floral shirt looked ready to push through and up the gangplank, but he stopped himself. He pointed at Roo directly. "Who are you?" he called out across the no-skid steps.

Roo looked to the left and right, as if not realizing the question was directed at him.

"Who are you?" the man repeated. He unbuttoned the top of his shirt, threatening to reach for the gun. Roo held up his camera and started recording the man. The man stopped himself, and then said, "We need to talk."

"Sorry." Roo shook his head. "Like that man said there: no more tickets."

He stepped back into the throngs of noisy partiers. They were hurricane chasers from Europe. They'd fly down right before a big one with duffel bugs of emergency rations to watch the storm from a sturdy hotel, excitedly sharing clips of them leaning into the wind or daring each other to go outside.

The pontoon boat loosed its ropes, and the electric engine burbled away as they kicked back from the dock. The man swore, pulling a phone out of his pocket and shaking his head.

For several minutes Roo scanned the area for other boats, or a helicopter. But the tail wasn't being backed up at that level. If Roo had been rushing to get here, it made sense that anyone else had trouble getting resources to the ground quickly as well. And with a hurricane about to hit, most of the equipment they could rent would be tied down for the weather.

Roo picked up his phone and listened to the message from Zee one last time. Then he called Delroy.

"I'm on the booze cruise paddling through the middle of the harbor," he said. "Bring the dinghy after it, come get me off this damn thing, okay?"

He waited until he saw Delroy's lights, his nephew gunning the engine to close in with them. Then he looked down at the phone in his hands.

Roo dropped it overboard into the dark water.

5

In the quiet still of predawn, they slipped out of Road Harbour, putting the multicolored buildings dotting the brownish-green hills to *Spitfire*'s stern. The dinghy swung in the davits behind them, and the wake from the silent electric engines churned gently as they headed back west along Tortola's rocky coast.

The world was ghost-quiet, except for the crack of sails and the burbling of water against hull. Roo watched as Nanny Cay marina slid past, filled with bristling masts sticking over the breakwall.

Early morning traffic buzzed along Francis Drake Highway, following the coastline with him.

When the sun rose over the hills and humps of Virgin

Gorda farther east, it was baleful and grim, sliding behind a wall of dark clouds.

They sailed under an ochre light between Little Thatch and Frenchman's Cay on the West End of Tortola, the catamaran jibing against the gentle wind as Roo turned northeast toward Jost. Roo ran the engines hard, chewing through the batteries to help keep the pace up, leaving the mainsail up for the occasional puff to help drive them along.

As they passed out from the protection of Tortola's West End, the swells rose again. Delroy woke up, staggering out of his cabin with loud thumping footsteps that came natural to all teenage boys. He climbed up the stairs out of the right hull and into the main cabin and blearily fumbled around the galley.

The smell of coffee filled the air around the cockpit as it leaked out of the main cabin's sliding door.

When Delroy came out with an extra cup for him, Roo nodded toward the bows. "Jost up ahead. We sailing right for Great Harbour, so just watch out for lobster traps." Most of the buoys were smaller than a soccer ball and, although brightly colored, hid in the dips and crests of waves and swells.

If the propellers caught on one they'd get snagged. Most of the work sailing up between St. Thomas, St. John, and Tortola consisted of keeping an eye out for the things.

A lot of them were chipped with solar-powered beacons and popped up on the navigation display. Most fishermen didn't want to lose a pot and paid a little extra for the newer buoys. But some still used old plastic bottles filled with air to tie the lobster trap lines to, and those required old-fashioned attentive human eyeballs to spot.

Delroy grunted, still not at the part of the morning where he was going to speak, and sat on the captain's chair. He squinted out over the main cabin ahead and sipped his coffee.

Roo left him to sit himself down at the chart table near the galley. The dark blue of the ocean shifted around the windows of the main cabin as he pulled up a screen and plugged the frog drive into an adaptor.

He didn't look up until Delroy shouted that they were in Great Harbour, and the sparkling white sands of one of Jost Van Dyke's largest beaches was up ahead, with the colonial-era brick-and-stone buildings gleaming in the early morning sun.

It was odd to sail into this harbor and not see it filled with ships at anchor. Jost Van Dyke was a popular sailing stop.

They cleared customs to officially enter the British Virgin Islands, even though Roo had done that already late in the night by sailing to Tortola. He'd conveniently arrived after customs closed, and left before it opened. The Virgin Islands, split down the middle by a border between St. John, U.S.V.I., and Tortola, B.V.I., required all the usual passports and customs hassle to travel between.

The customs official processed their "entry" into the B.V.I., and then Roo thanked him and promptly asked for the paperwork to also leave. "I needed to help a friend for the storm," he explained to the suspicious official.

"Why didn't you just take the ferry?"

Delroy laughed. "See, I asked him that. But he won't listen to me."

The official looked out the window at the lonely *Spitfire II* at anchor by itself in the harbor. Any other day, Roo had the feeling he'd want to search it. Or maybe hassle him more.

"I told you," Roo said to Delroy. "I have all my tools and everything I want on the boat. I'm particular."

Delroy rolled his eyes. "Too cheap to buy anything you need here on Tortola. Have to bring it all over. How much a hammer and some wood cost? Really?"

The official relaxed at the family bickering, and cleared them back out quickly.

There were no other boats or traffic as they got back aboard, winched the dinghy back up the davits, and secured it in place.

Now midmorning, the wind was starting to kick up as they left Great Harbour. The tips of the swells foamed slightly as the wind whipped the sea into a slight salty spray.

Roo didn't have to gun the electric motors. The sails filled taut with the wind. He pointed them southwest to get into the channel between St. John and St. Thomas's East End on an easy broad reach. It didn't take long before they slipped back out of the B.V.I. and close to St. John, easing back into the U.S.V.I.

"So your dead friend's present?" Delroy asked. "What was all the fuss about?"

Roo leaned against the fiberglass side of the cockpit, standing to look out over the catamaran's cabin-top and narrow pair of forward decks as they sliced through the waves. The port hull was getting slapped at a slight angle by the growing chop coming down through the islands. A coating of salt crusted Roo's clothes.

The ocean was getting angry. This wasn't brisk fun, there was a darkness uncoiling over the gray humps of the distant easterly hills of Tortola and Virgin Gorda on their stern.

"Right now, all I see is research," Roo told his nephew. "I don't know what it all is. Not yet."

It looked like Zee had spent a lot of time obsessed about privately owned space launch programs in Florida, Guyana, and Barbados. Financials, analytics, employee lists. He'd clearly been investigating three companies there, hunting for something.

But there was a lot of other random crap, Roo thought. Like files on atmospheric particulate data for the Atlantic. "You know how you always complain about scrubbing Sahara dust off the deck?" Roo asked. Several times a year the skies over the Virgin Islands turned slightly ochre, and a faint dust would settle down on everything.

Delroy grimaced, obviously thinking about having to clean the dust out from the many nooks and crannies of the *Spitfire*. "Just because we came once from Africa don't mean Africa should be dumping dust here all the time. And definitely not radioactive dust."

"He was looking at that," Roo said. "The Algerian plant failure. He had a map of the radiation dispersal."

It hadn't been life threatening, but the Cherynobyl-level failure had prompted a huge backlash against Chinese nuclear power installations throughout the North African region, and there had been a major push to launch the Destertec project: massive solar development all throughout the sun-rich Sahara regions that now made North Africa an energy exporter to much of Southern Europe via the Gibraltar Connection.

And Zee had been digging through the worldwide impact of the vented gases.

"That's as far as I got," Roo admitted. He held the frog up on the end of a necklace he'd attached it to. He was going to keep it next to him. Almost like a talisman. "I'll dig deeper after the storm, call a few friends. See what I can do. For now we have to get ready for the storm. After . . . I owe Zee following up." Particularly if someone was skulking around the mailboxes.

Delroy caught the look on Roo's face as he rubbed the green frog. "He was a good friend?"

Roo looked up. "I told you I was trouble, wasted my youth. Didn't make many friends. I was never there for . . . family. The Caribbean Intelligence Group, that was the first time I turned it around. And Zee was someone always there for me. I lived for it. Until I found out about you."

The two of them didn't talk about Delroy's father. Roo kept avoiding it, and Delroy wasn't in that place either. Delroy knew there'd been a falling out, knew that they hadn't been close. In some ways, they didn't know much about each other's past, because Roo certainly didn't ask Delroy about the foster family or his time spent without family. And Delroy could never get much out about the CIG, and the boy was never really sure if he believed his uncle had been an agent.

But Roo knew Delroy had seen some tough times before

he'd gotten to him. When Roo'd come back and offered Delroy a room on the *Spitfire*, along with a chance to start new on St. Thomas, the boy had started crying. And for a year or so, whenever Roo'd moved too quickly, Delroy would flinch.

So they both left the past behind them as best either of them knew how.

Until now.

A gust of wind hit them hard. The rigging keened.

They both jumped slightly and Delroy looked over nervously at the ever-darkening clouds advancing on the islands.

Roo tapped the screens of weather data, pulling up wind maps and satellite video of Makila. "It's just a tropical storm, we fine." He smiled. "I sailed worse winter storms up north than this."

But Delroy shook his head. "Storms is storms," he muttered. "And you can't say for sure it won't turn on us and get worse."

Roo didn't disagree. "I'll reef the sails." He tapped the roller furling controls on the jib. It spun, the sail wrapped itself up, and the amount of exposed canvas shrank a bit. They slowed, but the gusts would be less likely to blow the sail out.

He nudged the mainsail in as well.

Better to be cautious, even if he had been secretly enjoying the feel of the *Spitfire* sprinting beneath him.

"We'll be okay," Roo said, seeing Delroy looking at the black clouds on the horizon. "Storm hits tonight."

The wind speed indicator spun merrily away on its perch at the top of the mast, the readout down in the cockpit's glass indicating it was topped out in the gusts at forty knots. The sustained winds were high twenties.

They passed back along St. John, and then eventually put St. Thomas on their starboard. Delroy waved as they sailed on by Red Hook. They ran downwind hard, wing and wing with the catamaran waddling from side to side a bit. The mainsail was let out all the way to port, the triangular shape of the jib was shoved out to starboard with a pole, the whiskerpole, to keep it locked into place.

Spitfire preferred a reach, the wind against her side. She didn't point to wind as tight as a monohull, and she was a little more fiddly when running downwind. But if you were willing to sit at the wheel and pay attention, correcting the catamaran's quirks, as tiring as it was, you could get her to move quickly.

Roo sent Delroy into the cabin to watch a movie and relax as the gusts got snappier, angrily dive bombing them with a mild taste of what was still off beyond the horizon.

Spitfire ran before the gusts as she sailed toward the eastern tip of St. Thomas, moving along the reddish cliffs of the eastern southern coastline that eased, sloped down, and turned into muddy mangroves, then into the greater Charlotte Amalie harbor area. Roo took them past the bright towers and condos of Frenchman's Reef. Unlike the great ships of old, he didn't enter Charlotte Amalie harbor, instead passing the mouth of it until he was south of Water Island, which lay just past Charlotte Amalie to the west, across from Crown Bay Marina and the merchant docks stacked high with containers.

He hauled the sails in and went back to using the electric motors as he pulled into the lee of Water Island, then pointed them in to Flamingo Bay on its southwestern tip.

The farther into Flamingo Bay they coasted, the muddier and more stagnant the water got. Through the outer harbor and then the cut, and into the shallow and fully protected inner harbor.

The hills on all sides of the bay kept the wind out. And the currents and swells struggled to get in. Mangroves everywhere, hungry for the nutrient-rich muck and silt, also helped regulate the storm surges. In short, as the cluster of other ships here indicated, it was a natural hurricane hole.

Roo got the catamaran right up close to the mangroves, then kicked the starboard side prop into reverse while gunning the port to spin the catamaran neatly around.

Delroy dropped an anchor from each of the two bows. Roo set them, pulling against them in reverse for a bit, then they paid out anchor chain until he'd reversed right up to the mangroves. They were churning mud with the propellers now; the low draft keels of the catamaran scraped the soft muck. Just a few feet deep here.

They used spidersilk-weave dock ropes to tie off to the mangroves. And after an hour of work, the *Spitfire* now sat cradled in a web between her anchors and the ropes leading to the mangroves just thirty feet away.

But Roo wasn't done yet.

They ran a third and fourth anchor out lateral to the catamaran, with more chain. Sweaty work in the late afternoon. The air had been still in the harbor as they started, only the trees on the hills around them swaying to show how windy it was. By the time they finished the wind was shoving its talons down into the usually mosquito-rich and still atmosphere of the hurricane hole.

"See," Roo said as they sat and watched the wind start to kick up the water around them. "No worries."

He checked over the forecasts on the chart table's screen. The bright white swirls of tropical storm Makila were beginning to occlude Anegada, the most easterly island in the Virgin Islands, as seen from live satellite feeds on weather sites.

Outside the sun hit the horizon; orange and ochre twilight pulled after it over the gray and foamy white seas.

This was their fifth time bolting into Flamingo this year. Now that they had all the chain down, the stern fastened to the nearby mangroves, he could see Delroy relax into the routine.

Still, neither of them could sleep once settled down inside. Delroy read a few books, the ghastly backlight of his reader bathing his face in an eerie glow. Roo dozed on the settee, looking out the windows away from Delroy so his night vision wasn't harmed.

The wind passing through the rigging of the all the ships in the hurricane hole began to keen and wail.

It didn't let up for hours. By midnight the sound had become mundane to them. Roo paid more attention to the shift of the catamaran, the jerk-crack as it reached the end of an anchor's pay out, or as it yanked against the stern ropes.

At two thirty in the morning, Roo saw something move out in the dark.

He stood up, grabbed a pair of binoculars, and flipped them to night vision.

In the gray and green he saw a forty-two-foot Grand Banks motor sailer moving unchecked across the harbor water.

"Shit."

Roo said it with a half mutter, but Delroy woke up right away, eyes wide. He started breathing heavily. Damn, Roo berated himself. He was going to scare the kid if he wasn't careful. Delroy was always nervous about storms. And Roo couldn't blame him. They'd taken almost everything from him.

On the other hand, Roo was a bit nervous as well. Cut loose, a wild boat was going to do damage in the anchorage. It was going to hole other boats. Probably sink them. At least break some of them loose. If it came for them, they might end up mangled by it. Their lives were in danger from it. It didn't do Delroy any favors to try and hide him from the truth. The truth was going to be slamming around them soon enough.

"What's wrong?"

"Loose boat." As Roo watched, the motor sailer struck a single-hulled yacht. They couldn't hear the crunch, but Roo could imagine it well enough. He winced.

"The wind's pushing it up toward the dock," Roo said. "But when the storm's winds spin around it's going to be all over here down by us. And bringing any ships it cuts loose with it."

The other boat's mast shivered. Roo squinted and saw flakes

of fiberglass fly off with the wind. The motorboat wallowed and scraped on, and he saw that it had gored the fiberglass hull of the yacht a few feet above the waterline.

"It's bad?" Delroy asked.

"It's bad," Roo confirmed.

6

Roo opened the sliding door out to the rear cockpit. The winds had rotated with the shifting structure of the storm. No longer roaring in from over the hills around the bay, now they swept around and threw waves against the protected spit dividing the inner harbor and outer bay.

The catamaran wasn't bucking too hard, but he still staggered as it hit the end of its ropes and unbalanced him. Water slapped and churned in the mangroves behind them. They'd dragged a little bit closer, and normally he'd winch them a bit away.

But he wasn't as worried about the mangroves as he was the other dark shapes moving around near the docks. Shapes headed their way any moment now that the wind had changed direction.

He untied the rear ropes and tossed the lines free. The *Spitfire* was now held in place by the wind coming at the harbor and the four anchors off her bows, two out in front and one off to each side.

Roo pulled survival gear out from the cockpit lockers. "Delroy! Did anyone answer?" They'd been on the radio, calling to see if anyone was aboard the motorboat.

His nephew paused at the border between cabin and cockpit. "No."

Roo grimaced and gave him a bright orange survival suit. "It's cold weather survival gear," he shouted. "But at night, in the water, even here you can still get hypothermia. So stay zipped up, and stay in the cockpit, okay?"

Delroy swallowed and nodded.

"Do not get on deck to help me," Roo ordered. "If something happens to me, you get in the dinghy and head for the mangroves. Get as deep in as you can. The roots will protect you from the worst of it, the suit from the cold."

Once Delroy started pulling the suit on, Roo left him and crossed through the cabin as he zipped himself up. Bulky, plastic, overly warm, the survival suit was designed to be a personal lifeboat to anyone who fell overboard. Filters in the suit could suck in and desalinate ocean water. It floated. It kept you warm. It had a beacon to call for help. If you pulled and sealed the hood completely over your head in heavy waves, you could breathe inside the suit, it had oxygen scrubbers inside to recycle air for forty-eight hours.

Some models had a snack pouch. Enough calories to keep you going for a week.

Teflon and Kevlar fiber weave in the material supposedly helped with sharks.

And so far, Roo had never had to use one of the damn things.

"They coming right at us," Delroy shouted through the cabin at Roo, right before he reached the door leading out to the front decks.

Roo zipped the suit up. "Shut the door. Do *not* come out front."

Delroy did so, and then Roo slid the door leading out front open with a grunt. The wind hit him, shoved him back off his feet for a second as it battered the bright orange suit.

He leaned forward into it. As usual, it felt like sticking his head out of a car on a highway. He had to strain to slide the door shut behind him, then he leaned into the driving rain as he staggered up the deck.

Forty-mile-an-hour raindrops stung his face. But it was the gusts that he had to watch out for. Sudden blasts of air that would knock him back on his ass if he wasn't careful. Take him right overboard if he was unlucky.

He crouch-walked his way along the netting and looked up through the howling, painful rain as he got to the starboard bow's windlass.

A bowsprit glinted, catching light cast by still-standing streetlights from the road leading down to the bay. The bowsprit was a stainless-steel spear of platform and railing that jutted out from in front of the motorboat coming right at the *Spitfire.*

"Not this ship," Roo said as he gauged the direction of the incoming, storm-powered missile. "She ain't yours to have."

He pulled a carbon-fiber machete out from where it was strapped in a holster next to the *Spitfire*'s own stainless-steel bowsprit. The edge, microscopically thin and diamond hard, could cut through anything on the ship. He kept it up here to cut through fallen rigging, even a mast, in weather like this.

Roo cut through the anchor chain on the deck with a hard chop. The metal links parted and rattled off across the deck into the water.

The anchor off to the side, stopping them from swinging around, took up the tension. The spidersilk rope snapped tight and threw off drops of water.

The motorboat lolled, drifting with the surge of roiling water coming in through the cut. The bow dipped and the ship yawed, not quite making up its mind where it was going.

Roo stared at it. Waiting, waiting. Watching the ship grow larger and larger, waiting for that gut feeling . . .

. . . there. He chopped the rope, burying the machete into the deck a little and swearing.

Spitfire, no longer held in place by the starboard anchors, swung in an arc to port. Roo yanked the machete free of the deck and sprinted back to the netting. He bounded over and across to the port bow and windlass.

He let the chain out, leaving the port anchor over to their side take the full brunt of holding the catamaran in place.

The maneuver swung them even farther away from the wild boat in the dark. It roared past, fifteen feet on the starboard side, a ghost ship that madly flung itself into the mangrove roots just behind them. And that was where it remained, waves holding it in place as they slammed against the side of its hull.

Roo relaxed for a moment, until he saw the forty-foot monohull coming in next. It was driven toward them by the same waves that had hurled the motorboat at them.

For a moment it looked like it would swing right on past them as well.

But then it shifted course. Almost like it knew where to go.

"No no no no." Roo tried to will the yacht away from them as the red hull, lit up by the jagged streaks of lightning, swept closer.

It turned at the last second, giving Roo a stupid sort of hope. It crossed their bows, a sleek sailing ship out of control and ungraceful with its sides to the waves.

And then hit the anchor chain.

"*Ras* . . ." Roo swore.

Spitfire jerked and shivered. The spidersilk, strong as it was, still twanged and shot apart, cut clean by the other ship's keel. Then it snapped loudly enough to rival the thunder.

But the chain held.

The other ship, its rudder tangled up in the chain, spun so that it faced the mangroves. Side to side, the *Spitfire* and the monohulled yacht slammed against each other. Fiberglass shrieked and tore. Crunching sounds shivered through the portside hull of the catamaran as Roo ran up to the bowsprit.

It was three seconds, and an eternity, before he reached the anchor chain and cut it loose.

The chain yanked free, a section of it flailing back like a mace and striking him.

The wind knocked out of him, ribs bruised or possibly worse, Roo fell back into the netting between the catamaran's hulls. Freed of all restraints both ships spun as they swept toward the mangroves, still locked in their creaking, hull-ripping embrace.

He needed to get back to the cockpit and use the engines to pull them free. They could spend a night up against the mangrove roots. But not with another ship on top of them, he thought. But Roo struggled to draw a full breath.

And then, Roo saw the two masts above him strike. *Spitfire*'s shivered and gonged. But the other ship's mast had had enough abuse for the night. It just splintered.

It broke in a half, upper section dropping right for the net.

Roo scrambled back, machete still in hand and held out like a shield as he got clear.

This was bad. This was really bad.

The mast punctured the netting. But Roo was already up and on the port deck. Shattered glass exploded from the front-facing parts of the cabin. One of the spreaders on the mast punctured the port deck.

Bound together in the embrace of rigging and mast, they all swept into the muck of the mangroves.

Roo shoved his way along the railing, rabidly chopping with the machete at the debris on deck. The rigging was easy, on his hands and knees he got most of that cut away and thrown over into the now-empty space where the netting had been. Getting the mast was like chopping down a tree, though. He hacked at it for a solid minute, lost in a world of piercing rain, wind that slammed and howled at him, and the steady sounds of violent crunches, until the damn thing parted with a screech.

Roo slid mast and rigging off the deck and down into the water between the two bows where the netting had once stretched.

As he pushed the last length of mast away, the other boat slammed into them again. Roo, leaning hard to push debris, fell forward. He grabbed the ruined remains of netting dangling from the deck to stop himself from plunging into the water between the *Spitfire*'s hulls.

His feet dangled for a moment, and he strained, trying to pull himself back up on deck. But it was wet, and slippery. Every time he got a good handhold the ships collided, knocking him back down.

His back ached from all the cutting and shoving. His fingers quivered.

Maybe, Roo thought, he should let go and spend his strength swimming for the mangroves.

A hand grabbed his wrist. Roo looked up as Delroy pulled him up onto the deck. The boy had pulled the top part of his survival suit off and was soaking wet, but he'd done that to put on a pair of gecko-finger gloves.

"I told you to *stay in the cockpit!*" Roo shouted at him. He grabbed him by the collar of his shirt.

Delroy held up both gloved hands in reply. "Even this wind couldn't knock me off the mast if I climbed up with these."

Roo pushed him toward the cabin.

Delroy was right. The bio-mimicry in the gloves kept you stuck hard to anything, as long as you pressed the gloves to the surface in the right way. Delroy was always using them to goof around, climbing the mast to jump off into the water.

"You need to listen to me," Roo said in the main cabin. The soaking wet main cabin. The wind blew rain in through the shattered front windows.

"I could see you in trouble," Delroy said. "Say what you want; I couldn't just stand and watch you hanging there."

And they didn't have time to argue further. They were staggering around as the other ship slapped hard against theirs. Roo passed into the cockpit and flicked the engines on.

In full reverse he scraped and shuddered away from the other boat. Once free, it blundered into the mangroves, and Roo let *Spitfire* do the same.

The mangrove roots, though, had give and flexibility. The catamaran bounced off them as the waves shoved them.

"Pull your suit all the way on," Roo warned Delroy. "Leave the gloves."

And then he ran down into the *Spitfire,* flicking on lights and destroying his night vision as he looked for leaks. None of the sensors scattered all throughout the bilges were pinging the cockpit with alarms, so that was good.

Most of the damage looked like it was above the waterline. A puncture here or there. The plastic weaves mixed in the fiberglass on the modern hull had flexed, most of the horrible sounds had come from the other ship.

Roo let out a deep breath and climbed back up to the cockpit.

The winds had fallen. The storm, just in the last hour of madness, moving on.

Then the water alarms started pinging with gentle urgency. In the cockpit a schematic of the ship showed leaks in the port hull, forward and middle.

"We taking on water?" Delroy asked. "Should we get in the dinghy and head for the mangroves?"

The catamaran began to automatically pump water out of the bilges. Roo squinted at the readouts.

They'd spent a night in the mangroves once. Last year. In a full hurricane. Far more windy than this. And it hadn't been fun. Roo had resented every minute away from the ship.

"We're in shallow water, already up against the roots with *Spitfire*," he said finally. "Let's keep the pumps running and stay put. We'll figure out what to do in the morning, once the storm finishes blowing itself out. Come help me board up the cabin."

Even taking on water, the catamaran had a lot of natural flotation built in. It would take more than a few holes to sink the *Spitfire*.

7

The worst of the tropical storm passed. The winds had died back; they'd screamed themselves hoarse.

Aboard the *Spitfire* the pumps strained, not built to keep up with this much water. There were two holes punched into the inner part of the port hull, a present from the end of the mast Roo had cut up and shoved overboard. It had gotten trapped in the shallow mud just under the two hulls, one end buried and the other waiting to skewer his boat.

But all that flotation built into the hull kept the hull buoyant. And the flow of water rushing in had a stabilized a bit.

"The wind died out," Delroy noted. "What you want to do?"

Roo looked out at the harbor. Three yachts lying against

the mangroves, and the motorboat half sunk in the mud. The calmed water looked safe.

"Motor us out into the middle of the inner harbor, and hold the position," Roo said. "I'll get the patch kit."

Once he came back out from the storage lockers in the starboard hull, Roo found that Delroy had moved them away from the mangroves. It was risky, he thought, as he got into the dinghy with the duffel bag holding the patch kit. By the mangroves, the catamaran couldn't sink more than a couple feet before grounding. The boat could always be rescued.

Out here, now, the only thing above the water would be a mast if the ship went all the way down.

Roo clipped a few emergency lights onto the side of the dinghy and pulled himself along the hulls.

He unzipped the emergency patch kit, and jammed the nozzle of what looked like a fire extinguisher into the two gashes. When he triggered it, foam gushed in, expanding quickly until it spilled back out of the broken hull and Roo stopped pumping it in.

The foam hardened up in minutes. Roo knocked at it with his hands, checking to make sure it was solid.

"How bad is it?" Delroy asked when Roo came back up and slid the door into the cockpit.

Roo grabbed his shoulders and smiled for the first time in hours. "We still afloat, right?"

Delroy grimaced, not quite playing along with Roo's heartiness. But Roo could feel his nephew's shoulder's relax slightly.

He clapped him on the back of the neck. "It's calm enough.

We have a dinghy we can jump in if she starts to sink. Let's see if we can get *Spitfire* up to Independent Boatyard in Brenner Bay."

"The patch'll take it?" Delroy asked, still seeking assurance.

"I don't know," Roo said, honestly. "We won't know unless we try, and if the patches get knocked loose, we'll turn back into a harbor and tie up. But I want to get *Spitfire* out the water. I want to start working to fix her. It might be the wrong decision, but it's a decision. It's better than sitting here waiting to see what comes next."

He nudged Delroy out of the way and took the wheel, pointing *Spitfire* out of the inner harbor.

This time out he didn't head back out to open water, but stayed between Water Island and Crown Bay, pumps still working at full capacity as they started emptying the bilges instead of struggling to keep up.

He spent all morning staying close to the coast as he passed Hassel Island and through Charlotte Amalie harbor itself. People were out, checking around. Cars moved along the harbor front road. Dinghies began to leave docks to motor out to anchored boats, concerned owners checking them over.

Damage on shore didn't look too bad. Some downed trees. Power lines. Roo noticed some roofs missing solar tiles. The worst of it seemed to be the leaves, stripped bare of the trees. It left the island looking somewhat grayish.

Then it was past the cheerfully painted pastel-colored condos and the gleaming white hotel complex of Frenchman's Reef, and farther along the coast, pumps and motors straining, until they reached Brenner's and navigated through the increasingly browning water into the boatyard.

Roo greased a few palms ahead of time via e-mails and shuffled money, and by the time they arrived a massive crane on wheels waited by the haul-out slip for them.

By sunset *Spitfire* was up on wooden blocks in a corner of the boatyard, batteries all but dead from lack of sun and overuse, dripping water out from around the pieces of now dislodged foam.

An older man, hardly much thicker than the mast of the *Spitfire* and wearing gray jeans coated in daubs of different-colored paint, approached Roo in the late morning to watch him chipping the last of the foam out of the hull. He folded his arms across his armless shirt after running his hands over a shaved head.

"Where's your boy?" the man asked.

Roo stopped and wiped at sweat with a rag in his shorts. "School." He'd called an automatic cab to pick Delroy up.

"The day after a storm like that?"

Roo stared at the holes in the inner side of the hull. "Wasn't that bad of a storm for anyone on land," he said. "We used to them by now, right?"

The man chuckled. "You know, when I first moved down here as a kid, there were a bunch of wooden-built houses. That's back when the big hurricanes only hit every five years or so. And when the next one hit, those stick houses just blew away. And for a while, the land would just sit there empty.

Then these state-side contractors would show up, get all excited, and build another bunch of wooden houses that would stand a few years. Until the next one hit."

The fiberglass guy would be here later this evening. Before he came, Roo needed to scrub down the hull and get all the scum and barnacles blasted off so it was clean enough to paint. He nodded absently as the man continued talking.

"Eventually the insurance companies stopped insuring anything other than hurricane-ready houses," the thin man, who introduced himself as Samuel, said. "All bunker houses now. Concrete roofs and concrete walls. Brick if you can afford to ship it. Extra strong tie-downs for your solar panels."

"There was a reason people who lived here a while used to build just concrete and storm shutters," Roo said. Though, he thought bitterly, even building with concrete wouldn't help much in some situations. Like living too close to the water.

"Uh huh," Samuel agreed while eyeing *Spitfire*'s hull. "Look, you ever try the shark-based bio-paint for your antifouling?"

Roo looked over at him. "No."

"You got that old copper-based shit." Samuel walked over and scraped at a bit of it with a thumb. "It's soft. Copper stops some of the growth but you still end up having to jump in the water and scrape barnacles off your boat's bottom every month. I used to like the lead-based bottom paint, much more effective. Illegal up here, though. But a nice, hard paint. Didn't ablate off too much over time, kept the shit from growing on your hull and slowing you down. But regulations didn't let us little people have it, even though large shipping companies had their exemptions to put it on their container ships. But the shark paint's good. Expensive, new to market, but good."

Roo eyed the man much the same way he was eyeing *Spitfire*'s hull. "And you're selling?"

Samuel smiled. "You buying?"

There was a marine supplies store right here near the boatyard. Roo wondered what toes he'd be stepping on here. "What does the bio-paint do for drag?"

"Oh, bio-paint reduces friction. You're adding a couple knots to your ship's speed, as well as keeping the crap that grows on the bottom of your boat off for a couple years. Like owning a whole new ship. I mean, these are real sharkskin cultures, mixed in with the bonding agents. Once you get that coat on and it solidifies, the bottom of your boat is an oceanic creature."

This was like buying a joint off the first person you met coming off the plane, Roo thought. Shark paint was military, still not for general sale. Definitely illegal for civilians.

Not that it stopped offshore factories from producing it and kicking it around marine yards around the world for sailing enthusiasts looking to get more speed out of their ships.

And it was going to be expensive.

Roo picked up a hose attached to a power sprayer. "I have to clean off the hull so they can repair the damage," he said. "When I'm done, you can buy me a beer at the bar and tell me what you think it'll cost for you to paint that on." That'd give Roo time to feel the man out a bit more. Make sure he wasn't getting entrapped. Though the man's sunburned, scaly face indicated he all but lived here in the scorched, gravely boatyard.

Samuel's answer was drowned out in the whine of the compressor and blast of water as Roo started stripping mossy seaweed and barnacles off from below the waterline with each wave of the power sprayer.

No man was truly an island unto himself. But nowadays on a boat you could get pretty damn close. Roo had been sailing around the world aboard a catamaran for long enough to feel fairly comfortable as a modern vagabond.

There was a 3-D printer and a supply of plastic and metal raw feed for it. He could build basic parts for the ship. Emergency sealant foam took care of most quick emergencies, like the puncture they'd taken. The watermaker used reverse osmosis to create drinkable water. Solar panels along the cabin top, and extras that folded out of the davits on the back and on the top of the mast, meant that they were usually well charged up.

Some cruisers wandering around the world had small meat stills along with their refrigerators. Steaks grown inside by feeding microbes seawater, which then laid down and reproduced cloned meat from some long-lost original sample.

But those machines broke down too much, and Roo wasn't good at keeping them going. Better to just find a port of call and buy what you needed. He wasn't going to go through the hassle of trying to turn the netting area in the front of the catamaran into some sort of square garden, or dabble in aquaponics.

He was just too damn lazy for that shit.

But he liked knowing he could pull up the sail, with a larder full of a few months of canned goods and frozen foods, and head out where his whim took him.

This summer, Delroy and he were supposed to sail south. Down through the Caribbean to see Martinique. And then a long stretch out in the Atlantic to get all the way to South America. The great cities down there were something Delroy should experience.

But the boy'd been struggling with classes. That was the main reason Roo'd sent him back to school right away after the storm, instead of asking him to help get the boat ready over the last few days.

They fell into a rhythm. School for Delroy and work on the boat for Roo. Delroy helped paint the hull when he got back, which was tricky business. Laying down lattice for the biopaint to adhere to as it slowly bonded with the hull rewarded patience and precise fingers.

Later in the week, the two of them worried over tracking another powerful storm brewing in the Atlantic, but this one headed for Florida.

There was always a bit of guilt about being relieved the storm was off to hit someone else. But at least state-siders could still use vehicles to retreat along the highways and wait out the storm.

Roo had thrown himself into refitting the ship, and dropped into bed each night tired. Bone-deep weary.

And, he knew, ignoring the data hanging on the chain around his neck.

I'm not ignoring you, Zee, he thought. I just can't face it all just yet. He needed to get everything sat back in place, shipshape, before he could take on the heavy weight of figuring out what was in the damn tree frog drive. He'd charged in too quickly in Tortola, instead of playing it safe. That left him making things up in the field.

If the person had been less worried about public violence, the whole scene in Road Town could have ended very badly.

Maybe that was an excuse for his delaying. But Roo had always worked his way sideways toward things.

And with the tree frog hanging just inside his shirt as he worked, he felt like he still had a piece of his old friend with him. When he really dug into it, he was going to probably have to let it go. Come to terms with Zee being dead.

Roo had never been good about that sort of stuff.

With *Spitfire* back in shape and just a few days left in the boatyard for them to relax, Roo made a trip to the Tutu Mall area a couple miles down the road, with an electric Haier hatchback he'd rented for the afternoon, to pick up more deep-frozen food for the catamaran and an extra set of batteries.

They'd come close to draining the ship's battery bank in the storm. And the last few days of clouds hadn't helped; they were still running a bit low. Last night the virtual talking heads had started chattering about yet another storm that could possibly turn and start coming for the islands. One of three forming up in the overheated middle of the Atlantic.

Better to get prepared for even worse, everyone said. No breaks this year in the constant summer-long hammering of storms up through the middle of the Caribbean and lower East Coast of the U.S.

Roo parked the car, picked up a battery in each hand, and walked across the gravel of the boatyard, through the sporadic forest of boat hulls with their masts towering overhead.

A table saw kicked up a whine in the distance, a bit of vibrato kicking in as it bit metal. Someone else blasted music as they painted a hull.

Always a handful of people working on hauled-out boats. Other boats were still and quiet, some wrapped in polypropylene. In storage. Waiting out the hurricane season.

Roo'd gotten used to the rhythm of the boatyard already. He'd been in enough of them.

So the two men in jeans and shirts off near one of the boats caught his eye.

Casual wear. But clean clothes. Not covered in paint splatters, barnacle slime, or dust from sanding. No oil or grease.

Roo kept walking toward the *Spitfire*. He'd already gotten halfway through the yard. It was a point of no return. He'd keep walking to the boat.

And maybe they weren't there for him.

He thought about the green tree frog drive hanging from his neck, suddenly pressing hard and sharp against his chest. Thought about the man in the floral shirt glaring at Roo as he pulled away from the dock.

There was a woman waiting by the *Spitfire*'s stern. Pale-skinned, slightly freckled, blond hair ponytailed back, and wearing a gray pantsuit. She looked a bit flushed in the boatyard's heat. The air hung still over the mangroves and bay here, and it cooked everything. Worse: it was midday.

Two bodyguards flanked her.

They were heavy and serious-looking, but more bouncers than killers. Because killers was the vibe Roo got from the two angular men out in the shade of the ancient Pearson 42 a couple hundred feet away.

"Hello!" she said, as he approached the boat.

Roo put the batteries down. "Hello," he said, warily, looking up at the largest of the two bodyguards. The man could have been in one of those Strongest Man competitions, representing Iceland and picking up massive logs to throw across a field in feats of strength. A real-life Viking.

The man could break Roo in half with his bare hands.

"You're Prudence Jones," the woman said.

Roo looked back from the Viking to her. She had, he thought, very sad green eyes.

"You're Prudence Jones," the woman said. She knew it. It wasn't a question. She'd found what she wanted.

And nothing had happened. The Viking hadn't attacked, or done anything. Just stood there, scanning the yard.

"I'm Zachariah's sister," the woman said. "I know you're the last person he called."

Zachariah . . . Something in Roo wanted to correct her. No one ever called Zee Zachariah. Not that Roo had known of. But that was his first name.

"There was a lot of encryption on my phone," Roo said at last, and carefully. "How'd you find out about that call?"

"I paid a lot of money to Heimdall Incorporated here to crack the last call he made. And find out where. I flew down here the moment they tracked you down, along with two of their bodyguards."

Two.

Roo glanced briefly at the shadows under the chocked hull of the other boat down the yard. The other two men were leaning against the keel, faces in the shadows.

Well, he thought. She was either lying or hadn't realized she'd picked up a few extra guests for this meeting.

"My brother's dead, Mr. Jones," she said, her voice quavering slightly, getting his attention back. "My brother's dead, and of all the people in the world, he called a stranger right before he died. *You.*"

"Come on board," Roo said, picking the batteries up and moving for the stepladder on the back scoop of the port hull.

The other bodyguard, who had a more Hell's Angels sort of look going, but cleaned up with a suit and mirrored sunglasses, moved to block him.

Roo looked incredulous and the woman shook her head. He stepped back while Roo moved up the ladder onto his boat. "Leave the muscle to guard the boat," Roo told her as he turned and held out a hand.

She looked dubious, for a second. Then nodded.

He glanced back and around, then waved her in past the cockpit into the *Spitfire*.

"Your brother called to ask me for a favor," Roo said, closing the door behind her. "He left a message. He was a good friend, not a stranger. I'm sorry to hear he passed, Miss . . . ?"

"Kit," she said.

"Kit Barlow?" Roo asked, making sure of the last name.

She nodded. "Mr. Jones, I recently got a phone call saying Zachariah died of a hemorrhagic fever. From the CDC. They didn't let me bury him. He was already cremated, and handed over. I never even got to . . ." She took a deep breath. "I never even got to see him one last time."

Roo pulled a seat cushion off the bench near the table and pushed it up against the side window. All the curtains were already drawn against the sun. A sort of twilight filled the main cabin. "I'm sorry," he said.

"You're sorry," Kit said in a monotone. "The CDC was sorry. Everyone's sorry. Do you know what I do for a living, Mr. Jones?"

Roo stopped and looked at her. "What do you do for a living?"

"I work for an insurance company in Boca Raton. Do you know what the statistical chances of a fit male in Florida dying of hemorrhagic fever are?"

The bench had a small catch. Roo unsnapped it and opened the lid. The bin under the seat bench was full of emergency supplies. Medical kits, water filtration straws, rope, expanding foam, and whatever else Roo thought might come in handy. "I don't know," Roo said.

"Zachariah traveled a lot. I know he worked, sometimes, for the Caribbean Studies Institute doing research all over . . .

but . . . he told me once he really worked for the Caribbean Intelligence Group. Mr. Jones, what are you looking for there?"

Roo pulled out the bright orange revolver, and three cartridges. "Flare gun," he said mildly.

"A flare gun?"

"I don't usually keep firearms on board. Got a teenager living with me." He cracked it open and slid a flare in, much like loading a shotgun. "But this'll have to do."

He snapped it back shut, pocketed the other two flare shells, and turned back toward the door.

8

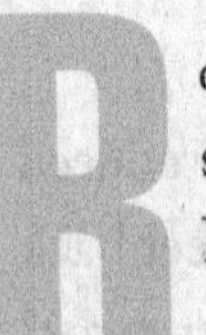

Roo glanced out past the cockpit by the door. He couldn't see the Viking's long blond hair out there anymore. Nor Mr. Motorcycle and his tattoos.

Not a good sign.

"Are you worried about my bodyguards, Mr. Jones?" Kit asked.

Roo retreated farther back into the dark cabin. "Your brother and I used to work together a long time ago." He slid over to one of the windows and peeked through a gap in the curtains to scan the yard. "With the CIG. He was calling in a favor. He talk to you much about what-all he used to do for CIG?"

"No," Kit said. "He kept me out of it. But . . . one has imagination."

The reason people at CIG recruited agents with no families, or desperate to walk away from their own.

"We used to work together, a while back." Roo pulled out his phone and took a quick shot of her face. He set it to run facial analysis, curious to see what it showed up on the public record. "Was a good man."

Kit was a pale blob in the darkness of the main cabin out of the corner of his eye. She shifted uncomfortably, but he had her covered just slightly with the flare gun, though it wasn't too overt. He was still trying to get a good scan of the boatyard.

Was she a lure? Or an unsuspecting lure? Was this a setup? She sounded, and looked, genuinely upset and curious.

"Why did you lie to me about the extra bodyguards?" Roo asked.

"What?"

"There are four people out there. The two you introduced to me as bodyguards, and two others a few hundred feet back under nearby boats watching us. Who are the other two?" Roo looked at her, the flare gun pointed down at the floor but ready to come up when needed.

But Kit shook her head, and Roo looked into widening eyes the same color as the varnished teak trim in the cabin.

Not lying. Or a damn good actress.

Either way. "Call out to your two bodyguards, let's get them up in the cockpit," he decided. "But stay right where you are."

She squinted, looking a bit dubious. But she leaned forward a little and called out. "Olafson? Brewer?"

They didn't reply.

She opened her mouth again, but Roo grabbed her arm and pulled her with him. "Follow me," he whispered.

He pulled her with him down the stairs into the port hull, past the chart table and Roo's old flatscreens on hinged arms. "Is it safer here?" Kit asked in a frightened whisper.

"Nah," Roo said, shaking his head, dreadlocks tapping the back of his neck. "Hull's just fiberglass. Won't stop a bullet. But we're harder to spot."

He walked her back to his cabin and, very, very carefully, shut the wooden door behind them. There was a starboard hull for the men to have to search, and two ends in each hull. There was a decent chance that if they boarded the catamaran, and Roo was betting they were just seconds away from doing just that, they wouldn't come at this area first.

There was a hatch on the inner hull here. Catamarans occasionally flipped. And if that happened, unlike a monohull, they pretty much remained upside down. Like a turtle on its back.

The hatch allowed you to get out when everything was upside down.

Roo turned the latches that kept it tightly sealed against water and, ever so carefully, quietly, lifted it open, to look out. He listened as footsteps creaked, the sounds of two men trying to stealthily move up the wooden ladder and onto the rear starboard scoop on the back of the hull.

The two men carefully walked across his cockpit, still trying not to make a sound, but failing. Roo's ears knew every squeak and creak of the boat.

He put a finger to his lips and slipped out of the hatch

headfirst. In a slow motion somersault Roo kept his hold on the lip of the hatch in the air over the gravel until he had carefully lowered his legs to the ground.

Once standing he reached up for Kit and helped her down.

He heard the sliding door open above them as the men entered the main cabin.

Roo held Kit firmly in place with one hand on her upper arm, the other aiming the flare gun into his cabin.

A deep breath. Another. A third. He listened to the sound of boots tramping around inside his boat. A sound that curled the corners of his lips with annoyance. They'd be tracking dirt all over his varnished floors.

They were headed forward, and down into one of the hulls.

"Now," Roo said, and yanked at her. She didn't want to move, though. Roo looked over to the rear of the port hull. Her two bodyguards lay underneath a tarp, hidden from the midday sun in the shade underneath the *Spitfire,* their faces exposed as the end of it blew slightly up into the air. Their throats had been slit; the blood had pooled under their necks and stained the gravel black.

"We have to move," Roo hissed.

Gravel crunched as she let him pull her along. Roo steered her toward the long keel of a nearby yacht, with patchy gray paint and dried seaweed caking the bottom of its hull.

They ducked underneath, panting and inhaling the smell of dead ocean as they skirted around the rudder.

"They're dead," Kit murmured, swallowing hard. "Who did that to them? What's going on?"

"I don't know."

Those were all good questions. But not for now. Because they'd end up dead, too, Roo figured, or worse, if they didn't loop out to the parking lot to get out of here. He was breathing heavily now. The adrenaline ramping up, making him focus on random things that his jumpy mind thought important.

He forced himself to take a slow, deep breath.

Calm down.

"Let's keep moving," he said. They crossed the yard, ducking from the shadow of one hull to another. "My car's on the other side of the gates."

A tall wire mesh gate ran around the whole boatyard. During the day there were large gates left open so people could drive in and out. And in the parking lot just past the gates: Roo's rented hatchback. A way out of this messy situation.

Shadows moved along with them as they ran, but on the other sides of the chocked boats. Boots slapped the gravel hard. Roo, suddenly chilled in the hot sun, glanced over at a nearby hull as a thin man in black boots and gray cargo pants suddenly rounded a rudder.

He'd assumed that were only just the extra two other people out in the yard here. A stupid mistake, Roo thought, yanking the flare gun up and steadying his aim by resting his right arm in the crook of his left as he skidded to a halt.

For a moment both men stared at each other.

Roo pulled the trigger.

The flare gun kicked, spitting smoke. The flare dazzled the space between them, even in the bright midday, then struck the man in the leg and ricocheted madly off down the yard as he fell over.

"Go." Roo grabbed Kit and pulled her along.

The man rolled on the ground, screaming and trying to shake off the glowing magnesium that was scattered over his pants. Roo carefully reloaded the flare gun as he kept moving.

He glanced back and saw the man ripping his shirt off to beat the flames out. Pale muscles rippled under intricate tattoo work.

And then Roo didn't have time to focus on it. Bullets kicked fragments of gravel up as someone else in the shadows of the boat hulls fired at them.

"Faster," Roo snapped. They were in the open, now. Running past the fence toward the parked cars. Metal twanged, the gate getting hit. More dirt hissed, but the worst of it was over. Hard to hit a moving target with a pistol at this range.

He fired the flare gun back behind him, though, to dazzle and startle.

They got to the Haier hatchback and yanked the doors open. Roo clicked into drive and stamped the accelerator as they both ducked low. Roo didn't even close his door, no time for it, just let it slam closed as he took off.

The back window cracked, safety plastic splintering as a bullet struck it, suddenly opaque with impact veins as Roo ripped them through the gravel and then onto the road.

He swerved to avoid a sedan that almost hit them dead on and wobbled the hatchback onto the right side of the road, facing traffic for a second. Kit, for the first time, screamed. Her palms were shoved hard against the large sticker on the dashboard with an arrow that said REMEMBER: STAY LEFT IN THE VI!

Roo glanced up at the rearview mirror. "Shit."

"What?"

"They're following us." A sleek, matte-black sports car accelerated out of the yard. The angry grill on the front seemed to sneer as it passed traffic to catch up to them.

Kit turned around to look at their pursuers. "Mr. Jones?"

One of the jackbooted men leaned out and started firing at them. "Prudence!" Kit shouted.

Roo looked down at the flare gun he'd dropped on the floor. Just one round left in his pocket.

That wasn't going to do any good right now.

"Don't call me that," he said to Kit. "Call me Roo."

He yanked the steering wheel and tore them off the coastal road, heading uphill.

9

The rickety hatchback tore up increasingly potholed roads as Roo used his shaky memory of the interior of the island to try to find higher ground.

Somewhere up here, Roo thought, there was a road that would do the trick. For a moment they got stuck behind a dollar cab trying to chug up the inclined road ahead. Ten or so passengers sat facing one another on benches bolted into the back of the modified pickup truck, an open plastic roof over their heads, groceries and bags at their feet.

"What are we going to do?" Kit asked, craning to look behind them again.

The road straightened and Roo zipped around, glancing out of the car to the steep drop just a few feet from the car's tires.

And right behind them came the lean black sports car with its two gunmen.

Roo almost spun the hatchback out taking another hard turn, down onto worse roads carved into the steep hill. Pocked holes jarred the car. He could see the lower-slung sports car behind them smack even harder against the rough road.

"Almost there," Roo said.

The little Haier hatchback was light, designed specifically for islands or for countries where speeds never got much over thirty or forty miles an hour. And its high wheelbase was meant to handle potholes.

"Here." Roo grunted with satisfaction. They zipped through roads where concrete and plasticblock houses on stilts leaned into the hillsides.

Kids who should have been at school, sitting on steps and liming around, scattered at the pop-pop sounds of gunshots. Roo accelerated the little hatchback as fast as the electric motor's could scream.

"Hold on."

The four wheels lost their grip on asphalt as the turn came. It was almost a switchback turn, with a tin-roofed outdoor store selling fruit nestled deep into its leafy elbow. A pair of old, gray-haired rastas with long locks jumped up from their chairs to shout at them.

Roo slammed the car over a rain gutter at an angle with a shudder and screech, using momentum to bounce over it. Then he pointed the car up the steep, half-dirt road, and climbed.

They tore uphill again, the hatchback shuddering and

wobbling, something in the axle or wheels knocked out of alignment.

Behind them he could see the sports car try to take the hill as well. But at this speed, and with no warning, it bottomed out even harder on the gutter. Sparks flew, and the chassis screamed as it broke itself on concrete. The car came to a complete stop. They reversed, this time slowly approaching the dip at an angle.

Roo pulled into a concrete driveway next to an explosion of pink frangipani plants. Again he used momentum to make the turn into the bend in the driveway, just out of sight of the road. He slammed on the parking brake and kicked the door open.

"Stay here."

He grabbed the flare gun, hopped out of the car, and slid down the dirt alongside the road. He loaded the flare in just as he made it to the bottom and the sports car came wobbling up the road.

They saw him and slammed on the brakes. Roo tracked it, aiming calmly and taking a breath, then fired down into the open window of the car. The gunman, in the middle of reloading his weapon, raised his hands and tried to duck as the brilliant flare flew between his legs to strike the floor by his feet.

The car filled with hissing and sputtering red smoke. The entire interior glowed, filled suddenly with hell itself, and the car wandered wildly, then pitched off the side of the road.

Roo walked across the road and looked down over the steep edge. The car rolled twice, picking up momentum as it bounced down the hill, then struck a thick mango tree. The carbon-fiber roof shattered and revealed aluminum ribs beneath it.

It lay bent around the tree's trunk, vomiting red smoke.

Roo's lip curled. He tossed the flare gun down the hill and walked back up to the Chinese hatchback. Kit stood at the passenger side, her door open. "Are we okay?"

"Just about fucking anything *but* okay," Roo said, getting in.

"I didn't know there were other people following us," she said.

Apparently she didn't know a lot of things, Roo thought. But he chose not to say it. "Get in. I'll take you somewhere safe."

She looked down the hill, seeing the red smoke slowly rising out from around the crooked trees downslope. And then came to a decision and got back in.

"They followed you," Roo said, thinking out loud as he popped the parking brake and rolled backward down the hill. "To get to me. I don't know who they are, but they weren't professionals. Or in the trade."

The fucking amateurs had been leaning out of windows shooting in a public area. Who the fuck was stupid enough to do that? Cheap, low-level chickenshit. Roo slammed the parking brakes on and spun the wheel in a textbook J-turn. The car whipped around to face downhill.

He released the parking brake before the car fully spun and floored it. They bounced out of the driveway onto asphalt.

At the bottom of the hill he eased them over the gutter this time, and they passed the now-flaming wreckage of the sports car as he accelerated westward.

"The first man I shot in the yard." Roo was replaying everything in his head, hunting for details. "He had tattoos. Swastikas. All of those men were white. Like European white. Nordic. None of them seen the sun in a while." One of them had been already starting to sunburn . . . he'd been in the car. He'd be well past sunburnt now, Roo thought.

"I swear, I don't know who they are," Kit said.

Roo rubbed his forehead in frustration.

"I shouldn't have kept the phone," he said out loud, more to himself than to her. But it was convenient to have someone to talk to, because he all but needed a therapist at this point. Stuff was bubbling out from deep inside him.

"What?" Kit looked over.

"Should never have kept a phone." Should never have remained connected.

It was hard to do, though. Hard to ignore the allure of a burner. Of anonymously forwarded old mailbox numbers through some routers so that he could keep in touch with a few people from the old days.

Before he'd retired from it all. Found Delroy.

Roo hit the wheel. "Damnit."

He should have known better.

Kit put a hand on his elbow. "Does all this have something to do with Zachariah?"

He looked over at her. Her blond hair had escaped her ponytail to fly every which way, her eyes were narrowed. Movements jittery from the adrenaline come-down and stress. He wondered when the tiny shakes would creep into his fingers as the reality of the firefight let go of him.

"Maybe," Roo said. "Maybe . . ."

He still had the data on the chain around his neck. The tiny tree frog just under his shirt. Maybe he should just give it to her and let her walk away. She'd braved enough for some answers.

Best thing to do was to walk away from all this himself. He'd done his time, been in the service. Roo owed the world nothing. He'd given it enough.

"Both you and them are after me because he called me."

"What did he want?" Kit asked, her voice suddenly sharp.

He looked over at her and she looked out of the window. In a low voice she said, "I just got shot at. And I don't know why. And he's dead. And I don't understand why."

"You think someone killed him," Roo said.

She nodded.

Roo tapped the wheel for a moment. "Well, hard to argue with you now that people are coming and shooting for us, yeah? I think you're right."

"Then what the hell did he ask you to do?"

"Nothing," Roo said.

Kit looked dubious. "Nothing?"

"He did give me something," Roo admitted.

"What?"

"Information. Stuff he'd been working on. Had it in a lockbox in Tortola."

Kit leaned over. "And now?"

"Now we have other problems," Roo said, and slowed down. He pulled into the Bolongo Bay Resort, stopped just by the entrance, and looked at Kit. "Do you have cash on you?"

"I do."

"Go in there, enjoy a rum coke. In fact: have a couple. Until you stop shaking, or wanting to shake. Then have a good meal. Then go sit on the beach, and forget this happened until the police come and ask you about it all. You tell them everything; they'll be able to piece it together with public cameras and the vehicle logs anyway, no profit in lying. Tell them the truth and hire yourself a good lawyer. You haven't done anything wrong. When it's over, go back to your office job in Florida and put this all behind you. Let your brother go. Let me go. Live a good, uncomplicated life."

She looked in the direction of the hotel's entrance and considered his advice for a second. "Roo, I'm an insurance patterns analyst, basically. There isn't such a thing as a good, uncomplicated life. Just life. I know that if I get out of this crappy little hatchback, I never see you again. But I'm now responsible for leading two men I hired to their deaths, because they had no idea my brother was into some serious trouble. And if I leave, I never find out what really happened to Zachariah. And that will eat at me from the inside until I'm just a hollow thing, going through the motions of life. Do you understand? I can't get out of this car. Not after everything I've gone through to get here."

"I can't promise it won't get worse," Roo told her. "I have no idea what level of shit we're deep into, understand?"

"Something is *wrong* here." She clenched her jaw. "I want justice for Zachariah. I can help. I have money. If Zachariah gave you some information, I can get analysts to help us with it. No matter the cost."

Roo nodded. So she was going to stick next to him, no matter what. "Zee," he said, coming to a decision.

"What?"

"That's what we called your brother," Roo said, putting the car back in motion as a confused bellhop stared at them as they looped on by. Roo smiled. "Well, except when we were training with the SIS in England. We changed his name to Zed for half a year."

Kit let out a deep breath she'd been holding. "Where are we going now?"

Roo pulled out the new phone he'd picked up while out shopping for groceries, a simple prepaid set, and tapped away a message to Delroy: Do not come back to the boat. Stay at school, or go to a friend's. Let me know you received this. IMPORTANT.

He sat in thought after he looked at the time. Delroy wouldn't be getting out for a few hours yet. He was safe at school.

Roo made a decision and pulled back out into traffic, heading toward Frenchman's Reef and into Charlotte Amalie. "It's time for me to call in a favor," he explained.

A single flare gun was not going to be enough. Not if people were threatening his home. Not if Delroy might be put in danger due to this whole, messed up situation.

Time to go into the lioness's den.

10

Roo swung them past the cruise ship docks as they came down from the hill by Frenchman's Reef Hotel and its brightly colored multistory condo-complexes. St. Thomas was fourteen miles long and a few miles wide, a little larger than Manhattan, but mountainous. Crown Mountain, at fifteen hundred feet, meant that most of the island's roads and inhabitants were clustered near the sea or perched on a hillside. Driving was always upward, down, or around the mountain, and the few miles from the yard to Frenchman's Reef still took twenty minutes. It was a busy day, with three mega-ships docked, looking for all the world like gleaming white starships fitted snugly into their slots. Seven stories high, they dwarfed the shopping complex they were tied next to.

The road was miserable with sunburned tourists and their sunhats, but the herds thinned out when Roo turned toward the hospital. A couple of them mistook him for a taxi and waved him down, but he continued right on past. The high-end jewelry shops, restaurants, and souvenir shops faded quickly. So did the crowds they catered to. The shopping complexes turned into plazas aimed at local needs: grocery stores and fast food. A quarter of a mile changed the air, even though a few straggling and increasingly confused tourists were still doggedly walking along the sidewalk.

Smaller Caribbean islands like St. Thomas were dense, particularly near the harbors. They looked tropical and green, houses spilling over the mountainside as you approached by a ship. But Charlotte Amalie had the density of human population of a major continental city.

Tourists filtered through alleys and roads, looking for interesting ways to spend money. But just like any city, take a few turns, move a few blocks in the wrong direction, and you weren't in a place for snapping pictures or looking lost. Turn the wrong corner and you were likely to get mugged.

Past Pearson Gardens and the new Indonesian-manufactured high-rises and back into the area near the hospital, Charlotte Amalie had been rough for as long as Roo knew it.

A few turns, dredged up from deep in his memory, and Roo stopped down the road from a plasticated-brick apartment complex. Two Dominican teenagers in crimson windbreakers stood near the courtyard gate. Cut-off sleeves revealed elaborately inked biceps.

Well, the Dominican Reds still held up here, Roo thought. Hopefully Jacinta was still inside.

"This isn't the sort of place they're expecting insurance adjustors," Roo said, looking at the two teenaged guards. He reached back, grabbed two of the larger foil-covered freezer bags full of groceries still in the back of the car that he'd never had the chance to unload, and dumped the contents on the roadside between the car and the sidewalk. "Or anyone else in a suit."

Roo opened the car door and both guards swiveled to regard him as he stood up. "Just keep yourself cool," Roo told Kit.

"*Que deseas*?" the nearest teen asked, stepping out onto the street as they approached.

"Jacinta," Roo said, and relaxed when he saw the flicker of recognition in their eyes. "Tell her Roo's here to call it in."

They stood in the street, eye to eye. The teen on the right looked Roo up and down coldly. "Who the fuck you think you are? You don't smell street to me."

"I took a shower," Roo said.

The guard on Roo's right snickered. The one blocking his way sucked his teeth. He moved a hand to a holster under his left arm. He might have been young and amped up, but he wasn't some wannabe gangster sticking a gun in a pocket or down his pants. Because, of course, Jacinta wouldn't put idiots on her front porch. Just young and tough. "Don't fucking—"

"Tell me," Roo interrupted. "What's your favorite hand?"

"My favorite hand?"

"For wiping your ass. Writing. Shit like that. What hand you use?"

He looked at Roo as if studying an idiot, then pulled the gun free. "I like this one," he said calmly to the other guard. No bravado, no nothing. Just the realization that Roo knew what he was talking about.

Roo had gotten through. He leaned in a little. "Don't tell her that, then."

"Tell her what?"

"When Jacinta asks you what your favorite hand is, don't tell her it's that one. If you turn me away and she finds out. You know what I mean."

The guard reholstered his weapon.

"Ain't exactly a trade secret," he told Roo.

"Yeah, but I'd be stupid to use it as a threat when you know what Jacinta would do to me if I'm full of shit," Roo replied.

The guard stared at Roo, then nodded. He stepped back a few feet and used a phone from his pocket to call someone inside the house.

"What the fuck was that?" Kit asked.

"You know that kid, sitting in the corner of the room reading the big, adult book that's a bit beyond them. They don't mind the teasing, they're so caught up in the place they went?" Roo looked over at Kit. "That was little Jacinta with the coke-bottle government-issued glasses, back in the Dominican Republic, reading James Clavell's *Shōgun*. Before her parents were murdered. Some of the things she read inspired her vision of leadership and organizational principles."

Of course, Jacinta had updated a few things to account for modernity. And she'd also realized some of what she'd been inspired by was just authorial bullshit as she tested it out in real world circumstances.

As far as Roo knew, she'd never convinced any of the Dominican Reds' foot soldiers to commit suicide for screwing up, like the possibly fetishized, honor-obsessed warriors of Clavell's fictional Japan. Lower order gang recruits were even reluctant to cut off their fingers or hands for offenses as if they were TV Yakuza.

So Jacinta did it for them.

"Follow me," the guard said, putting the phone back in his pocket.

They walked into the green-cemented walls of the apartment complex. Two more guards, older and more grizzled, stood with submachine guns hanging from straps on their shoulders.

They pointed Roo toward a first-floor door; one of them was missing a ring finger.

Inside, another Dominican Red member politely led them through a corridor into another room. There were leather couches arranged near colorful potted plants. A half-opened Dutch door led to a small kitchen on one side. The other door looked like it belonged in a bank: thick metal and dogged tight: the entrance to a high-security vault.

A guard with carefully plaited hair stopped Kit with a raised palm. "Jacinta knows him, but I'm afraid you are new to us. This is as far as she gets."

Kit glanced at Roo, who nodded. "Everything's cool," he said.

The guard smiled smoothly. More maître d' than security,

he continued in a businesslike tone. "We have beverages, and a tray of appetizers will arrive for you shortly. If you have a cocktail preference, just inform the two men at the door. They will get it for you from the bar upstairs. Mr. Jones, if you would follow me?" The giant vault door rumbled ominously open.

Roo left Kit and stepped to the other side.

The vault door started to shut slowly behind them. Roo checked his phone quickly, before the signal was killed off. Damn fool of a kid, Delroy hadn't responded at all to him yet.

Stay at school. Do NOT go home. I'll pick you up, Roo repeated.

The vault door sealed shut with a final thud. And the signal faded with it.

"Prudence *fucking* Jones," Jacinta said from the other side of the room. Her brown eyes twinkled behind a set of glasses. Roo could see a flicker of data reflected on her eyeballs. She was as well connected as he used to be, using a highly encrypted dark cloud network piggybacked on a popular photo-sharing site to coordinate her empire. And she had a knack for keeping a pulse on the outside world. The better to know where her wares were needed. "Not even a phone call or e-mail ahead of time? Just in the hood, thought you'd drop by? Maybe ask to borrow some sugar?"

"Here to call it in," Roo said.

"You sure about that?"

He held up the two grocery bags. "I'm sure."

The vault they stood in went back several rooms. All the walls had been knocked out and the high security area built into the shell of most of the house's first floor. The open space, lit brightly by fluorescents, featured racks and racks of weapons. From sidearms to rocket launchers. Machine guns to grenades.

The bodega, she called it once, laughing. As if it were some small mom-and-pop grocery store in Queens.

Jacinta waved an arm. "What do you want, Roo?"

He didn't waste any time. He'd been mulling the list over in his head on the way over. Grenades. Half a bag. Two Uzis. Light, easy to aim. On TV idiots with Uzis sprayed them all over the place and didn't hit anything, but there was a reason the Israeli Special Forces invented them.

Ammo to top that bag off.

Jacinta followed him, marking off the details of what he packed on an old ledger in a script only she could read. "There's a new storm coming. Normally you get gallons of water and some groceries, Roo. Not guns."

"A new storm?" Tear gas grenades, another half bag. A gas mask. Some pistols. More ammo for that. Roo thought about it a second. Then remembered the name of the next storm. "Njema, right?"

"You know American scientists are feeling it when they run out of names for hurricanes that haven't killed anyone and start using African names," Jacinta said. "Njema's coming for us; they just firmed up the forecasts. You probably should lay up nice and tight and come spend some time in the vault. Catch up on old times."

Roo finished. The two oversized freezer bags, still slicked with ice water and the muddled smell of various groceries, barely closed over the arsenal he'd quickly packed up.

"You're looking to start a war?" Jacinta asked.

Roo set the freezer bags down between them, back at the front of the room. "I think one came to me," he said grimly.

Jacinta held up a finger, and the other hand tapped the air quickly. "The boatyard? That was you?"

He nodded.

Jacinta made a face. "You could get guns up near Red Hook, so those aren't the real reason you came." Not much escaped her attention.

"That woman outside in your waiting room, you have a good picture of her from your cameras?"

"Yes," Jacinta nodded.

"Find me out who she really is," Roo said. "She's claiming she's Zee Barlow's little sister."

"Zee has a little sister?"

"That's what she's saying." They looked at each other for a moment. "But I knew Zee for years and years. And you know one thing Zee didn't have?"

"A sister," Jacinta said.

"No sistren, no brethren," Roo confirmed.

"She's very light-skinned," Jacinta said.

"It's the Caribbean," Roo said. Jacinta shrugged in semi-agreement. "Zee passed for white when we trained in the UK. She *could* be his sister."

"Could be a half sister he kept protected," Jacinta added.

"Yes. Either way, I need for you to tell me how the fuck she's sitting out there when there are no records of her. And the picture I took on my phone comes up with nothing when I search her face against publicly available images. The woman's a ghost. Not many people are ghosts these days."

"I know she's a ghost," Jacinta said. "That's why she's sitting out there, even though she's your guest. Someone shows up to my door and I can't figure out who they are, I get nervous."

Roo rubbed his forehead. "I know you have some CIA on the take, guns for drugs to get you into the old country. Use them."

"That's a big favor," Jacinta said.

"More than the one you owe me?"

"Even for that." Jacinta crossed her arms. "But those two freezer bags, that shit ain't free. That's extra in the ledger."

"I'll pay bills or heavy metal for the guns when you tell who the woman standing out there really is," Roo said.

"Heavy metal?" Jacinta looked interested.

"Platinum."

"Seriously, man, what are you doing with *platinum*? You got all high roller on us." Jacinta's eyes gleamed behind the data projected from her glasses. "Did you get that up in the Arctic, right before you 'retired?' A lot of people up there are still diving the area with ROVs in radioactive water, looking for the *Tellus* and the treasure it sank with."

Roo interrupted that line of thought, not willing to let her follow it through. "Just tell me who the sister is."

Jacinta scratched her lip, annoyed at getting bumped back to the business at hand. "All right. You need someone to take your bags back out to your little car?"

"I'll manage," Roo said.

11

he waited until they'd climbed up Raphune Hill and higher up onto the mountainside, where the air cooled and the occasional floral scents beat out the smell of hot asphalt. She must have realized he wasn't in any mood to talk; Roo was driving without thinking, just following routes laid into the back of his memory. He kept trying to call Delroy. "My clothes and laptop are back at my hotel," Kit finally murmured.

He looked over. "If you go back, you're probably dead."

She digested that, looking down at her knees. Smoothed the pants fabric out unconsciously. "Shit."

That was that.

They snaked their way back through the heavy shopping areas around Tutu, and then off to the Clarence Henry Center.

"What is this?" Kit asked, looking at the gleaming five-story, solar-power windows of the Henry building and the geodesic dome of the Academic Hall.

"School," Roo said. "Wait here."

The student-designed and -maintained gardens were full of tiny robotic gardener balls that fled Roo's quick steps as he hurried to the Academic Hall. He was looking for anyone he recognized, like lecturers for any of the recent student-created classes or friends of Delroy's.

"Pablo!" Roo shouted by the edge of the car park's grass and low-bushes that marked out each parking space.

A young Puerto Rican with locks looked up from playing with some three-dimensional object in the air only he could see, and waved.

Roo walked up to him. "I'm looking for Delroy."

"He left for home already," Pablo said.

"I've been calling him," Roo said, despair suddenly creeping into his voice.

"He's been deep in this week's project," Pablo said. "Shut down all outside interruptions to get it done for the group. We're test launching a balloon that should be able to get us some pictures from the edge of space, but the uplink won't work. Delroy left early to go home and work on it alone. Plus, he left his phone in his room and wanted to get it back. Don't worry, he's headed straight home, I promise you!"

He yelled that last bit out as Roo ran back for the car.

Roo slammed the door shut and reached back for one of the insulated grocery bags. He unzipped it, pulled out a pistol, loaded it, and put it on his lap.

That done he swung them back out on the road.

"If I can't go back, what do you recommend I do next?" Kit asked, breaking Roo's concentration a few minutes later.

"What?"

"What do I do? Where do I stay? What are my options . . . woah!" That was a response to Roo zipping around a large water truck, again facing oncoming traffic, and then pulling in just front of it.

She released her death grip on the door handle.

"Get on your phone," Roo said. "Get a reservation under a fake name. When you get there, pay cash. Tell them an ex-husband is stalking you if they insist on seeing your ID. You'll get a room. Particularly if you add a little to the cash."

"I have a few thousand on me," she muttered.

"That'll do," Roo said curtly.

He tore through traffic as best he could, though being careful not to get pulled over. Minutes counted.

The gun was still on his lap when they approached the boatyard. Emergency lights flickered and strobed between the masts. Virgin Islands Police Department cars blocked the gate, yellow caution tape fluttered in the wind along with courtesy flags on the rigging throughout the yard.

"They could be here for the other men," Roo said, his voice scratching his throat as he slowed down.

Kit cleared her throat. "Give me the gun," she said.

One of the policemen approached them, wiping sweat from his brow, motioning them over to park away from the gate. As Roo guided the car in, Kit slid the pistol back into the silvered, bulging cooler bag and zipped it closed.

They still bulged in odd places, but the thick panels didn't betray what was inside thanks to the gas masks and ammunition Roo had packed against the sides.

Another member of the VIPD looked over at them, then back at a small screen on the sleeve of his wrist. "Eugene, that's him!"

The nearer cop, suddenly more alert, hand on the gun at his waist, motioned Roo. "Can you get out of the car, please?"

Roo nodded, keeping his hands obviously clear of anything.

"Are you Prudence Jones, the owner of the catamaran *Spitfire II*?"

Again, Roo nodded.

"We need to talk." He seemed both nervous, and a little sad.

There were people around the gates of the yard. Curiosity crowds. Trying to see what had happened. Part of that human urge to see the story themselves.

It made Roo nervous.

Then he saw the body on the stretcher by the boat. The dark brown hand on the white plastic. Roo lurched forward. "No."

Kit's feet crunched on the gravel as she got out as well.

"Hey . . ." the cop said. But Roo didn't care. He staggered past him, through the caution tape and into the boatyard.

"Stop!" someone else yelled. The voice cracked with authority and broke through the whirlpool of grief beginning to suck everything inside of Roo down into itself.

Roo dropped to his knees and stared at the sheet-covered body a hundred feet away. He should have left Delroy alone with that foster family. Because now Roo's own past had come back and killed the boy.

Hadn't it been the right thing to do, though? Look after family?

Roo buried his face in his hands and stared at the gravel by his knees. It was covered in reddish paint flecks scraped away from a boat's hull.

The wind swept them away in a gentle whirlwind of hot dust.

12

They recorded Roo's lies with tiny cameras embedded in their shiny hats, taking his statements. He mumbled through the haze of it all. Spinning a story about grocery shopping and shock.

Soon enough they'd find out he was involved in this. Cameras from across the street subpoenaed, the GPS in his rented car. Face recognition would create a timeline and they would realize Roo lied.

But if he told the truth right now . . . he would lose his options. They'd start looking into who he was, and right now the false identities he gave them should hold up to a first pass, but he didn't want to get caught up in the mess that would happen under deeper investigation. He wouldn't hold up under a deeper dive. They'd know he didn't kill Delroy, but the false identity would end with him being location chipped and asked to stay put while it was all resolved.

And right now, Roo was starting to think he didn't want to get stuck.

Officer Standish Simpson, according to his badge, had Roo sign an old tablet, then thumbprint it as he finished the interview. "These people who attacked your nephew, they flew in just yesterday."

"You should call someone to make arrangements quick," another officer informed Roo in a soft voice. "Don't have much time before Hurricane Njema hits."

"Will you even have time to look for Delroy's killers?" Roo asked bitterly. They would be preparing for Njema to hit. And she would be worse than just a tropical storm like Makila.

"We hunting," the officer said. "We hunting." He put a reassuring hand on Roo's shoulder and left.

Kit stood in front of him now with the two oversized shiny freezer bags of weaponry. Roo stared at her, speechless for a second.

"Are you done searching the boat?" she asked Officer Simpson. "I need to put these in the freezer for Roo. For the hurricane. I've been standing here this whole time with them. I know this is a horrible time, but they need to get put away."

Roo looked back at the car, then at her, and blinked. All this would have fallen apart if a single officer had looked in the bags she'd been holding patiently all this time.

"Yeah, yeah, go on," they told her, and Kit headed confidently for the *Spitfire*.

She climbed the ladder, stepped around the edge of the

cockpit to avoid a blue tarp, and went inside with the freezer bags of guns.

"Don't leave the island, Mr. Jones," Standish said, jolting his attention back over. "We will be following up."

They weren't thinking he'd leave. Certainly not by boat on dry land in a dockyard, not with a hurricane on its way shortly. But as they all faded away, Roo noticed that a single officer remained in a car parked just a little bit up the road from the gate.

They'd taken his information, they'd pieced together a small part of the story. But they weren't naïve. They were keeping an eye on him.

When he got back to the *Spitfire,* Roo yanked the blue tarp away and stared at the now-browning blood hardening on the fiberglass floor. Some of it trickled down the port side.

"You shouldn't have stayed with me," Roo said into the dark cabin, staring at the pooled blood.

Kit didn't say anything.

"Now they'll suspect you as well."

"Those are my bodyguards that died; they'll figure out I'm involved soon enough," Kit said. "The question is: what do we do now?"

Roo still hadn't looked in toward her.

"There's a scrub brush, and some soap, under the sink in the galley," he told her. "Please bring it out here."

The fiberglass on the cockpit's deck surface wasn't smooth. Artificially pocked and texturized, it gave feet and shoes traction. Even when slick with ocean water. And that same texturized surface meant the blood clung to the nanoscale pits and cracks.

Roo got on his hands and knees with the bucket and scrub brush and put his back into it. Five times he scrubbed and rinsed, each time the cockpit floor releasing more and more blood, then dirt, then grime.

But every time he got down, nose to the fiberglass, he would see something.

Maybe not reddish, but it seemed like it.

And the scrub brush would come out, and he'd start again.

Five times, scrubbing until his back ached, the tips of his fingers burned, until sweat dripped and burned his eyes.

Kit sat inside quietly for the hours of scrubbing. Roo ignored her presence. She didn't belong. This wasn't her grief, and she was smart enough to know that anything she did would be the wrong thing. She was a ghost in the ship as he moved around, cleaning, clearing things out.

Someone knocked politely on the side of the hull.

Roo slid the gun he'd hidden under a seat cushion out. He held it against the side of his thigh as he leaned to look out back toward the rear scoop of the port hull. "Hello?"

"Pastor Thompson here," said the rail-thin man in the suit, his tightly curled, graying hair visible through the scuppers. He carried a satchel against his hip, and looked at all the bags tossed on the ground.

He caught Roo's eyes. "What's in the bags?" he asked.

"Delroy's things." Roo quietly flicked the safety of the gun back on. He placed it on the cockpit floor, out of sight, and sat down to look at the pastor. "He doesn't need them anymore."

Thompson took a deep breath. "You reached out to me to prepare Delroy's memorial. But I am not just here for him. How are *you* doing, Mr. Jones?"

Roo stared at the man's slim, brown leather shoes. "I'm numb. That's how I am." Everything felt silly and profound at the same time. Like the little silvered tips on the pastor's shoes.

"Not angry?" Thompson asked.

What good was anger right now? "My soul was cauterized," Roo murmured. "I was his only family. He, mine. When I came back to the islands, I found him in foster care. My brother had died. A neighbor's whole roof landed on their house. Hurricane winds. Crushed the whole family, except Delroy, pinned beneath his parents. I came back to him so late, because I had left my family. I hadn't even known he was orphaned until he'd been with other families for . . . too long."

"It was a good thing you took him in," Thompson said. "That was the right thing."

Roo squinted. "I *thought* so. Three different families, he'd been with, when I came back and took him. But what good is that? What did I spare him from? A tough life. All I gave him was a decent life and then death too soon."

Thompson reached up from where he stood on the ground and put a hand on the deck by Roo's wet feet. "I'm sorry, Mr. Jones."

Roo looked off past him into the shadows cast by hulls throughout the boatyard, lengthening due to the sun's low angle.

"I guess," Roo said, biting a lip. "I guess it wasn't a bad

way to die. Bullet in the head, they said. He didn't have time to even realize what was happening. I've seen worse deaths."

The pastor pulled his hand away from the deck, as if Roo had slammed a knife next to it.

"I visited someone in a cancer ward once," Roo said. "Saw these kids dying of cancer. Terminal. That fucked me up something bad for weeks, seeing that. All those long, slow days. The suffering. Maybe I'm saying that to make me feel better. I just don't know. I just don't know."

He saw the pastor thinking of something to say, caught off guard by the direction of Roo's thinking out loud. Roo realized he should shut up and keep his thoughts to himself.

But that was the man's job, wasn't it? To listen? Wasn't that why he'd come. Surely he'd heard worse?

Or maybe Roo would need to talk to a Catholic priest. The sort that heard the darkest confessions on the other side of a partition. Not a sunny, friendly, God-is-nothing-but-goodness-and-shiny-happiness pastor. The kind that wanted to provide comfort, and ease, but not really examine the crevices of the human condition. And Roo was digging around some crevices right now, that was for sure.

"So there won't be any family at his memorial, Pastor," Roo said.

"Other than you," Thompson confirmed, pulling out a small pad from his satchel to write notes on.

"His friends will come. And others who knew him. I may not be there, so you will be making all the arrangements."

Thompson finally dug his heels in, moving away from his role of being a comforting ear. "Mr. Jones, I can make the arrangements. Tasteful arrangements. I can talk to his friends and look at what he has left behind online and do that. But you need to come to the memorial." He said it with a firm conviction.

"Look . . ." Roo stood up, but Thompson interrupted forcefully.

"I'm not here to give you a sales pitch, but everyone has some kind of moment where they need to say good-bye. It is important. Whether you are a believer, which you may not be, or just angry. As human beings, we all need to mark a moment, and come to terms with what has happened. Remember the person that was, even if you don't believe they continue on. Honor that, for them. And maybe, to find a small measure of peace."

Roo took out his phone. "No peace to be found here, Pastor," he said. "But I'm going to give you an unlimited line of credit. I want a good memorial. That is how I will mark the moment."

"You can't run away from it," Thompson said, slipping his pad away.

"I'm thinking about running toward something else," Roo said.

"The middle of grief is not a good time to be making major decisions."

Roo laughed sadly. "There's never a *good* time to make a major decision. Mister Thompson, there's another damn hurricane coming. There's no time for waiting around. There never is, in the summer, here." Roo could hardly remember a time when hurricanes let up. Too much heat in the atmosphere. Too much carbon dumped into it. And now they bore the brunt of it. Storm after storm slamming into the islands, the hurricane season extending ever longer. The sea rising up over the beaches, threatening the reason tourists came to visit the islands.

A huge wave of loss threatened to unmoor Roo as he thought about the past and then tried to cut it away.

Thompson got his attention back to the moment. "A big one coming. A lot of families will be hurting in a week's time."

"Then don't waste time out here with me," Roo told him. "Go back to those who need you. And do good by my nephew."

"I will," he said.

Roo looked back down at his phone. And then sent a massive donation to the man's church.

In Delroy's name.

He wasn't sure if it was enough to help with any future sins, but it would be enough to help anyone in Thompson's community about to suffer from the next explosion of weather-related fury coming their way. He picked the gun back up.

Downstairs he reached past Kit, who was sitting in the chart table area near the VHF radios, paper navigation charts, backup RDF units, and Roo's wall-mounted screens. He ripped an old map of the Caribbean with pins stuck into various islands and angrily threw it in the trash.

A senior summer trip that he would not be taking with Delroy.

He stalked past Kit, who sat so still it was as if she was afraid any movement or words would destroy him, like a hammer to porcelain.

In his cabin, the door locked and the gun resting on his bed, Roo stripped off his wet clothes until he stood naked. Nothing but the chain with the tree frog on the end.

That damn frog.

The damn forwarded voice mail.

Roo looked through the slats in his room door into the corridor. Kit hadn't stirred. Silence hung heavy throughout the catamaran.

He pulled out a pad Velcroed to the wall. Plugged the tree frog into it, and flipped through the data again.

More of the same bullshit. Charts of average hurricane formation data for the past century. Growing activity. Nothing you couldn't snag from any weather research site.

And more of that esoteric stuff about particulates riding high in the atmosphere.

"What were you trying to leave me, Zee?" Roo asked the wall.

But the smooth fiberglass had no reply.

Zee was studying dust in the Saharan Air Layer. As Roo had told Delroy. Storms would rip across the deserts of West Africa and whip the dust up high into the air. And above the wetter, colder Atlantic air a dryer layer would hold the dust and sweep out across the ocean to rain softly down in the islands.

With the jet stream wobbling to dip down into the Americas, changing wind patterns due to colder Arctic air constantly battling and changing everything up and down the East Coast, secondary layers often took the dust up into Florida nowadays. Sometimes farther.

Roo pulled the data out. Zee died to protect it, and there was more. But Roo had never been a researcher. He'd ridden desks, true. Back when he'd been up to no good, Caribbean Intelligence Group pulled Roo out of house arrest, cut the GPS chip out of his ankle, and told him they could use a grifter.

Social engineering, they'd told him. There were some hackers that could dig into code, or find vulnerabilities in the programming. But the weakest link? The people actually using programs. And Roo had a knack for exploiting the link between the keyboard and the screen.

You could dress up in a pair of khakis and a blue dress shirt with a name tag and fake company name and show up to fix almost any network or computer. You could frantically call someone and tell them they needed to access a certain security site. You could get anyone to give over all sorts of personal information to fix a problem with their file in HR, if they thought you were HR.

Fifteen minutes on a phone, and Roo could usually get what would take hours to force one's way into. Roo read people, figured out how to follow the threads up the chain. Took action.

Zee, on the other hand, he would dig and dig until patterns came. They'd worked well together. Zee, the bloodhound. And Roo, moving pieces around the board based on Zee's research.

He could read Zee's raw research until his eyes bled and not spot what was obvious to Zee.

Roo needed to tackle this in a people direction.

Or he could turn his back on all this shit and put the boat back in the water. Run before the hurricane, like a Viking of old on a longboat before the storm. Lose himself. Start over.

One of the boards creaked outside.

Roo, still naked, picked up the gun and aimed it right at the door. "Yeah?"

"I don't . . ." Kit said, her voice breaking slightly. "What happens next, Roo?"

He looked at the broken outline of her silhouette through the slats in the upper part of the door.

That was the question, wasn't it?

Gun still raised, he moved until the barrel almost touched one of the wooden slats. "Are you serious about justice?" Roo asked, his voice cracking slightly. "Ready to risk it all to find out who did this to Zee, to my Delroy? No matter where it takes us? Because your brother and I, we didn't sit behind desks when we first met, you understand?"

Kit shifted on the other side of the door's slats. "I'll go wherever it needs to go. We have no parents, no other family to mourn us. It was just him and me. I'm willing."

"I think they found me through you," Roo said, leaning his forehead against the door. "So let's turn this around, yeah? It's time for you to go back to that hotel room you told about."

She stopped moving forward. "You're going to use me as bait."

More like chum, because those men were sharks. And if she was naïve, she wouldn't know it. She would trust him and say yes and walk willingly into a line of fire. But if she was in the business, like Roo, then she knew it was going to be dicey, and ugly, and that this was a stupid move for her.

So, Roo thought, let's see how committed Zee's possibly fake sister is to this.

"Yes. See that police car up by the gate? It's going to keep trouble away. So we're gonna get real up close and personal."

"And then?"

"Going to kill the clot-bastard-fuckers for Delroy. And find out why they came up on us. I'm going to tug on this line and see where it leads. Because it's this, or . . . I go become someone else. Someone more broken, and tired, and alone. And always I'll wonder, who did it? Why? What was it for?"

Kit took a deep breath, then sighed. "I'll be your bait. For Zee."

"For Zee," Roo said. "And Delroy."

13

Frenchman's Reef Hotel stuck out of one of the corners of Charlotte Amalie's harbor. From it you could see the whole town sprinkled along the curving bowl of the mountain-made amphitheater of the harbor. Everything stretched around that curve. From Frenchman's Reef, to Yacht Haven, which was clustered with gleaming mega-yachts for the unbearably rich, all the way to Frenchtown, where fishermen still pushed out to sea in wooden, brightly painted fishing boats.

Roo, flamboyantly out in the clear air in his camouflage as a tourist, walked by room after room. The doors to his left, railing to his right. And behind the rails, the nighttime lights of Charlotte Amalie twinkled.

At the pool, an overweight, pasty woman in a mumulooking bathing suit had handed Roo an armful of wet, sunscreen-smelling towels.

"Here you go," she'd said, with an air of casual expectation.

Kit had opened her mouth to object, but Roo had just nodded and taken them. At the edge of the pool he had pulled on a pair of swimming trunks, doused himself sopping wet with a hose, and pulled on a Hawaiian shirt that assaulted anyone passing by with its tropical colors.

"You go ahead," Roo told Kit. "Let them grab you. Fight them, but let them take you. I'll be right behind."

He had draped one of the towels over his head to obscure his dreads, wore wet, squeaking flip-flops, and had wrapped the other towel around his waist.

A bright red duffel bag, the last towel casually drooped from the space between the handles, bumped against his hip.

Kit now reached the stairs ahead of him and, after a deep breath, started up.

Roo watched her go until her feet were all that were visible. A pair of professionally efficient pumps, scuffed from the gravel, that ticked up one more set of stairs and disappeared.

He kept moving toward the open stairs. Found his first target just around the corner, down the stairs just in the shadow. Smaller muscle, keeping an eye on the stairs and pulling the trap closed. He was paying more attention to Kit and getting ready to follow her up.

Roo broke his attention. "Hey, can you tell me where to find the ice machine . . ." He dropped the duffel bag with a heavy clunk and cracked the towel at the man's sunburned, heavily stubbled face. There were tattoos up and down his forearms, more swastika bullshit.

"What the fuck?" The lookout seemed confused, not expecting a swimsuit-wearing tourist to snap a towel at him, so he instinctively grabbed at it. Roo let go, and as the lookout focused on balling it up and throwing it aside, Roo ran into him and flipped him over the rail.

It was four stories down to the ground, and then tumbling as the body snapped its way through scrub along the steep incline the rooms were perched on.

Roo hadn't waited to see the outcome, he'd already unzipped the duffel bag and started up the stairs. He pulled out a two-foot-long speargun and paused to pull the bands into place, forearms straining to get them on the release catch.

A silencer wouldn't do shit. It was useful for disguising where you were shooting from, or cutting down on mayhem. But out here, the supersonic crack of the bullet was going to give everyone a head's up.

Bullets were loud. That was always a constant.

A spear, on the other hand . . .

When Roo cleared the top of the stairs he could see a guard standing outside the door. All muscle. Slavic and with shoulders so wide he probably had to turn sideways to slip through a normal sized doorway.

Muscle on muscle, like an over-bred bull. Thanks to steroids, human growth hormone, maybe even some sequenced DNA spliced up, and reinjected with new markers from top muscle builders. You didn't need to be born with lucky genes, you could always steal them from black market sequencing shops.

Whether the person who created the new viral DNA strain you were injecting into yourself was any good at his coding, that was another story.

Shooting a slab of meat this tall wouldn't even guarantee his silence. Not unless it was a direct hit to the heart.

But, Roo knew, shooting him in the lung with a speargun was a good way to shut him up. The speargun twanged.

The mountain of a man grabbed the end of the spear embedded in him and opened his mouth. Blood sprayed the air as he hoarsely tried to shout a warning. But with a pierced lung he was reduced to little more than grunting. Roo yanked on the long string still attached to the spear.

It came out in a sickly ripping gasp and a tiny rush of air. The barbs were designed to keep the spear in place, but Roo had yanked it back so hard it came out anyway.

The effect was dramatic. The giant dropped to the floor, gasping and struggling to handle a suddenly collapsed lung.

He held a hand up, trying to push Roo away, but there was no pity left in Roo. He drove a knee into the center of the man's chest as he dropped onto him, then slit his thick, corded neck with a shark knife pulled from the end pocket of the duffel bag.

Now there wasn't even gasping. Just blood.

"There was a boy," Roo whispered to the man, leaning forward and looking into the pale green eyes. "You shouldn't have killed him."

There was no comprehension. The eyes focused on something far away from Roo.

He reloaded and listened to Kit scream. There was a slap of a hand from inside the room, faint, but audible. Roo stepped toward the door, then grimaced.

There would be one more guard. With a deep breath he rubbed his hands on his shorts. Inside his head, he was on the edge of a cliff and wobbling. It was good to be scared, it heightened his nerves. What he had just done would sink in later. For now, he needed to keep moving. There was no turning back. The decisions made in anger were solid. He was here for retribution. He was here to do this the messy way.

He turned away from the door.

Stepping out of his flip-flops, Roo ran silently for the other stairwell. Around the corner he pointed down, sighted, and shot the other posted guard in the chest before the elaborately tattooed, muscled neo-Nazi could reach for his gun.

This one Roo didn't kill. He knocked the gun free from the man's hands and yanked him up the stairs by pulling on the wire still connected to the spear. The guard tried to scream, sprayed blood in the air instead, and clutched his side. Holding the spear in place and groaning, he stumbled upward until he was close enough for Roo to lean in. "Walk," he said.

The guard shook his head, so Roo stepped behind him and pushed him forward by gently tweaking the spearpoint to repeat the request. The guard jerked forward toward Kit's room while Roo wound the spear line around his arms to bind him.

Blood dripped on the ground as they moved forward.

Enough that Roo knew the guard wouldn't be standing upright for much longer. He prodded the man forward. "Faster."

In front of the closed door, Roo pulled the duffel bag further open, his bloody hands shaking. Another spear, another reload. He pulled on a gas mask and reshouldered the duffel bag. He yanked out tear gas grenades from the bag now under his arm, pulled the pins, and then shoved the guard up to the door.

"Knock and enter," he hissed. "Now." He twisted the spear again, and the reluctant, bleeding man obeyed.

The door creaked open, and Roo kicked the guard forward while tossing the tear gas grenades in past him.

A stream of nasty swearing in Russian and Hungarian filled the room as two men scattered from the spitting tear gas like startled cockroaches.

Roo shot the nearest one in the stomach with the speargun, the twang of the released cable filling the room. The other man Roo hit with the duffel bag, the weight of the guns and ammo inside cracking him hard in the head and knocking him onto the large queen bed in the center of the room.

He pulled the bloody shark knife free of the bag and crawled up onto the bed. He was breathing heavily in the gas mask, struggling to pull air into his lungs.

The other man, reddened eyes streaming with tears, blinked as Roo crawled onto the bed. For a moment he managed to get a hold on Roo and pawed for the gas mask.

A moment passed. One that stretched as they strained and grunted at each other.

But Roo'd had some training at the dojo with bigger,

stronger instructors. He wormed his way out and buried the shark knife deep into the man's neck.

He lay for a second, panting, staring at the white speckled ceiling and the unmoving fan.

Not a single shot, he thought dizzily.

The first man he'd speared as he entered the room crawled around, trying blindly to find his gun. Kit held it now, aiming it in his general direction as she squeezed her bloodshot eyes shut in pain and tried to wipe tears off with a shoulder.

Quick thinker.

Roo jumped up, crossed to the door, and pulled the big guard inside. Then he grabbed the duffel bag, Kit's elbow, and pulled her in the bathroom.

"Keep looking up." He tilted her chin and used a bottle of liquid antacid to flush her eyes out. She thrashed for a bit, unused to the sensation of the chalky liquid.

He handed her a gas mask and an emergency scuba bottle.

"Hopefully we have some time before all that blood outside is noticed," he said. "But why don't you get your things together, take them down to the car. Catch your breath. I'll be down after I have a quick chat with the man still crawling around on the floor."

Roo pulled a desk chair over to the tied up, bleeding man with a spear still in his stomach. He leaned close, so that the man could hear him through the gas mask.

"When I was just so," Roo held his hand up off the floor to indicate the height of a young boy. "I worked for this dealer named Vincent. Tough yardboy, sent from Kingston to make sure we did it all just right. He told me once, you kill someone's blood, then you might as well kill them, too. Because there's no way to settle that, no way to work past it."

There was no response. Roo picked up the bloody dive knife he'd used earlier and began to cut the man's shirt off to look at the tattoos underneath, poking at the swastika.

"This don't exactly make you the most sympathetic person," he said. "Seems like a favor to the rest of the world to get rid of you."

That got a response. "Fuck you!" The man spat at him. The spittle ran off the water-repellent glass of the gas mask almost instantly.

"Whatever you wanted," Roo said. "You wanted it from me. Why did you drag my nephew into it?"

The man shrugged, then grimaced as the motion caused the spear in his gut to shift slightly. But he bore the pain like a soldier being interrogated, with some hint of pride that went along with the defiance. "We were looking for a black man with a data chip," he said in a thick English accent. "A black man showed up, we shot him. He didn't have the data chip."

Simple as that. Roo's eyes were wet, and it wasn't from what little teargas had leaked around the edges of his mask.

He sat back and stared at the Golden Dawn tattoos, the swastikas, the double lightning strikes. Hungarian fascist bullshit. The man was a walking billboard for failed twentieth-century fascism. An easy-to-use foot soldier.

"Who wants that chip?" Roo asked.

"Fuck you," the man said, in such a way that they both

knew he wasn't going to give that up easily. His eyes dared Roo to do something nasty and horrible. "Do your worst."

"I'm not fucking CIA. I already shot you, not going to torture you. Seen enough of that in my life. But you killed an innocent. A civilian," Roo said. "My nephew. There is a price for that."

"His death is just a taste of what comes in the war," the neo-Nazi hissed. "The clash of civilizations is coming. The rising tide is here."

Roo sighed. Well, there was another hurricane coming, he thought. That was about the only tide coming anytime soon.

He got up and rifled through the pockets of the dead men on the floor and found a passport. Thumbing through, he looked at the last date stamp on the paper. Thank goodness for old, paper-oriented passport systems and tourist nostalgia for having a stamp in their passport to memorialize their travels.

The Aves Island CARICOM non-exclusive trade zone was the last place the man had been. "You can't know where you going, if you don't know where you're coming from," Roo said.

"What?"

Roo held up the passport. "A week on Aves Island before coming here, when you could have come straight from . . ." He flipped through. "Budapest. What were you doing on Aves?"

"Fuck you."

So. Something interesting.

"It took me four hours to scrub all my nephew's blood off

the cockpit floor where you killed him," Roo told his captive. "I had a lot of time to do a lot of thinking. Thinking about what I would do next. And I've decided this: you and your men here, they killed Delroy. But it didn't start with you. Someone else further up the food chain did that. So I'm going to kill you, and then start working my way up to find out who caused this. And then I'm going to kill them, too."

Kit waited for him in the car. He handed her a small baggie with a phone sealed inside. She looked at the flesh-shaped bulge at the bottom. "Is that an index finger?"

"I want to find out who they really were. The passports were fake, though helpful."

He put the duffel bag in the back. He used one of the hotel towels to clean blood off the spear he'd pulled free of the last man.

"Spear fishing?" an older man in a maintenance uniform asked.

Roo looked up. Nodded.

"Catch anything big?"

"Not big enough to keep," Roo said.

"Better luck next time."

He got in, shut the door, and sat for a moment with his hands on the wheel. There was blood in the crevices between his cuticles.

"Did you kill the last one?" Kit asked quietly.

Roo shook his head slowly. "No. Pulled the spear out the back and let him scream a bit, but no." Killing someone tied up in front of him . . . he couldn't do that. Not even in the middle of all that white-hot rage.

"So . . ."

"Left him holding a sheet to his stomach wound. The harder he presses, the slower he'll bleed out," Roo said. "Figure the cops'll roll up on him soon. Even if you and I disappear following this lead, we'll leave a fairly obvious path for anyone behind us to follow."

He crept the car forward and put the gaudy condos and hotel block of Frenchman's Reef in his rearview mirror.

14

The blue articulated crane, a two-story-tall spider of a contraption that glinted here and there in the midnight dark, gently lowered the *Spitfire* into the water with its padded metallic claws as Roo stood on the bow. Once in the water and settled, Roo tied them off to the concrete walls, then clambered out onto the dock.

Tinker climbed out of the cab of the crane and smiled when Roo handed him a thick brick of paper money. "Fuck me," he said, flipping at the ends of it absently. And then he realized how much Roo had just handed him. Once more, with a mild awe in his voice, he repeated, "Fuck. Me."

"That should get your engines up and running," Roo said. "Maybe see you down south some time?"

"This is too much," Tinker said, his beard blowing in the wind.

"Hide it good," Roo said. "If they figure out you helped me they'll hassle you for serious."

Tinker shrugged. "Weren't here. Saw nothing. Boatyard's gonna be pissed I hot-wired their crane, though. It was a quick, dirty thing. Good thing it's electric, not some damn engine. Start an older one up everyone for miles would have known what we were up to." And it had still been loud enough as it was, making Roo nervous about getting caught.

"I left an envelope of cash in their mailbox," Roo said. "They're taken care of."

Tinker slipped the cash into a pocket in his dirty overalls, and frowned. "You gonna be okay, Roo?" He glanced at the *Spitfire*'s cabin. Wondering, no doubt, who Kit was. "The memorial . . ."

"Good-bye, Tinker. See you down south, some day. Okay?"

Tinker nodded, and grabbed Roo's forearm in an awkward shake. "Some day," he grunted.

Roo watched him amble out of the yard, a ball cap pulled firmly down over his face.

"Will he be okay?" Kit asked softly. Roo knew what she was asking. A camera, somewhere, would tag him. He would get questioned. But Tinker knew that.

"Cash will keep him out of trouble," Roo said. And let him mess around with his boat for another year.

He'd never end up down south, Roo knew. He'd buy some other half-working contraption. Come up with some other crazy dream that he would get to half work and half spectacularly fail. He'd grumble about it to anyone who'd listen at the Sand Dollar.

And be one of the more content men Roo had known.

The wind kicked up a bit. Hurricane Njema was making its presence felt. Still a little over a day away.

After a half hour of checking the bilges and the hull patches, Roo untied them and motored out from the docks, using the heads-up display on his cockpit windows to navigate them through the deep black, cloudy midnight. Ghostly green charts plotted his blind course out to sea. The blinking lights of harbor navigation buoys were highlighted by the heads-up display.

"You still have a chance to get in the dinghy and go back," Roo told Kit. "You sure you want to run a hurricane at sea? Njema is turning this way. I'll head south for Aves Island, but Njema might turn and follow us."

"Roo, I'm in this to find the people who killed someone I loved dearly. If you think that means we sail to Aves, we sail to Aves."

She'd hardened a bit since the hotel. Her jaw still set in determination, her eyes a bit weary. It was always like that, Roo thought, after action.

In the formal days, he had to give up his weapon and spend time coming down. The CIG would put him up somewhere quiet and give him a therapy program to talk to for a few weeks. Get his head sorted out. Because taking a life was never an easy thing.

Except this time it had been almost too easy.

He thought about the killing as the moon broke the clouds

and the dark silhouettes of island hills filled in around him as his eyes eagerly adjusted to the light.

No, shooting each of those fuckers who'd been waiting for Kit had been easy. No harder than shooting a fish. Because they'd killed Delroy. And nothing could make him feel guilty about bringing Delroy justice. Maybe his mind would sort it out differently later on. But there was a reason vengeance was a basic human emotion. It was real. It was understandable.

That visceral identification didn't come with some of the other things he'd been asked to do, long ago. Or even the things he'd done when younger, before the CIG had put him to work.

It felt more like self-defense. Bloody, horrible, but with no doubt in his mind that it was the right course.

He would pay. He knew the shakes would come at some point.

But the torturous second-guessing, the existential fear of creeping evil. Not this time, he thought, gunning the engines. He was charting the right course.

"Okay," he said to her. "Okay."

Roo didn't put up the sails for almost an hour, not wanting to be seen from shore. He spent that hour watching the charge on the ship's batteries drop until he was uncomfortable, then rolled everything out.

The strong winds yanked at the sails. The mast shivered, and then the *Spitfire* surged forward happily.

This was better than trying to fly to Aves, or taking a ferry. They would have been flagged and arrested. The cops wouldn't assume Roo would ship out the day before a hurricane made landfall. Too stupid.

Very stupid.

He leaned back out of the cockpit's roof to look up through a clear plastic window at the mainsail overhead. It bellied out a little, but was fairly taut. The familiar creaks of stays, the hull shifting, and the waves slapping the hull made him smile briefly.

And then the smile faded due to guilt at the happiness and familiarity of being at sea.

Kit had left him alone for all the prep and casting off. But now she moved to stand next to him. "You going to sail us all the way to Aves by yourself, or do you want me take a turn?"

"A watch," Roo said automatically. "It's called a watch."

She folded her arms. "Do you want me to take a watch?"

Did he want to go down to his cabin and sleep with her wandering around the *Spitfire*?

Why not? If she was after the data, it was hanging from his neck with her none the wiser. As long as he slept with a gun in his hand and the door locked, he should be safe.

A younger Roo would have just slammed some methamphetamines and done the whole trip wired. But he wanted to show up to Aves rested and ready.

So Roo hopped down from the captain's chair. He started to show her the basics, the sheets for the roller furling and the mechanized windlasses. She nodded patiently, slipped into the plastic chair, and then trimmed the mainsail slightly, adjusted the jib.

The *Spitfire,* ever so slightly, sped up a quarter of a knot according to the heads-up display.

Roo stopped patronizing her. "You've sailed before," he muttered.

"In the Keys," she said.

Respect. She didn't give him grief for assuming otherwise, but he should have asked first. She disconnected the autopilot and steered with her feet on the stainless-steel wheel rather than her hands, settling her back against the chair with a satisfied grunt that Roo knew well.

He gave her a brief overview of the nav software. "Do you want some coffee?"

"God. Please," she said.

It felt strange to go downstairs leaving a stranger sailing his boat out in the inky black seas. But she had a good hand.

He came back to find that she'd created a personalized account on the nav software and rearranged the heads-up displays on the cockpit windows to suit herself. "Thanks," she said, taking the steaming, bitter mug he handed her.

She'd called up a satellite picture of Njema and for a moment they both stared at the concentrated swirl of cloudy energy. The barest of its edges, a single wisp, seemed to be reaching out for a small dot on the map. She pointed at it. "What's that?"

"Anegada," Roo said. "Where I grew up."

"Small island," Kit said.

"Underwater island," Roo replied. "They leave the name up on the map out of habit. And because the big ships still get stuck on it sometimes." The rest of the Virgin Islands were mountains thrust out of the ocean. They curved, the weathered and eroded edges of an ancient volcanic rim. Anegada was a reef, though. With some sand on top. Some coconut trees and brush. By the time Roo was a kid, most of the houses left on it were on stilts, and tourists came to visit a "Caribbean Venice."

By his teenage years, it was a Caribbean Atlantis. One of many islands all over the world lost to the rising oceans.

"Oh," Kit said. "I'm sorry."

Roo shrugged. Old history. "It's not too different from Aves."

"What do you think we'll find there?"

"Trouble. It's Aves Island. It's always fucking trouble," Roo growled.

There was a second curve of Caribbean Islands farther west of the islands everyone could see on the map; an underwater chain of mountains that didn't quite reach the surface. If you looked at a topographical map of the world under the Caribbean Sea you could see the peaks and valleys lurking in the blue depths.

Less than a couple hundred miles south of Puerto Rico, and a hundred and fifty miles west of Dominica, one tiny tip of this chain breached the surface of the Caribbean Ocean just ever so slightly.

That was Aves Island. Decades ago, little more than a small spit of sand in the middle of the north basin of the inner Caribbean Sea. For much of the twentieth century, Venezuela effectively claimed it for themselves. An interesting claim, as Venezuela lay more or less four hundred miles to the south in South America. Claiming Aves, however, extended Venezuela's international maritime borders absurdly far north and allowed it to bring most of the Caribbean Sea within the dotted line. To further cement the claim, Venezuela built stilted structures on Aves to garrison soldiers and paid several families to live on the island.

Dominica had protested in the past. World law claimed that nations owned areas out to within two hundred miles of their borders, and Aves fell into the borders of Dominica. But what was Dominica? A small independent Caribbean nation of a hundred thousand.

Venezuela, a medium-sized South American state with a standing navy, a large military, and its own air force, could squat on the island. The long-standing disputes over who owned Aves that went back to colonial times were settled by their presence, and Dominican politicians had kept the peace by affirming Venezeula's right to own Aves.

So Venezuela hunkered down there, because the inner Caribbean Sea held a wealth of oil resources in the deeps, much of it becoming more attractive as other wells throughout the world dried up. And the benefit of drilling in the Caribbean was not having to dodge the occasional iceberg like one had to do in the mostly melted, but still often dangerous Arctic seas.

During the Caracas riots several politicians in CARICOM with ties to international energy companies saw an opportunity: take Aves, and they would regain the Caribbean Sea and the wealth underneath it.

Like the European Union, Caribbean Islands had been slowly opening up economically at the turn of the century, creating common passports for travel, and even creating shared currencies over the decades. But it was Aves Island that created the modern pan-Caribbean state.

It began with lawsuits in the world courts from Dominica against Venezuela. With their leadership tied up in the riots, the maneuver went ignored. At the same time, the Caribbean media went on the offensive, decrying the stealing of Caribbean wealth by the South American country.

The second stage happened with the secret backing of French and U.S. intelligence agencies looking to blunt Chinese and Venezuelan cooperation and control of the Caribbean basin: a small CARICOM Force Squad used a captured narco-submarine to land on Aves Island in the middle of the night.

They overpowered the Venezuelan forces, deported the handful of civilians, and "returned" the island to Dominica.

Venezuela mobilized half its air force and most of its navy: ten smaller ships and a troop carrier. But the rest of the army remained busy at home. The re-invasion failed as ad-hoc Caribbean intelligence networks tracked the attacks and flew single-use drones into Venezuelan planes to neuter their air force.

Then, halfway to Aves Island, four hundred toy planes flew into the Venezuelan naval fleet. Each one equipped with IEDs or homemade napalm, they sank the troop carrier after a whole day of radio-controlled toy drone kamikaze attacks launched from St. Lucia by expatriate controllers linking in via satellite from all over the world.

When the Venezuelan Navy turned back, they rendezvoused off of the coast of Grenada. The implicit threat to Trinidad and Tobago, Barbados, and Grenada created even more national Caribbean solidarity. In three days, the generation's long experiment of trying to bind the dozens of major islands together into a larger identity had been cemented by the Southern threat.

When Caribbean Sea deep oil rigs appeared, the oil royalties were set up similarly to the North Sea Norwegian and Alaskan methods. Half the money went directly to citizens as cash payouts. A bid to avoid direct corruption.

The other half went to governments, many of which began to use the money for infrastructure.

And the Caribbean Community, now suddenly of serious interest to the larger world, began to invest in military and intelligence. Beefing up Aves Island. Building a drone air force that could reach into Venezuela. Building the Caribbean Navy's automated fast-attack hydrofoil gunships.

Aves, not forgotten, grew. At first a large garrison to protect it. Then the floating airport to house the larger drones. And the people to feed and house them. Then came the stilt homes for living. And boardwalks. And floating gardens to feed them. The docks. An economy. Oil development money.

A CARICOM free trade zone, it became a port of call for docks and ships traveling through the Caribbean. A beacon of Caribbean strength.

A powder keg, because it was the fulcrum on which so much depended.

"Something fucked up is always going down on Aves," Roo said to Kit, looking out at the dark, windy seas.

15

A phone buzzed.

For a split second Roo couldn't tell where he was. He was alone in the dark, the world shifting and tilting around him.

Sleep had struck him hard, and not stayed nearly long enough.

He blinked. The *Spitfire* heaved, shuddered down a wave, and struck the trough. Things clattered and fell, bouncing off shelves or knocking around inside cupboards.

The phone buzzed again. Rattling away against varnished wooden rails where it had fetched up.

Roo still clutched the gun in his hand. He faced the door to his locked cabin.

With a deep breath he grabbed the phone. "Yeah?"

Jacinta answered. "It's getting full shit here, man. Already flooding coming up over Yacht Haven and into the streets through the barriers. How's Njema treating you?"

Roo unlocked the door and peeked out a larger porthole in the corridor. They were riding fifteen-foot swells. Which explained the beating he'd gotten while sleeping. He'd been tossed all around his bed. He checked the wall clock. Almost time to relieve Kit from sailing.

Kit and he'd taken turns sailing all night, and now for most of the dark, stormy day. He'd let her take a spare room in the starboard hull for when she was off her watch.

With the waves crashing hard against the side of the ship, they had started zigzagging their way toward Aves so they could either sail into or with the swells. If they let the waves come at their sides they would flip the catamaran. Which meant it was going to take longer than he wanted to get to Aves.

"It's okay," Roo mumbled, bracing himself against the wall with one hand to keep wedged in place. It was disconcerting to feel the catamaran rocking from side to side, as it was usually so stable. But they were sailing south. The wind and waves coming from the east were large enough to rock the catamaran, though already clocking slightly more northish as trailing arms of the hurricane would be reaching them. That's why it was still dark out. The sun was lost to them, the sky covered in ominous clouds as if the apocalypse had begun.

"Police scanner says your boat's up and gone," Jacinta said. "Where you holing up?"

"I'm not," Roo said.

"You at sea?" Jacinta was shocked. "Where you headed?"

"Jacinta . . ." Roo said, rubbing his eyes. "You have something for me or not?"

"You never sent over the heavy metal you promised," she said. "You know how I feel about broken promises, Roo."

Shit.

Roo put his back to a wall and used a leg to steady himself. "Delroy's dead."

"I know," Jacinta said. "I'm sorry."

"I had to go after them," Roo said.

"With a speargun?"

"Delroy's dead." Roo repeated that flatly.

"I'm not a corporation," Jacinta said. "You don't get billed by me for my services. You either pay me, or you don't. I didn't demand it up front because . . . you know."

"Then I will either owe you a favor, or pay you the heavy metal when I'm next in town. You need the favor before I can pay you, I'll settle up," Roo said, knowing damn well he was going to pay her before she could call it in.

He could almost hear the predatory smile on the other side. "I know who your little *mamacita* is." She was vamping a bit, now, enjoying the moment of holding something over him.

Roo looked down at the gun in his right hand and rubbed the flat space around the safety thoughtfully. What, he wondered, was going to happen next?

He suddenly realized he wanted to hang up. Not to find out.

Somewhere, something deep inside him wanted to believe

that Kit was Zee's sister, hidden away in Florida all this time. A secret that Zee had managed to keep.

"She's French," Jacinta said. And Roo let out a puff of sad air. "A DGSE agent stationed out of Guadeloupe and Martinique. Popped up a few times in French Guyana. She trained in the Thirteenth Parachute Dragoons, so . . . don't get any ideas, Roo. She'll probably kick your ass. And she's most definitely not Zee's sister, or related to Zee in any way. Her name is Katrina Prideaux."

"Thank you, Jacinta," Roo said.

"Roo," Jacinta's voice softened, "I went to the memorial service this morning. Before it got too bad. . . ."

Roo ended the call quickly.

Gun in hand, he walked up the steps and into the main cabin, then out into the spray-filled cockpit. Katrina sat in the captain's chair, a rope serving as a quick and dirty seat belt.

They were moving with the waves: surfing down them a little as they caught up to the boat, then the bows pitching up as the swells swept on by. Katrina was no longer using her feet to steer, now. Her back muscles strained to hang on to the wheel under a seawater-soaked blouse. She'd pulled her hair back into a ponytail, and was shivering.

Salt crusted everything. Water droplets beaded every surface in the cockpit, including the waterproof heads-up display windows.

"*Bonjour* Katrina Prideaux," Roo shouted. "*Je suis très heureux de faire votre connaissance.*"

The *Spitfire* slid down the back of a wave. The next towered ten feet over the cockpit behind them. In the trough it felt like the entire world was suddenly glassy oceanic gray and full of spray. The wave threatened to envelop them. The cockpit, with windows on the front and the main cabin in front of it, was completely open to the rear. Any waves coming from behind the catamaran would dash themselves right against anyone standing in it. But the slope of this wave caught the stern first. *Spitfire* rose with the giant wave. The deck pitched down as they began to rise and move with the wave, instead of it dashing against them.

There was a rhythm to it. A wet, dangerous, constant, exhausting rhythm.

Kit set the autopilot, tapping on the salt-encrusted glass of the cockpit window. "I didn't know you could speak French," she said. In English, but an English without the flat Midwestern accent she'd been adopting earlier. Now her own slight French accent replaced it.

Without her hand at the wheel, the autopilot struggled to smoothly handle the massive swells on its own. The rudders kicked, following digital instructions that were not as instinctual as a human hand.

"Delroy and I had plans to visit Guadeloupe," Roo said. "I was taking lessons."

Kit pointed at the gun held loosely by his thigh. "Do you need the gun?" she asked.

Roo looked down at it, then back up at her, still tied tight into the chair. "Probably not," he said.

Kit untied the rope. "You knew I was lying, a long time ago. I'm fairly sure of that," she said calmly. She held on tight to a handrail and stepped closer to him. "And you haven't felt

I was a threat. Now that you know who I am, do you think it's all changed somehow?"

Roo flicked the safety back on, but didn't say anything.

She stepped closer. "You let me on this boat because, deep down, you think I might be able to help you. You have good instincts, Roo. Listen to them. Let me help you."

He looked at another massive wave dominating the horizon behind the catamaran.

This was all such a bad idea. But then, he always went for hooking into people. Whether virtually or in real life, it was about following the chain of people.

Kit was another link.

"So you're DGSE?" he asked.

"Yeah." The wave struck, and the back of the ship dipped below the surface of this one instead of rising with it. A steeper wave, it gently grabbed the back of the ship. A foot of water suddenly rose up to boil around Roo's knees. Kit's eyes flickered with a moment of panic as she gripped the nearby rail with both hands.

After the wave passed by and the *Spitfire* pulled free of the fingers of ocean water, as the scuppers hissed and gushed leftover water over the side, Roo looked at the soaking wet French agent in front of him.

"How much further were you going to take all this?" he asked her.

"My orders were to pretend to be Zee's sister to see if we could find out what your part in all this was, and why he reached out to you. But then I ended up in the middle of a running gun battle within minutes of meeting you. Everything since then has been me making it up. It's been a mess. I'm hoping we can still find a way to work together."

She hung tight as another wave struck. The autopilot systems were coping remarkably well.

"You stayed with me," Roo said. "But how do we get past suspicion and toward trust when you never told me who you were that whole time?"

"You and I," Kit said, "have to start all over again. I understand that. I broke your trust. But you knew something was wrong with me and kept me close. So just trust that. Let's see if we can build on that."

They braced and let another wave sweep through the cockpit.

Kit started shivering. Even in the Caribbean, the water was just a few degrees colder in the storm. Enough to start sucking away your body heat.

"Roo. This storm . . ." she said. "We're in trouble, aren't we?"

He could see what she was thinking. A man in grief, taking to the sea. She'd been caught up in the moment and running away toward some solution. Now she was wondering if he was out here to push the edge, maybe nearly commit suicide by storm. She was wondering if he'd dragged her down with him.

And maybe, somewhere deep inside of him, in a place he wasn't going to look too carefully, it was true. If they died out here, he'd take his revenge and grief down in pieces to the lightless abyssal mud thousands of feet below them.

Where it truly belonged.

This was why, whenever he killed someone in the field,

they took the gun and sent him to a beach for a few weeks, he thought. Meeting the therapists. Getting your head straight.

Roo cracked open the cockpit locker. "I should have shown this to you," he shouted. "I'm not thinking straight."

He pulled out Delroy's survival suit. That's why he'd been avoiding getting the equipment out. Avoiding one last thing of Delroy's because he couldn't face seeing it. And because of that, all the while he put her at risk of getting swept off and dying.

Shit.

They weren't in the worst of the hurricane. It was just a bad storm right now. But that was still no excuse. The swells were tall, the wind strong, and the cockpit awash with water. And it would be getting a little worse, though Roo felt they could weather it just fine.

"A survival suit," he said. And gave her the same exact rundown he always gave Delroy as he helped her suit up. "It's the closest thing you'll ever wear to a spacesuit. It gets bad enough, just zip up, jump off, and leave me. You'll get picked up once the worst of it all blows past. Understand?"

Kit nodded. No recrimination in her eyes, but a strong look of relief. Roo got suited up as well, tucking the gun away deep within one of the many inner pockets.

It was time to get his head in the game. He strapped himself into the captain's chair and motioned Kit over. "What were you hoping to find? What happened to Zee? Why are the French all up in this?"

Kit staggered over and shoved her back against the cabin so she could face him and keep herself secure. Roo offered her a harness clip, and she snapped on. Even if a wave knocked her clear off the boat she could pull herself back aboard.

If she chose.

"For the past few years I've been assigned to a team specializing in genetic terrorism," Kit said. "Two months ago in Bordeaux two families died of a particularly virulent hemorrhagic fever."

"Like Ebola?" Roo asked. He imagined people dying, blood leaking out of their orifices. People in masks and cleansuits standing around.

Dying like that was horrific. And not something you associated with Bordeaux, France. But the superflu that hit ten years ago caused redesigns of major airports to include medical testing facilities and quarantine hospitals. Bugs could travel anywhere within a half day.

"Ebola would have made sense in a larger city. Still, people travel, Bordeaux is easy to get to by rail from Paris and an international flight. But these families hadn't traveled anywhere. They were immigrants, but long since settled in their routine. The house was in the country, a retreat with a fully stocked automatic bar. It was supposed to be a rare, much needed, quiet vacation for them. They had the place stocked with groceries ahead of time, planning to stay in and cook for themselves. They were infected on a Friday evening, by Sunday leaking blood from around their eyeballs and barely strong enough to call for help. An emergency quarantine of the whole town locked the situation down."

Roo shook his head. "You think it was a test run of some kind?"

"Yes. A minor test. A taste of things to come. It was a strain of the Marburg virus, originally discovered in Eastern Europe and cultivated by the Russians last century."

"There are European hemorrhagic fevers?"

"Eastern Europe. It's very old, and the vector was likely African monkeys. But yes. We've always been haunted by them. No one's been comfortable that the Russians canned it and kept it alive. But then, the E.U. and U.S. keep some very nasty viruses alive as well."

That was the sort of apocalyptic, mutually assured destruction sort of thing that appealed to paranoid, large nationalistic militaries. Last solution bullshit. And, Roo thought, whenever something like that was left around, someone would decide to use it for something. "That's what killed the two families in Bordeaux?"

"There was MARV-like code in the DNA. First we thought it was just that. But the more we sequenced and poked around the more worried we got, because we found elements of an aerosolized Venezuelan hemorrhagic fever grafted in. Had we not assumed the worst and quarantined the area, it may have spread via emergency support personnel. DGSE treats it as an unknown bioterrorist attack."

"But I haven't heard about it," Roo said.

"We kept a lid on it and declared it Ebola," Kit said. "No one claimed the attack, so we refused to give them the satisfaction of terrorizing anyone. But Roo, it's important we catch these people. If they release it in a big city anywhere . . . hemorrhagic fever is bad enough. But if all it takes is a sneeze to spread it, it will spread like a flu. But one where you vomit blood. That has a fifty percent mortality rate. That's Black Death all over again. Worse."

"Is that how Zee died?" Roo asked reluctantly.

Kit looked down. "The same virus. DGSE shared information with all the agencies about the attack. CIA found Zee dead in Miami. He'd taped all the ducts and air gaps in a hotel room shut with garbage bags and tape. He called you. Then he called the CDC and told them he was dying of an aerosolized Marburg virus and to treat the hotel he was in as a biohazard. He died halfway through the call."

"Without telling you who did it to him," Roo said, puzzled.

"He wasn't sure," Kit said. "That's what I'm here to find out."

Roo took a deep breath. Then he pulled the tree frog necklace off and handed it to her. She looked down at it. She could tell it was something important. "That's what Zee left me," Roo said, tightly. "Go down, stay dry, see what you can figure out. I'll sail."

Kit's eyes were wide. "Thank you, Roo."

He shut the cabin doors behind her and zipped his survival suit up tight against the increasingly large waves and stinging wind.

The autopilot was struggling. It was too dangerous to run with the waves, now. He was going to have to turn them around to face the waves so that they could break over the ship's bows. And he'd have to turn the catamaran quickly, without tipping them over. He would spend the rest of the night staring Njema down, eye to eye. Let the violence sweep right past him, through him, or wait until it headed north again.

Roo clipped in and glanced back at the towering swells. The wind whipped spray off their tips, creating a violent storm of white that filled the air above the dark green gaps of the ocean.

He spun the wheel and triggered a command to reef the sails further.

16

Somewhere around midnight the tip of Njema's southernmost spiral passed them by. The winds shifted, and while the swells remained building-sized, their slopes were gentle and predictable.

While pointed into the wind, Roo's reefed sails hadn't done much to propel them forward in any way. They'd just kept him pointed into the howling wind. So each battering wave had shoved the *Spitfire* backward. Time and time again. The GPS plot showed they'd continued to move south all through the night. A good forty miles.

At three in the morning, Roo'd felt comfortable turning them southwest toward Aves and letting out some sail. By five he was letting the autopilot take control again.

At sunrise Roo washed his face with some freshwater via a

deck hose in the corner of the cockpit, scrubbing away caked-on salt and letting the cold water shock him.

There was a danger in sailing. The ocean looked infinite from the cockpit. The horizon hundreds of miles away. But the truth was that you were only actually seeing a few miles in any direction. With radar, a camera at the tip of the mast sweeping for objects, and modern collision alarms plugged into a distributed navigation system, the chance of stumbling over something was small.

But you still needed to stay alert. For other small craft. For something floating in the water.

Yes, you could let your eyes sink closed for a few minutes. And open them to find something large coming over the horizon. No alarms because the software was glitched.

Container ships couldn't swerve to avoid you, even if they wished they could.

So after washing his face Roo got back into the chair and kept on for Aves, leaving Kit downstairs.

By the afternoon the sunlight glinted off the waves and the rhythm of the swells changed. They weren't in the deep ocean anymore; the depth finder was able to find the bottom underneath them.

The first hint of Aves were the tops of the office buildings. Communications equipment and whip antennas appeared, as if floating on the ocean surface. A distant helipad rose from the horizon.

As they got closer, the glinting metal windows of the main cluster of high-rises loomed over a tiny spit of sand.

Roo made a phone call. "Hey, Elvin! It's Roo."

A moment on the other side. "Prudence?"

Roo made a face. He wasn't sure if Elvin had refused to use his nickname to keep needling him, or just out of a strange sense of formality. He'd last sat on the deck of the *Spitfire* with Elvin a few years back when he'd sailed around St. Vincent a bit. Helped Elvin fix a broken 3-D printer.

He kept in touch because Elvin worked private security gigs up and down the islands. The kind of person you wanted to know, because Elvin knew who was up to what in terms of larger corporations. It was an old habit, because Roo wasn't in the game anymore. But he couldn't help himself when it came to collecting contacts like Elvin.

And now . . . it came in handy.

"Been a while," Roo said. "But I need to ask you a favor. I'm coming into Aves. Need your help feeling my way around."

As he talked to Elvin about what Elvin had been up to since they'd last seen each other in general terms, the expanding lower mass of Aves filled out. A horizontal blotch of a city on stilts, surrounded by more sturdy platforms rising out of the sea on rusted, rotund legs. Some of them oil platforms, moved to create more open space where the sand no longer existed. But later, the floating piers and homes systems had been added to Aves that were commonly found in more and more coastal cities throughout the world.

No one on Aves ever planned to try and keep the roaring seas back. It was a futile gesture. Instead they used the tip of the island peeking up from its submarine mountain range as a base to bolt everything to.

Even the sand around Aves's pylons was a fiction. The

original Aves Island had long since been swallowed by rising seas. The sand had been imported to continue the fiction that Aves Island was still a *thing*. A physical spit of *something* that people could continue to threaten a war over, countersue about in courts, and generally get upset about or use.

Twenty thousand people lived out here, naked to the ocean's power, clinging on stilts to what lay underneath.

"So, you need a favor?" Elvin asked. He didn't know much about Roo. Roo figured he suspected Roo worked Caribbean Intelligence, though that hadn't been true since he'd left the Arctic. But the impression meant that Elvin wouldn't turn him down.

"You willing to let me buy you a meal?" Roo asked.

"I'll send you the location," Elvin said. "Let me know when you feet hit ground."

Roo saw several ships thrown up onto the floating docks and barges around the outer ring of Aves now. Many more shattered and half afloat inside the hundreds of thick stilts.

A beautiful house leaned dangerously over, its legs half knocked out from underneath. Some of the roads between the apartment complexes and barges had collapsed.

But Aves was already buzzing with activity. Large oil tankers were docked near the industrial section, vomiting their liquid black gold into barges that would be using it to spit out plastics that could be airlifted by low-cost blimp throughout the Caribbean basin. A hydrofoil ferry from somewhere down island was docked on the main floating dock, people in bright white shirts walking up a steep ramp to get into the main thoroughfares of Aves, high off the water and safe.

Aves was less a tourist attraction, more of a manufacturing and industrial park. The sort of metallic carbuncle of density and frenetic human energy created by trade, oil, and power. But like every Caribbean island, there was somewhere to dock and for sailors to gather. Roo eased them into a harbor created out of a large concrete floating barge that trailed docks behind like squid's tentacles.

Once secured, he checked on Kit. She was asleep in the spare cabin, her arms wrapped around one of Roo's old tablets, snoring softly. There was a big bruise on her forehead from a violent toss from sometime in the night.

He closed the door quietly.

Elvin had gained heft, the result of desk jobs and easy consulting gigs. But he wore the extra weight well, particularly in his sharp, shiny black Gucci suit, silver Oakley glasses, and vaguely cowboy-ish looking boots. His shaved scalp beaded with sweat as they met for a late lunch.

"This is a view to kill for," he said, sweeping gently between chairs and tired-looking business types hunched over mutual paperwork. The smooth movements seemed at odds with Elvin's frame, but he'd spent years working front lines before moving his way away from the action.

A dancer often kept their grace, an athlete a banked fire at their core.

Elvin picked out a table near the glass railing at the edge of the open-air restaurant. "We're getting good at this," he told Roo.

"What?"

"Recovery. Just this morning Aves is hit by a powerful hurricane, and by late afternoon, here we all are." He swept a hand around the business lunch crowd. "When I was kid, each storm would destroy everything. Billions of dollars lost, homes, people's lives. In some places, it's still a catastrophe. But Aves is built from the start assuming we'll get hit by several a year. The new normal."

The restaurant perched on a half side of an open floor area three quarters of the way up one of the handful of twenty-story core buildings clustered at the heart of Aves. A small botanical garden wafted the smell of fresh flowers at them. Birds of paradise, ginger, and lots of hibiscus. Thick plastic windows had rolled out from tracks to protect them from the storm, and had been rolled back into place afterward.

From here they looked out South over all of Aves.

And Elvin was right. Roo had seen the worst of the damage on his way in. In fact, that damage had been swept by the surge and sea under the city into its pilings. From up here, Aves was streets and buildings.

The core lower areas assumed flooding and battering seas. The pedestrian walkways and bikeways weaved in and out of carefully maintained greenspace. Most of the roofs had gardens and more greenspace, making Aves look like more of an island from above than it had from the gritty, rusty forest of pillars at sea level that Roo had seen as they approached.

Some of the island's walkways were at the same height as the top of *Spitfire*'s mast.

And already the cleanup of downed trees and solar shingles knocked loose was finishing up.

It was survival of the fittest, really. Buildings not able to handle the hurricane-force winds were not even allowed to be built. Add near-bulletproof glass in windows. And anyone building new construction out here demanded roofs with wingtips designed to shove them down harder onto their houses, rather than flip up and fly away into the wind.

Other designs had long since been swept away and given up on as useless for survival here in Hurricane Alley.

With Caribbean basin oil money, a lot of rebuilding for rising oceans had been done. Rebuilding that would have bankrupted the small Caribbean nations back when Roo was little.

"The green tower," Roo said, pointing out the newest, almost thirty-story spiral to the north.

"That's a Beauchamp vertical farm," Elvin said. "Beauchamp Holdings is all over Aves now. They're trying to wrangle their way into building another farm specializing in hard-to-grow fruits, and then supplying the nearby islands from here."

"They have one on St. Thomas," Roo said. Some islands had room for agriculture and markets fresh with produce. But lots of things had to be shipped in. Used to be everyone just shouldered the doubled cost of basic foodstuffs. The vertical farms dropped the price slightly and kept the food locally made.

Roo slid the passport he'd stolen across the table to Elvin once their drinks arrived. "You're working security for Aves now, right?"

Elvin flipped through the passport with a single hand and

sipped at an alarmingly yellow-colored Carib beer with the other. "Who's this?"

"The favor I was talking about. Delroy's dead. This was one of the crew that did it. They're Golden Dawn leftovers, or maybe just more generic general Eastern European neo-Nazi types. I'm not sure which. They passed through here. I'm hunting them down."

Elvin wiped his scalp with a napkin and then used his glasses to snap a photo of the passport for reference. He tapped the frames, then bobbed his head around as he navigated data only he could see.

"I'll pay," Roo said. "Gold. You work Aves Security. I need to know where your cameras have seen them, who they talked to on the island. Anything. They killed my nephew, Elvin. They killed Delroy."

Elvin put the napkin away in a pocket, and look at Roo over the rim of his glasses. "It's an ethics violation. The contract I have, I don't have no room for playing around."

Roo sat back and made a disgusted sound.

Elvin raised his hands. "Look, man. For real, the way you get around this is to get Interpol to call me. Or even Caribbean Intelligence . . ." He let that hang. "Go official."

"I'm hunting these fuckers down, Elvin," Roo said levelly. He couldn't play the CIG card. And now Elvin knew that. His position had just weakened.

"If you come causing trouble on Aves, it's not just me that'll be crawling down you throat. There is an actual CAR-ICOM garrison still on the island."

Roo leaned forward. "I have a French DGSE agent working with me," he said.

"Official?"

"Big enough player for you?" Roo asked. "Katrina Prideaux."

Elvin rubbed his temple and twitched his head. Searching. "DGSE. Here from Guadeloupe?"

"She came to St. Thomas to see me." Roo squinted. "Look, I won't lie, Elvin. I'm here for revenge. I'm following this chain, and I'm going to pull the house down around me to bring pain upon whoever did this. I don't expect it will be a good thing. I'll give you three years' income. If it blows up, you take a vacation and wait until it dies down and you can work again. If you manage to stay out of the mess I want to bring and don't get fired, keep the gold for retirement. Or whatever you want."

"Three years?" Elvin asked, looking around.

"Three."

Elvin sighed and pushed his glasses up. "Fuck it. I'll run facial recognition; see how well I can still manage old-school detective work. I'll come down to the docks to see you. Still the *Spitfire*?"

"Still *Spitfire*," Roo confirmed.

"I'll see what I can do."

17

Someone knocking on the side of the hull snapped Roo awake. He sat up, the net strung between the front section of the two hulls creaking as he got to his feet. Water lapped away underneath him, and the sun had been burning away at him. Or at least, it had.

Now it was gloomy dark outside. The sun nowhere to be found, just the last wisps of red and purple in the west.

"Prudence?"

It had been comfortable to lay there, soaking in the warmth and succumbing to a sleep deep enough he didn't keep surfacing to listen for something that wasn't ever going to come back to the *Spitfire*'s hull: the sound of Delroy's voice.

"Jones!"

Roo had a gun just by his hip. Fingers still tight around

the grip. He frowned at it, surprised he hadn't dropped it into the water when he fell asleep. He barely remembered getting it. But apparently he couldn't sleep without one in his hand now.

"Jones!"

Elvin stood on the end of the dock, even more sweaty than before. His nice shirt was blotched with wet stains. He fidgeted, moving from foot to foot, jaw clenched.

Roo moved across the webbing to the main cabin. "Come aboard."

Elvin hopped onto the side of the catamaran and over the railing. He followed Roo in and shut the door behind them.

When Roo set the gun on the galley counter, Elvin stared at it for a moment.

Roo opened the fridge and looked down. "Beer?" He was hungry, too.

"Oh good, you're up," Kit said, coming out of the port hull's corridor and climbing up into the main cabin with them. "I didn't want to bother you. You were very asleep, and very armed."

Elvin swiveled her way. "You're the DGSE agent?"

Kit shrugged, visibly annoyed. "Apparently." She grabbed one of the beers, wiped the condensation off on her shorts, and cracked it open.

Roo pulled out some cheeses from the back of the fridge: gouda, a sharp cheddar, some mild goat cheese. He looked at Elvin's reflection in the window over the galley as he quickly cut the bricks into slices and spread them out on a wooden platter. He also palmed a small wireless-spectrum sniffer as he did it, checking to see if Elvin was wearing a wire.

Nothing.

Roo slid a small panel open near the circuit breakers and flipped a solid switch. The whine of an interference generator let him know he'd dropped an invisible shield down over the cabin.

Elvin fidgeted with his beer and avoided Kit's openly curious stare.

When Roo set the cheese platter on the table between them, it was ignored by all parties.

"So . . ." Roo began.

Elvin jumped in. "I don't have the time, Roo, quit playing around."

Roo tipped his beer forward. "You're nervous, Elvin." And Roo wondered what that meant. He glanced outside the window and down the docks, but didn't see anyone there.

"Yes, I'm nervous," Elvin admitted. "Here's why."

He slid a palm-sized phone onto the table and pulled up video. "Backtracked and found you some Nazi bad boys, yeah?" Grainy black-and-white footage taken from some random pea-sized camera lying on one of the many surfaces of Aves showed Delroy's killers walking into the glass-walled lobby of one of the downtown skyscrapers.

Roo would have pulled up info about the skyscraper they were going inside, but he'd killed the connections in and out of the boat, so he looked at Elvin. "Where is that?"

"Beauchamp International Labs," Elvin said. Kit's jaw hardened, but she didn't say anything. Roo made a note of that.

"They make you nervous," Roo observed.

Elvin nodded. "Look, the Americans still are behind on

stem cell research, among other things they blocked and made law and are still struggling to undo. So a lot of American companies have set up research labs in the Caribbean and Mexico. They're close enough they can be easily inspected in person. And, Americans can fly down here for treatment. Medical tourism is a big deal. It's big money."

"Rich people make you nervous?" Kit asked.

"Stem cells aren't all the man has fingers in," Elvin said.

"What all is he in?" Roo asked.

Elvin looked at him with mild astonishment. "You know many legit enterprises that have neo-Nazis walking in the front door? You're the one sniffing after them. You fucking tell me!"

"What, you telling me you haven't heard any rumors?" Roo snorted. "You have nothing?"

"That man is more dangerous than most rich people," Elvin said. "Leave out Delroy, I seen people destroyed by him for fighting his projects to expand medical tourism here. More important people than me been broken. So, you need to cash me out. Because if he finds out I been snooping I am done. That man all but owns the island, Roo. Even worse, his ship ducked out for the hurricane. The man himself will be back on Aves soon, and I need to be gone by then, understand? I'm headed for the Pacific. I need to be leaving before his boat slides in here and docks for tonight's big post-hurricane party. So you're not just going to pay me, Roo. You gonna owe me big, okay?"

Roo leaned back and put down his empty beer bottle. "Yeah, all right."

He slid out of the settee and left them in the main cabin,

jogging down the stairs into the starboard hull. He glanced back, made sure they weren't watching, and dropped to his knees to pull open a bilge hatch. His bracelet snagged the edge of it, the carefully pleated paracord hanging up on a burr of fiberglass. Roo pulled it loose and made sure not to scrape his arm against the hatch's edge.

The interior of the bilge near the front of the hull had hoses running around for bilge pumps, but was dry. It gleamed white: Roo liked keeping it as clean as he could, as it helped him spot anything leaking.

Gray bars were stacked up against a pocket in a ridge. Weight that helped balance the catamaran and kept the hulls level for sailing.

Roo found a small canvas bag and put three of them in.

Elvin opened the bag and peered in when Roo dropped them on the settee table with a loud thunk and then a clink. He pulled one out and regarded it suspiciously, but Roo took it from him and peeled at the gray surface with a thumbnail.

After a few seconds the gray, rubberized paint peeled away to reveal the dull gleam of gold.

"*Ras,*" Elvin swore. "That's gold."

"Enough for the Pacific."

Elvin swore again and looked up at them both, words escaping him.

"Told you I look after you," Roo said.

Elvin slid the bar back in the canvas bag and petted it absently. "I gonna run," he said.

Roo watched him leap onto the dock and hustle away. Then he got up and shut off the interference generator.

"You have bars of gold in your ship," Kit said, slightly shocked. "Who does that?"

"I do," Roo said. "It was a gift."

"An incredible gift."

He started tapping on a spare screen near the galley. Beauchamp Labs. Construction. Aeroponic and vertical farm investments.

Roo stared at the image of the man he pulled up. A hawk-faced executive with a neutral expression and dark-blue suit. Shaved, balding head. Wiry. Did that face order the foot soldiers to come in and try to kill him? Or was he separated from it by a cadre of middle management who'd made the call?

Roo leaned against the galley counter and let out a long, deep breath. "I know you're DGSE," he said to Kit. "And I saw you react to the name of the company. It's a French name, so I'm guessing you had them as a suspect already. You're going to call this in. And you should. But before you do, I just ask you one favor."

Kit had been looking thoughtfully down at the table, not denying anything he'd said. She brushed her hair back and looked at him. "What is that?"

"Wait until tomorrow morning," Roo asked.

"And why," she asked, poking around at the cheese platter, "should I do that?"

Roo pointed at the screen over the galley. It showed video taken from the rooftop of Beauchamp Labs from a party thrown last summer. Rich men and women in tuxedos and shimmering cocktail dresses clumped around each other while attendants with silver trays and tiny hors d'oeuvres flitted in between.

"While most people are fixing hurricane damage or wondering how they'll handle being homeless, they'll be enjoying a rooftop party. I'm going to break into the labs."

"And find what?" Kit looked less than impressed.

"I'll bug it. I'll look around."

"Roo, how much experience do you have with infiltration?"

Roo picked up the platter and empty beer bottles. "Just give me a day, okay?"

"I can't go with you," Kit said.

"I didn't ask you to."

"This is a bad idea, Roo," she said softly. "A very bad idea. I have to leave."

Roo gripped the edge of the table and leaned forward. "They killed Delroy," he hissed. "They killed him."

"You need to keep your distance and gather evidence. When you go after him, it needs to be with people backing you up. In large force. Because this man is *dangerous*."

Roo threw the platter and bottle into the sink. The crash of broken glass was a release from the quivering feeling he had of energy building up everywhere inside him with nowhere to direct it. "There's no one behind me, Kit. There's just me. I'm all that's left. Surely you know the feeling?"

He looked back over his shoulder at her. She swallowed and looked away from him. Her voice cracked. "I know you're hurting, we're on the same mission, Roo. But you can't charge in there. Please believe me."

"And what has stepping softly around these people gotten

any of us?" Roo asked. "We're going to be careful, because, what? He is rich? Powerful? Has friends in high places? Because doing this can *hurt* us? I'm already hurt. I've already been broken."

"Roo . . ."

"I don't have time. I ran from St. Thomas, that will have repercussions. I'm no longer protected by the CIG. I have no family. I'm all there is. This is all I have."

And saying that out loud left him feeling hollow inside.

18

Aves's skyline glittered in the night. Roo tugged at his tux and grimaced. He'd last worn it a few years ago, and despite the weekly training, long swims, the pull-ups off the davits on the back of his boat, it still didn't quite fit right.

He wondered if anyone noticed, and then decided to shrug it off. Focusing on it would only bring attention.

"A drink, sir?" one of the attendants asked. Her overly short cocktail dress revealed rather muscular legs. A sprinter? Roo wondered. She held up a tray of delicate glasses and looked artificially chipper.

Roo stared at the tray for a moment.

"I have a Château Margaux . . ." she started to say.

"Is there any beer?" Roo asked. "Carib? Red Stripe?"

"No."

In last year's videos there'd been a temporary bar over at the corner. "Rum," Roo said.

"We have a wide selection . . ."

"Mount Gay Extra Old," Roo said. "No ice."

The rich, amber rum was easy to sip. The familiar semi-sweet of a good sipping rum with some fruity undertones and oak took the edge off as Roo began to circulate. The party was ostensibly a benefit. An eye-watering per-plate fee covered the overly pretentious finger foods, vat-grown steaks, and locally sourced vertical-farm grilled vegetables cooked by a chef flown in just for the occasional. Whatever was left over would be donated to a charity to help rebuilding efforts.

Mainly, Roo thought, it was a chance for the upper crust to enjoy the fact that they remained untouched by the storms.

He'd paid the donation via an offshore account, forwarded his picture and a false identity, and shown up in the gaggle of well-dressed partygoers down in the lobby.

Security guards and black-suited attendants guided them up into elevators that took them up to the roof, one load at a time.

"A super party for a super storm," a matriarchal lady with a perfectly sculpted nose giggled. She wore a shockingly white fur around her neck.

A younger man with dark brown hair was staring at the fur. "Can I touch it?"

"Of course! It's *real* Arctic fox. It's extinct," she said, excitement in her voice. They smiled at each other, and for a moment, Roo wondered what it would have been like to walk up here with Kit at his arm.

He shook that away.

"That must be impossible to get!"

"You have *no* idea."

"Is it hot?"

"No, it's soft and natural to the skin. Excuse me." She grabbed Roo's forearm with bony fingers as he slipped past her and the gathered clump of people to head inside toward the far side of the roof, near a clump of decorative tree-like solar arrays that had folded down their light-seeking leaves for the night.

He looked at her waxy perfectly taut skin and snow-white fur. "Yes?"

"Can we get some more of those little pickled things, they were absolutely delicious!"

Roo gently disentangled himself. "I'm sorry, we're all out."

The woman sighed dramatically. "Just my luck."

A minor tragedy, Roo was sure.

He circled around the party again, slowly edging further and further out, until he ducked behind the solar arrays. Alone in the dark shadows he pulled out his phone and swiped to one of his running apps.

The distant, grainy image of the rooftop wavered slightly. The quadcopter was fighting the wind to hover in place where Roo had piloted it before he'd walked into the lobby.

Now he aimed it through the air to him.

It buzzed loudly as it approached the edge of the roof and coasted into his hands like a wobbling, mechanical falcon. Roo glanced around. No one noticed anything over the sound of cocktail laughter and the live reggae band performing in the corner. The band was trying to find the right amount of laid-back bombast that left the donors comfortable.

Roo pulled three grenades off the hasty duct-tape harness, and pocketed the pistol.

He'd known there would be security in the lobby, including airport-grade scanners.

Inside his tuxedo's inner pocket were the deck gloves with the gecko pads. He hadn't put those on the quadcopter, because he'd been toying with the idea of breaking into the labs even if he wasn't armed and the copter had failed. Last time he'd used these, Roo thought as he pulled them on, he'd been in the middle of the storm with Delroy.

A lifetime ago.

Roo looked over the edge of the building. Twenty stories down. He'd never been a fan of heights. Never even been in a building more than a couple stories tall before the Caribbean Intelligence Group scooped him up and gave him something better to do with his talents.

He swung over the edge.

For a moment, feet dangling uselessly, Roo found himself second-guessing the glove's ability to hold onto his hands. The wrist strap, an advanced Velcro, bulged slightly. But after another long moment waiting for the long fall to happen, he calmed. He'd used these to go up the mast enough to know they'd hold just fine.

He began crabbing his way carefully down to the floor underneath, looking for the balcony he'd spotted when digging through public photos online of the building.

The lock to the balcony door yielded to a skeleton key that used brute force algorithms to run through wireless security until it told the door to open itself up with a satisfying click for Roo. While the skeleton key was running, Roo took the time to unwind his paracord bracelet and tied it off to the balcony.

Just in case.

He looked into the gloomy, half-lit offices and hallways, waiting for his eyes to adjust. He folded the gecko gloves and slid them into his jacket's pockets before he stepped in.

The lights flared on. He staggered back, hands still in his pockets, blinking, and three security guards with submachine guns snugged up shoulder-high and tight stepped forward. "Mr. Jones?" called a voice from behind them.

Shit.

There was no way he could run. One step back and they'd riddle his chest with bullets. He'd make it over the balcony. His dead body would hit the ground.

Kit had been right. This was a stupid move. They knew the ostentatious balcony was their weak point. They'd set up a trap and just simply waited for him.

Roo casually stepped forward. "You know who I am?"

Inside his pocket, he flicked the pins off the grenade in each hand.

Adrien Beauchamp, hard to miss in his cream-white designer tuxedo, stepped forward to stand just behind his three guards. They wore black suits, but Roo noticed a hint of some tattoos around their wrists.

Not professional security, these were more neo-Nazis.

"We were warned you might try and show up here," Beauchamp said.

"Get your hands out in the air, slowly," one of the guards shouted, not happy with the casual chitchat, suspicious that Roo was probably up to something.

"Okay. I'm pulling them out slowly." Roo stepped forward and held his hands out from his body. He let the grenade pins drop to the floor. "Shoot me, I drop the grenades."

"*Szar*," swore one of the men.

Adrien Beauchamp's lips tightened. "Would someone explain to me how he walked into *my* lab with grenades in his pocket?"

"It's impossible, they weren't there. He was scanned. Closely. Everyone was."

Beauchamp pointed at one of Roo's hands. "It's not impossible, because they're right there, aren't they?"

He turned around, but Roo stepped forward. "I wouldn't leave, Mr. Beauchamp. I still have the grenades."

The plutocrat slowed and waved at someone farther down the corridor. "I'm not leaving, Mr. Jones. Not yet. Besides, what will you do? Drop them and commit suicide? The fact that you still stand here in front of me indicates you're not suicidal."

"There's always a first time," Roo said, taking another step forward to keep Beauchamp close at hand. "And I'm angry enough to do something stupid on principle."

"Maybe," Beauchamp said. "But while you're willing to kill yourself, I wonder, will you be willing to kill your friend?"

He pulled a gagged and bound Elvin forward.

"Ah shit," Roo said, looking at his friend's broken nose and bruised eyes. Blood ran from his forearms where peeled strips of skin hung. He limped horribly on a leg where the trousers seeped dark fluid. "Elvin, I'm so sorry."

He'd dragged another soul down into this mess. Another person had paid the price for Roo's actions. Roo felt his stomach churn, and he bit his lip to remain focused. He felt like he'd stepped into quicksand. This had all gotten way out of hand.

Better to have remained the faceless puppet, gaining evidence, using his favors.

Gunplay didn't just get you or the assholes shot, he thought. It also gets the bystanders. The innocents. And the blood would remain on his hands forever, no matter the justifications he had.

Elvin staggered and wordlessly sank to his knees in front of Beauchamp.

Beauchamp sighed. "I take a very close interest in people snooping around my business. It's expensive to have a line into the local security systems, but it comes in handy when things like this happen."

"Let him go," Roo said. He twisted his hands, waggling the grenades. "Or tell me what you want from me to let him go. He shouldn't have to suffer for my mistakes."

Beauchamp smiled. "Mr. Jones, your first name might be Prudence, but you don't seem to be letting your given name constrain your actions, which is a shame. Now you're trying to ruin one of my favorite charity events."

"What you want?" Roo asked, impatient, struggling to keep the men around him in sight.

"What *do* I want?" Beauchamp asked. "Your island dialect might charm those vapid people upstairs, but I prefer precise grammar. Details matter to me."

Roo gritted his teeth. "What do you want, Beauchamp? What's all this about?"

The man waved the question aside. "No, you first, Prudence. I want to know what possessed you to climb down the *outside* of my building. Who's pulling your strings? Do you still work for the Caribbean Intelligence Group?" Beauchamp pulled a small silvered pistol out from under his suit jacket and pointed it at the back of Elvin's head.

Roo stared at him. "You really don't know why I'm here?"

"I'm all ears." Beauchamp stared at Roo, unblinking.

"One of your pet neo-Nazis tried to kill me. I imagine they were trying to get some information that an old friend of mine left me before he died in Florida from a nasty hemorrhagic fever. One someone designed."

"You know about that?" Beauchamp asked.

"Only," Roo continued, "instead of killing me, they shot my nephew dead."

One of Beauchamp's guards lit up with fury. "*You* killed the men at the hotel!" he shouted, stepping forward.

"They killed my nephew," Roo repeated. "The boy was the only family I got."

Beauchamp waved the man back and looked at Roo with sadness. "So you know loss, Mr. Jones. True loss."

Roo stared at him. "I know it."

"I lost someone once. My wife. Before I had the labs, I was a vertical-farm pioneer, did you know that?"

"No, I did not."

"She felt very strongly about trying to help people build infrastructure in the Democratic Republic of Congo. We built infrastructure in one of the northern cities. One of my farms could feed some forty thousand. I did it because she wanted it, and because she was such a beautiful human being, Mr. Jones. She wanted to make the world a better place. I wanted to make it a better place for her. But to live near the border of the Central African Republic and Congo . . . that was not a pretty place."

"Kinshasa is a beautiful city," Roo said.

"She didn't want to go to Kinshasa, where it was stable. No, it had to be where the need was greatest. And most dangerous. I'd never seen an entire fifteen-story farm torched before. The rebels dynamited it. They said it represented foreign interference. It was a symbol. So they dragged it down. But who cares, it was just material? What came next, that was worse. Because we were there to see it."

Beauchamp looked at Roo, and he saw the deep pain in Beauchamp's eyes.

"They tortured her, Mr. Jones. I listened to her scream *for days*. And then they killed her. But me, I was worth too much alive. So I lived. For three months, a captive. And I watched as the people she tried to save starved and died. Over what? A line drawn on a map? A city that was really more of a town? It wasn't enough that she died, all her work was gutted. They killed her, and they destroyed my entire world."

"Delroy was my whole world," Roo said softly.

"So you understand exactly how I felt when I got back to

Kinshasa," Beauchamp said. "And then, I watched the aid agencies swarm the country. You know what they did for all those homeless, starving people?"

Roo shook his head.

"They gave them free food," Beauchamp said, disgust in his voice. "Pallets and pallets of it."

"You act like that's some horrible thing," Roo said.

"And then I read a book that used an analogy that stuck with me: giving free food to starving people is just throwing fuel on the fire," Beauchamp stated flatly. "Combine the desire to give them free food so that you don't have to suffer the guilt of watching them starve, with the social conservative prohibition against also giving out free birth control, and you've basically got rabbits. They're just going eat and fuck and then all you have are *more* starving people."

"So better to let them starve?" Roo stared at the man.

"Yes," Beauchamp hissed. "Better that they starve just once, so that untold following generations don't live in misery and starvation."

"So you think you can shove that generation out in front the bus and save the others by doing it?" Roo said.

"Save them. Save other people on the planet. Mr. Jones, you know we barely have the farmland to support the people already on this planet."

Said the man who built vertical farms, Roo thought. "So all these poor brown people, after they die, what then?"

"When the black plague hit Europe," Beauchamp said, animated, "it changed everything. Moved whole economies out of feudalism! Because suddenly human labor wasn't cheap;

too many people had died. Midden piles outside cities showed nutrition improved. Because, Mr. Jones, we're like cockroaches. We just breed, with no acceptance of the consequences. With our planet overburdened, with civilizations looking at each other's borders, it's time we stopped throwing fuel on the fire."

"And you're going to solve that, with this plague? Reduce the population through sickness?"

Beauchamp cocked his head. "Plague?"

Roo's eyes narrowed. "The one that killed my friend, Zachariah."

"Was that his name?" Beauchamp asked levelly. "Well, he took something from me. And I don't like thieves, Mr. Jones. People don't get to take things away from me, not without consequences."

"I feel much the same," Roo said through gritted teeth.

"I'm glad we're on the same page." Beauchamp racked the slide of the pistol with a clack that echoed around them.

Roo stiffened. "Wait . . ."

Elvin had been on his knees, dazed, for the whole conversation. Fear flickered in his eyes for a second. Then Beauchamp pulled the trigger.

Blood splattered the carpet. That was what Roo focused on: the abstract splatter of it across polished black boots and the bottom of the wall.

Elvin slumped forward awkwardly, a lifeless sack of a human now.

Roo dropped the grenades to the floor.

For a split second the guards stared at him. No one had

expected him to do it. Roo stood rooted in place for a split second, not understanding what he'd unconsciously done.

Then everyone ran.

Three guards shoved Beauchamp behind a supporting beam and covered him with their bodies. One of them opened fire at Roo, who was already back out on the balcony and crouching behind the tiny sliver of wall for protection.

The grenades exploded. The doors shattered, glass raining down on the balcony.

Roo grabbed the end of the paracord bracelet he'd tied to the balcony and looped it around his ankles. He took a deep breath and chucked the third grenade in through the doors.

"Gránát!"

Roo leaped over the rail. The pop of small arms filled the air. Something smacked into his shoulder as he tumbled through the air.

The grenade made a crumping sound overhead. A sparkling cloud of glass and debris blew out into the air above Roo.

He reached the end of the paracord with a horrible smack. There was some give, built into it by the weave and because it had been designed for parachutes, but the arrest was still brutal at this length. He'd tried to jump off to the side to create a pendulum-like arc to absorb some of the impact as well, but now that meant Roo swung in an arc and struck a window hard enough to knock the air out of him. His right ankle had snapped, he realized. He could feel bone grinding on bone. Roo would have screamed, but he couldn't get air. He just croaked, hanging upside down as glass rained down past him, slicing at his clothes.

Someone leaned over the balcony and cut the rope.

The ground was fifteen feet below.

Roo managed to twist, like a cat, and land on his one good foot with a roll so bad he almost wanted to apologize. The stabbing pain up his femur hinted at another fracture, maybe even a break. Glass and debris punctured his hands and dug into his sides. Roo lay on the sidewalk, unable to think or move.

Pain hit him like waves furiously slamming into a reef. They covered him with a frothy stabbing as breakers of dizziness foamed and climbed over him to dash themselves against some inner point that struggled to remain firm.

There was a lot of blood on the ground around him, Roo thought.

And then that inner rock gave up and let itself get washed away.

19

Roo opened his eyes a few minutes later and fuzzily regarded the tilted lobby of Beauchamp Labs. He'd crawled away from the building at some point, he realized, looking back at the trail he'd made through the debris.

Through the floor-to-ceiling glass Roo could see two men in shredded black suits get out of the elevators. They motioned at the security guards near the metal detectors and pointed outside.

Roo pulled his pistol free of his inner jacket pocket and struggled to sit up, but it felt like all of Aves Island had suddenly been cut free of the coral it sat on. Everything rocked and moved around him.

He took a deep breath and aimed at the lobby doors.

This was it. His last stand. Sitting on the grass near the road in front of the lobby of the building.

When the men pushed the doors open Roo emptied the clip at them. The windows shattered. The guards scattered, seeking cover.

The high-pitched whine of an electric bike filled the air. Tires scrubbed on the street and Roo looked behind him just as Kit pulled to a stop, the back of the bike kicked slightly up into the air as she slammed the front brakes too hard.

"Where did you get that?" he asked, stupidly, loading another clip into his pistol and shooting back at the lobby to keep them covered.

"Stole it. Get on," she shouted. Bullets slapped the asphalt nearby. Too close. But Kit didn't flinch. "Let's go!"

Roo tried to stand. His ankle collapsed, bone puncturing through the skin. He wobbled, fell forward, and Kit caught him. He wrapped his arms around her waist as she gunned the motor, leaving a long track of rubber down the road. The popping sound of gunfire faded behind them.

"Left here," Roo murmured. The world tracked past him in jerky fits of images. His brain was struggling to handle the inputs as they moved out of the island's central core. He directed her toward the edge of Aves, closer to the water. Where canals ran between the skyscrapers on stilts in addition to the roads and bridges. "Right. Right again. The dinghy dock, right there."

"They're following us. I need to lose them." A pair of lights stabbed the turns behind them.

"No. Just get us to that dock." Roo could feel himself fading again, and jerked himself back awake.

"Roo, that's not where the *Spitfire* is."

"I know. We're not going back to the docks." He didn't want to lead them back to the boat, but to something else he had waiting.

They'd stopped.

"We're here. Come on," Kit said. She grabbed his shoulder.

"No," Roo protested. "I'm too heavy."

He tried to stand but she shoved him back. "*Merde*. You're not *that* heavy. And you can't stand." She slipped under his arm, ducked, and flipped him onto her back. A classic fireman's carry.

It wasn't as noble as having a comrade supporting you under an arm, but it allowed anyone to carry someone heavier than themselves. Kit easily walked down the slope to the dinghy dock, grunting under his weight but moving at a half jog. Every bounce against her shoulders sent pain shooting up through his core.

"That one," Roo gasped, pointing at *Spitfire*'s dinghy, tied up among a row of other small craft.

Kit tumbled them both ungainly into the inflatable, Roo biting his hand to stop from screaming as bones grated and shot pain up his leg.

"What now?" Kit asked.

Roo pulled the duffel bag out of the front storage locker and dumped the first-aid kit out in front of him. He stared at all the blood slicking the fiberglass bottom. That was his blood.

Shot in the shoulder. That was small caliber, in the flesh. Bleeding, but not as painful as his legs. Or the multiple shards of glass sticking through his jacket. Most of the blood came from his ankle, though.

He hit himself with several painkillers. Small aerosol one-shots that hissed and nipped his skin, but delivered a blanket of warmth. The pain ebbed.

The whine of an approaching engine grew. Roo handed her one of the submachine guns and pulled out the grenade launcher. He checked it over. He'd put everything he could think of in the dinghy ahead of time, loaded it ready for a hot retreat. Though this was hotter than he'd imagined.

One last piece of first aid: Roo slapped four patches on his arms. The rush of stimulants shoved the growing darkness back.

"I thought," he said, after gasping for air as his heart stammered into overdrive, "that you were leaving."

"I couldn't."

"I'm damn glad you stayed," Roo said. He raised the grenade launcher and sighted. The moment the car following them turned the corner he squinted.

Four guards.

Roo fired twice. With each thunk the grenades arced out over the other tethered dinghies and boats, over the dock, and into the street.

The explosions rocked the air seconds later, lighting up the night sky. The car swerved, then smashed through the protective railing down the ramp and onto the dinghy dock.

Roo took a steadying breath, then calmly fired another grenade into the car.

They cast off to the glare of the entire dock catching fire.

The platform under the car sagged, then broke. The vehicle sank into the water in a mess of bubbles.

Kit accelerated them away into the wide canal between the skyscrapers as Roo slumped into the bottom of the dinghy. He pulled out his phone, smearing the screen with blood. No signal. Interesting. He slumped back, staring up at the stars and the undersides of bridges, hugging the rocket launcher to his chest.

Kit found a quiet place in the pylons under an apartment complex that looked out over the main, crescent-shaped concrete harbor. With more sedatives, Roo found he barely had the coordination to set his ankle, so she helped, with a grimace. Then they bound it to half of one of the telescoping metal oars to make a crude splint. The bandages seeped blood, and the pain in his shoulder from the gunshot grew, but it was manageable with the field kit he had. The designer drugs were field-ready, combat-oriented military spec.

"We can't go back to the boat or the docks near it," Roo said, checking his phone. "I've fucked everything up. This is open warfare."

Kit didn't say anything.

"You can hide," he said to her. "I can drop you off."

"They'll have spotted me with public cameras," she said. "There's no hiding. I already debated that when I sped over to help you. I told you it was a bad idea."

"I know what Beauchamp plans," Roo said.

She looked at him sharply. "What?"

"To unleash the tailored plague on the world. Zee, that family: that was just the beginning. It gets bigger. The man's unhinged. He wouldn't stop talking about his dead wife."

Kit's face quirked. "We need to inform someone . . ."

Roo held up his phone. "Aves is locked down. The cell towers just shut off. It's a variation of an antiterrorist move after an explosion: kill the cell signals, only let official encryption through, and start jamming satellite signals. Trap everyone in place so you can sort through them all. I'm going to have to get out from under the jamming or I can't call out to give anyone the information. Neither can you."

"We're trapped," Kit said solemnly.

"I'm sorry," Roo said. "I'm very sorry. I didn't realize what I was really up against."

This was what happened when you didn't study what you were getting into. This was what happened when you ran in like a damn cowboy. He ran his hands through his dreadlocks and took a deep breath and looked out at the harbor. "Here they come."

Three Harbor Patrol boats idled through the water between gleaming white mega-yachts at anchor, their spotlights snapping around. Waiting.

"What are our options?" Kit asked.

"Been thinking we head for open ocean in the dinghy until we get a signal, then I call in help." Once he got out of the range of the jamming, he'd be able to call in favors. Risky, but doable.

"But not with those patrol boats?"

"No." They wouldn't be able to run that gauntlet. The Harbor Patrol in Aves had heavy caliber guns mounted on their bows. A holdover from the fear of Venezuelan retaliation. And there were other island defenses that could be used against them, if Beauchamp was particularly good at convincing people Roo was a threat. And that kind of money was a very good convincer.

"If you want to duck out now, I will understand," Roo said.

"You won't get far in your shape. And we need to get word out. Before anything irreversible happens."

Roo pulled the familiar tube of a rocket launcher out from the duffel bag of weaponry. "When I was looking at Beauchamp's parties, I saw a picture of his mega-yacht," he said. "I noticed it has a helicopter on the top deck."

"Is it still there?"

Roo pointed to the far corner of the harbor: the mega-yacht just visible, a helicopter perched like a dragonfly on a wooden top deck above the cabins. "Do you know how to fly one?"

"No," Kit said.

"Then you'll be the one shooting at anyone who tries to come at us," Roo said.

"What's the rocket launcher for?" Kit asked.

"To convince everyone aboard the ship to get the hell off before we board it," Roo said. "Right before we swarm over the side with knives in our mouths."

It was time to take the war directly to Beauchamp. No botched sneaking around, no bullshit.

He wasn't much of a field man. Roo preferred the dark. But when it was time for fireworks, he preferred to bring as much firepower as he could. And even more than firepower, explosions let you miss your mark and still bring the pain.

They bobbed in the dark under the apartment complex's pylons, safe and invisible to the patrol meandering around the middle of the harbor. The two boats were easing their way toward the mouth of the harbor to block any escape.

"You think we have a chance at this?" Kit asked.

"Full speed for the main docks the moment those patrol boats get out toward the mouth of the harbor," Roo said. "They'll be expecting us to try and leave. Not to try and board Beauchamp's ship."

"And then?"

"At the very least, I plan on sinking Beauchamp's very expensive yacht and his pet helicopter," Roo said. "It's the least I can do."

Harbor Patrol still blocked the harbor. They could hear a few smaller semirigid boats headed up and down the canals leading away from parts of the harbor as security forces tried to hunt for them in the watery fingers reaching deep into Aves. So far the dark-colored dinghy and their lack of running lights had kept them from being seen.

"The spotlights will get us soon enough," Roo said. "Don't worry about sticking close to the docks and going slow. Hit it."

He braced himself where he sat on the front of the dinghy as she gunned the engine. The water was smooth in here; he didn't get bounced too much as they skipped over the surface. He balanced the rocket launcher on his shoulder and looked into the small LCD panel flipped out of the side.

The screen included thermal imaging. Roo scanned the two-hundred-foot-long gleaming white mega-yacht in front of them. It looked like something dropped out of a science-fiction movie into the water: all gleaming polished curves, chrome, and tinted black oval windows.

It had its stern up against the dock with a gangway leading down from the concrete edge into its wood and brass-trimmed transom. Roo and Kit approached from the port side with the harbor entrance behind them.

In the thermal imaging display small human figures moved around or lounged. The rooms inside all seemed to line up with the portholes.

Roo aimed at the empty bows for the first shot.

"You ready? It's going to get crazy the moment I fire."

"Do it. I'm ready, Roo."

The shimmering reflection of the laser sight bounced off the bow's waterline, and Roo pulled the trigger.

Everything lit up with the blinding glare of the rocket's flash. It streaked out over the water, then dipped and struck the waterline with an explosive gush of fire and water spray. The hull of the mega-yacht rippled.

Roo reloaded. Out of the corner of his eye he could see the lights of the Harbor Patrol ships changing course as they turned for them.

"Get to the other side of the ship."

Roo fired a rocket into the waterline of the transom. Then another at the centerline of the ship, where the engine room sat idle, as the ship was no doubt connected to dock power.

Water poured into the gaping holes.

A spotlight blinded Roo, tens of thousands of candlepower creating a pool of artificial day around the dinghy. People shouted at them via crackling bullhorns.

Kit skidded them across the water and around Beauchamp's mega-yacht. "Duck!" Roo screamed.

He shot a final rocket into the waterline ahead of them and flopped himself down as the fireball shot overhead. He crawled back and grabbed the arm of the outboard motor that Kit had left as she'd scrabbled down to avoid the blowback. Roo gunned them right into the burning, five-foot-wide hole in the side of the mega-yacht with a lurching crunch that threw them both forward into the front of the dinghy together. Roo's ankle throbbed. He'd drugged the pain down to dangerous levels. That he could feel anything meant he was going to be in trouble later.

Burning curtains of fiberglass slumped into the back of the dinghy, hissing and crackling.

Roo picked up the duffel bag and clambered out into the warm water. The metal tube of the paddle he'd splinted his foot to worked like a peg leg, letting Roo grimace and hobble his way along awkwardly. But not quickly enough. Water from the massive hole swept him into a wood-panel wall and pinned his lower body in place.

"Where are we?" Kit asked, stumbling through the water to reach him.

Roo lit the room up with his phone's light and looked around. There was a massive bed up against the wall. "Master suite of some sort," he said.

Kit struggled to move along the wall to find the door until

they bumped into a gold-plated handle. She pulled the submachine gun he'd given her up to shoulder height as he opened the door with an explosive gush of seawater. "Clear," she reported from the corridor, legs braced against the water rushing past.

Roo limped out after her, his pistol covering the high ground near stairs leading out into a large saloon.

"Let's head up," Roo said.

Outside people shouted into the boat from bullhorns. The crackle of fire from the RPGs filled the air. Smoke started to haze the rooms of the ship.

A well-dressed man in a suit coughed and hacked as he stumbled out of the corridor in front of them. He raised his hands, eyes watering as he stared at them in shock.

"Get off the damn ship! It's sinking." Roo shouted. "Move!"

The authority in his voice startled the man into action. He spun and fled up the stairs. Kit and Roo followed him, Roo struggling to get up the stairs with his splinted leg. He had to lean against the wall and pull himself along the handrail while Kit crouched, at the top.

They burst out onto the deck with grateful gasps of clear air.

"Low, low, low," Kit whispered. The ship was surrounded by Harbor Patrol. Roo pulled himself along the deck, keeping his head below the rail.

They took the stairs up to the flat deck and helicopter pad. Roo slid inside and looked at the pedals as Kit cut the ties on the skids. He experimentally pushed at a pedal with his ruined ankle and splint. The splint kept jamming against the cockpit floor. Roo used a knife to cut the metal tube free. He cautiously tried the pedal again.

The world faded in a haze of pain and he gasped. Even with all the drugs, the abuse of the last few hours and the direct pressure was overwhelming.

"You okay?" Kit asked.

"Fine," Roo lied, blinking. He fumbled for another dose of painkillers and slapped them on.

He powered the displays up. The rotors kicked on instantly thanks to high-torque, high density battery packs. Expensive. And the range would be limited, a reason electric aircraft were still not as common as fuel-powered ones.

"Hey!" someone yelled, popping up on the deck. "Hey!"

Kit leaned out and waved the machine gun. The person ducked back down the steps.

Roo waited for thrust to build, watching the rotor RPMs climb.

"Are those boats going to be able to shoot us out of the air?" Kit asked.

Roo glanced over at the Harbor Patrol boats. The entire deck they sat on was beginning to pitch over and lean as the port side of the ship with its three holes took on water faster than the starboard. "The high-caliber guns are mounted for other boats. Probably not."

"Probably?"

"Pay attention to the smaller guns," he said. He focused on the controls. He'd never flown this model. There were commonalities between helicopters, but it was going to be shaky.

Most of his training had been on simulators. Part of the cross-training he'd gotten as a freelance troublemaker for the CIG.

The helicopter shifted and slid across the deck toward the railings.

"Here goes . . ." Roo grabbed the collective lever down by his thigh and pulled up. The electric engine surged and the helicopter rose off the deck.

Roo yanked it all the way up and tilted the helicopter forward, and then as they cleared the ship, he headed for the buildings of Aves. After a second of flight, he shoved down hard on the pedal with his ruined foot to turn them. He screamed as the helicopter's back rotor kicked around, and they curved to aim out for the open ocean.

"Roo!"

"It's okay," he hissed. They were rising, a few pings from lucky gunfire hitting the fuselage, but moving rapidly across the harbor and out of reach.

Glass shattered. A close shot. Roo winced and kept his hand steadily shoving the cyclic stick between his knees forward.

He glanced at one of the cockpit displays that served as a rearview camera. In the water behind them the yacht rolled over on its side in the water. It looked less like a spaceship at anchor and more like a dead whale.

You're welcome, Mr. Beauchamp, he thought, leaning back and closing his eyes.

"Roo!"

He opened his eyes. Kit stared at him, her eyes wide and

worried. She held the cyclical stick with one hand and shook him with another. "What?"

"You passed out."

Roo looked at the dark water suddenly just under the windshield. The helicopter blared an audible repeating altitude alert. They'd dropped down low enough to be skimming the ocean surface. A stray wave could kiss the skids, or worse, them.

He pulled them back up into the air. "How far out are we?"

"Just a few minutes. You stopped responding and the alarm went off."

Blacking out should have scared him, but he didn't have the energy for it. Blood dripped from his bandages onto the helicopter's floor. He'd taken way too many painkillers.

"I flew out in a random direction," Roo told her. "I need to turn us toward Dominica. I might scream again."

He eyed the old analog compass. Dominica would be eastish. Roo thought about it for a long, slow moment. Then he took a deep breath and pushed the pedal with his good foot, taking them in a long circle until they faced east.

"How you doing?" Kit asked.

Roo wiped sweat out of his eyes. "Look for a cloud in front of us," he said. "I'm having trouble focusing."

"A cloud?"

"I don't know how to access the maps function on these screens," he admitted.

"Shit." Kit leaned forward and squinted for a long moment. "There *is* a cloud," she said.

"Bearing?"

"Just a few points south of east."

"A few?"

"I'll call it out as we get further along," she said. "What is it?"

"Dominica," Roo said. "All the lights, reflecting off the bottom of any clouds passing overhead. Let's you see it over the curve of the horizon."

An old sailor's trick.

"ROO!" Kit slapped him across the face.

He jerked up. His shirtsleeve was pulled up and she'd applied the last two stimulant patches on his left bicep. His mouth tasted like seaweed, but was so dry he could barely swallow. "I'm sorry," he muttered. "I'm sorry. Just had to close my eyes for a second."

"It's getting worse," Kit said. "That's the fourth time."

Four? He didn't remember the second or the third.

Roo cleared his throat, but started coughing. He looked down at the blood on his hands from covering his mouth. "That's not good."

"I can get a signal on your phone, now," Kit said slowly. "Who do I call?"

"Anyone who can help you," he said. "DGSE."

"Of course I'll do that. But what about you. Who do I call at the CIG?"

Roo looked at her. "There's no one left for me, Kit. No one will touch me after what I just did. Get the word out, I'll get picked up by whoever. See if I can disappear, think about what to do next. You need to get the DGSE on Beauchamp."

He closed his eyes. He opened them up again to find Kit

screaming at him and holding onto the cyclical stick. The whole world was tilted wrong. Roo yanked them back to level with a gasp.

They were flying low, but Dominica would likely be scrambling small drones now that he was close enough to be tracked. He wondered if Beauchamp would be able to convince Dominican authorities to shoot them down. By flying off in the wrong direction they might have confused matters. By flying away, they wouldn't have been a direct threat to Aves, which was why they hadn't been shot down by drones on the way out. Approaching Dominica was a different story.

He checked the flight systems. Winced.

"Kit, there's a life jacket under your chair," Roo said, his voice slurring. "Put it on."

"Roo . . ."

"You're going to have to jump out. The helicopter isn't going to make it. Something hit the battery. The charge isn't there. Or maybe they didn't recharge it in time before we stole it." The batteries weren't the only things fading, though. He was going to accidentally kill them both when he tried to land. And if they were attacked by drones he was useless right now.

Roo squinted. He could see the distant shapes of lights. Houses on hills. An island just on the horizon. He slowed the helicopter's forward pitch, easing them toward a hover over the ocean. "Take the phone with you, put it in a plastic bag. Should be one in the duffel."

"What are you going to do?"

"Ditch the copter and float. Tell them to fish me out," he said.

"Roo, I don't think that's a good idea."

It was too late. Roo started dropping them down toward the water. The Caribbean Ocean glittered with smooth, large swells in the night air.

"Get the jacket on," he said. "Come on. See the capsule with the antenna? That's an emergency beacon. Trigger it by breaking the transparent seal, it'll call out. But if you can, get your people. DGSE. It'll be safer."

She hurriedly put the phone in the baggie. Roo dipped them lower still as she pulled the life jacket on, watching the swells. Just a few minutes of alertness more, he told himself. And then he could relax.

"Open the door, stand on the skids," he said to her. "And good luck."

She looked back him, her hair flying around in the rotor wash, face full of concern. "Roo. What about you?"

He winked. "Buy me a drink when we meet up on the shore later. Now: jump!"

She disappeared. Roo saw the splash below them a second later. She floundered in the kicked-up water from the rotor wash, so he quickly pushed forward and moved away from her.

A hundred feet. A few hundred. Five . . . Roo blinked. The helicopter dipped lower, wavered, and the tip of a wave struck its underbelly. The whole helicopter shivered. Roo tried to lower it into the space between the swells.

It gyrated, wobbling from the wave strike. He wasn't in control, every time he blinked the world shifted. Alarms bleated. Systems in the helicopter tried to take over and compensate for him, but he fought them. Down, down.

Roo was tossed as the entire world gonged, the rotors slapped water, and the dark ocean grabbed the helicopter and shoved its way through the windows to coldly embrace him.

He didn't have time to try and get out. He sat there, relaxing, as they sank through the darkness together. The water, initially shockingly frigid, now felt warm and pleasant against his skin.

Bubbles glopped and boiled around him, tickling the hairs on Roo's neck.

He was still buckled in, he realized.

20

Roo sat up on a comfortable bed surrounded by fluffy white pillows and under sheer cotton sheets. The breeze stirred gauzy curtains and Roo breathed in the smell of salt air, asphalt, and the distant smell of curry. His stomach roiled.

A medical monitor by the bed dinged softly. Roo twisted to eye it. The interface flipped through screens in standby mode as it sensed him watching, giving a series of summaries of his vitals.

Field-grade emergency surgeon's equipment stood in a semicircle around his bed. Roo spotted the folded-up capsule shape of a robotic surgeon, its spiderlike cutting hands folded away under the transparent shell.

A transparent stainless-steel device, shaped like a mini

whisky flask, had been taped to his right arm. An IV drip ran from it. Inside, Roo could see thumb-sized canisters of pressurized fluids. Blood, plasma, saline. A week's worth of vital fluids for a soldier, crammed into a palm-sized device.

This was all Special Forces shit, Roo realized.

His shoulder had been cleaned, the bullet pulled. There was regenerative skin already puckering under the bandage, mostly healed up. His ankle had been sewn up and a simple air cast covered it.

Roo limped across the room to the window, leaning against the sill as his muscles protested the abuse of walking around. He watched traffic swirl around the street below for a long moment, then turned back around.

A serious young man in full combat body armor and a very large, businesslike machine gun stood at the edge of the room. The body armor and uniform underneath were Caribbean Special Forces. He must have been waiting around the corner of the arches at the far side of the room.

This was a presidential suite, Roo realized.

"You're awake, sir. I'll inform the commander and the doctor."

"Wait." Roo held up a hand. He swallowed hard. The words hurt. His throat burned. Something had been rammed down it. Intubation tube, maybe. "Where am I?" he croaked.

"Fort Young Hotel," the soldier informed him. "You've been here for three days."

He disappeared back into his niche, just out of sight, murmuring an update to some unseen handler.

Roo stood at the window as long as he could. He was in

downtown Roseau, the capital of Dominica. They hadn't taken him away from the island he'd crash landed just off of.

His legs started buckling. He moved back and sat on the edge of the bed, watching the door at the far end of the lavish suite.

It opened. A tall man in a white suit walked in.

"Jesus Christ." Roo shook his head. "Aman *fucking* Constantine."

Aman smiled, handed his coat to the soldier like he was a doorman, and walked in. "Don't be so glad to see *me,* man. You should have kept sleeping in. Because now you up, the big boys is coming in to harass you."

"How bad?" Roo asked.

"Bad enough we being recorded right now. In case I try to help you out."

"Cold day in hell," Roo muttered.

Aman shrugged. "See, I actually think you're worth saving, Prudence. Because if anything you was saying before they shoved that tube down you throat to save you is true, then I vote we . . . fix you mess."

"Pushing the hills patois, Aman?" He came from up in the mountains of Jamaica. Push Aman hard enough, piss him off, even Roo didn't quite catch half the curses the man would sling at you.

"Want to make them big country boys listening in work for they bread," Aman said with a wicked smile. "What go on with you, you sound all Yankee American?"

"Too much time away," Roo said softly, and then changed the subject. "You have me hidden away. Not in a hospital."

Aman nodded. "Yes. If half what you say is true, then we don't want Beauchamp to know we have you. No hospitals, nothing. Just field medics and you bloody, drowned ass on the floor here. The best of the best of Special Forces medicine. And a beautiful hotel to recover in. Away from them prying eyes."

"You know something rotten with Beauchamp," Roo said.

"One big boy and one big girl coming in," Aman said, sweeping his hand at the door. "Save you breath."

Roo met his eyes. "Who?"

"One American, the other British. Draw a conclusion."

The doors to the suite opened. Two upper-level management types in nearly identical black suits walked in. They were sweating heavily, faces beet-red, their temperate-weather-styled heavy jackets no doubt overheating them.

The four of them sat at a small breakfast table in the corner of the suite. The man in the black suit set a phone down in the center, as did the woman.

He had a strong British accent, and after tapping the phone said, "This is a preliminary interview of Mr. Prudence Jones in reference to the Aves Island incident. Attending are . . ." He looked up. "Shit, I'm used to doing the formal one. Other than Mr. Jones, we're not really here, are we?"

Aman leaned over the table. "Roo, they just need the information confirmed so all of them can start digging. Understand? Nothing formal happening here."

Roo looked at the phone. "Looks formal to me, Aman. Am I in trouble?"

Aman smiled. "More trouble than Beauchamp tried to give you?" He spread his arms.

Roo nodded. "Okay," he said. "Here is everything I know right now. . . ."

When the door closed, Aman let out a deep breath. "And that is that, my friend. Beauchamp will be under a very large magnifying glass now. We know there are drums of something he moved out of his labs, we got the courts to let us get into Aves Island and review footage. We have people replacing the people running security now. Purging out the rot Beauchamp got in there."

"You don't know where he is?"

"We waiting for him to turn up."

Roo grimaced and looked at the door out of the suite. "What about the French?"

Aman looked blankly back at Roo. "What about the French?"

"No French agents are going to want to talk to me as well?" Roo was confused. They'd had an agent of their own caught up in all this. Why wouldn't they press for someone on the scene? "The DGSE doesn't want in on this, with their agent involved?"

"What agent?"

Roo swallowed. "Katrina Prideaux."

Aman flipped through his phone. "Our man in Guadeloupe is . . ."

"Man?" Roo's pulse jacked up. The monitor by the bed beeped a warning, and Aman glanced at it.

"There's no Katrina Prideaux representing the DGSE," he said slowly. "Not in the islands."

Roo felt his stomach lurch. He grabbed the table with both hands. "Aman . . ."

"But someone rescued you, Roo. Wrapped you in a life jacket and called for help. Gone when we arrived. That your Katrina?"

Roo opened his mouth, a sudden douse of cold water swirling through the back of his mind. "I remember getting free of the helicopter," he said. "Getting to the surface. I was angry."

"Angry?"

"I want Beauchamp dead. He killed Delroy. I wanted to hunt him down and make him pay. So I refused to give up. I got to the surface, I remember that."

He remembered moving up and down in the large swells, kicking off his shoes and jacket so that he could float in the water, his face turned up to the stars.

Just float.

"She gave me the jacket. Stayed with me," Roo murmured.

"And slipped away at the docks when we came and took over," Aman said. He held up his phone and turned the screen to Roo. "You said Katrina Prideaux?"

There she was. Younger, in a tailored dress that shimmered blue cut just above the knees. The diamond brooch on her collar looked fake, merely because the stones were too large.

"Who the fuck is she?" Roo asked.

"Katrina Prideaux," Aman said. Roo relaxed slightly. "Originally . . . Beauchamp."

"I don't . . ." Roo looked out toward the window, not quite able to process that. Beauchamp?

"She's his daughter," Aman continued. "And a recent widow. She used to be DGSE. They haven't been able to bring her in."

That didn't make any sense. Or had it? She had been using him to hunt something down. Hunt down Zee's information. Shit, she still had the tree frog drive, Roo realized, his hand automatically moving up to the empty space over his chest where the necklace had been.

Had she been trying to get at that for her dad?

No. Roo shook his head. She'd risked her life back on Aves. And in the storm. And while escaping her father's neo-Nazi gunmen. There had to be something else going on. "Widow? She didn't say anything about a husband." But she'd acted so grieved back in St. Thomas. He'd marked it as good acting, as she pretended to be Zee's sister. What if it had been something true?

"Two months ago, her husband, Hamid Prideaux, and his family went on a retreat in the French countryside. They all died of . . ."

She'd risked her life to get into the helicopter. She'd wanted to get word out. Wanted to stop her father. Roo looked at Aman as his words clicked into place for Roo. The French countryside. "Her husband died of hemorrhagic fever, didn't he? The plague her father designed."

She hadn't gone up to the party with him because she hadn't wanted to be spotted by her father. She'd chosen to wait in the shadows. To save him. Because she could have run with the drive if that's all she wanted. Left him to die outside the lobby of Beauchamp Labs.

Aman sucked his teeth. "If that was your friend, then yes. Her father killed her husband and his whole family. Left them to bleed out the eyeballs. Some cold-ass shit, Roo."

"Yeah. And she found out. You want Beauchamp, you go looking for Kit," he said to Aman. "She wants his head. Give me CIG clearance, a few agents, and some server cycles, I'll hunt Beauchamp down. They're going to turn up in Guyana, Florida, or Barbados."

"Why those three places?"

"We need to find out," Roo said. "That's where Zee was looking. Get agents out to those places, activate anything you can already out there. Get some computers searching through pictures tourists take, and get me in the game. . . ."

Aman was shaking his head. "You can't leave."

"What?"

"You're one of our cards. We keeping you close. And away from all this. You too close and personal, Roo. He got Delroy killed trying to come at you. You went after him. Blew up his boat. But remember, Beauchamp is filthy with coin. And we don't have anything for sure. So there are other men in suits, and politicians, pressing down hard on all of us."

"They want you to stop looking at Beauchamp?"

"Exactly. So we go look harder. Also, we got some others involved. People Beauchamp owns. We can't have you blowing them up. So we keep you under wraps from the higher-ups above CIG. Look for the surgical strike." Aman put a finger to his lips. "All hush hush. Besides, you in no shape to be gallivanting around."

"I feel fine."

Aman put a hand on Roo's shoulder. "That's just the good drugs. Roo, you under house arrest. Freddy here," he pointed at the soldier, "will be right up against you hip, watching you. Along with a few others scattered in the hotel. No phones, no computer. Even the TV in your room won't let you check e-mail or browse. That's my orders from above. Understand?"

Roo folded his arms.

Aman shrugged. "Take a few days, focus on getting better. Enjoy the unlimited bar tab. Look at them sunsets. Rumor say the weather will turn soon enough. It's hurricane season: enjoy the calm between the weather."

"There's no calm for me, Aman."

Aman reached into his jacket and pulled out a yellow box. He slid it across the table to Roo.

"Chocolates?" Roo asked, looking down.

"An assortment. A little gift. Glad to see you alive. I missed you, boss," Aman said.

"Haven't been your boss since I got sent north."

Aman smiled and got up. "Still miss you at the office. Enjoy the chocolate, Roo. I picked them out special for you."

Roo watched him leave, then tossed the box of chocolates onto the couch. Freddy closed the door behind Aman. As they'd been talking he'd gotten out of his body armor and khaki uniform with the Caribbean Curve insignia over the shoulder. He was wearing white shorts and a floral shirt.

"Casual Friday, Freddy?" Roo asked.

"Ready for dinner when you are, sir!" came the reply.

Roo sighed and put his head in his hands. I'm letting you down, Delroy, he thought. This is not vengeance. This is an unraveling mess that Roo had only managed to muddy up even further.

Maybe he should have stayed for the funeral. Passed on what he knew as he knew it. Not worked with Kit.

Who was Beauchamp's damn daughter.

Roo groaned.

"Sir?" Freddy responded.

Roo looked up at him through his fingers. "I want a drink, Freddy. And steak."

A dry, hot wind swept through the restaurant, which was perched on a deck over the concrete wall of the quay. Roo looked down the long pier thoughtfully as he drank a Red Stripe.

Freddy suddenly excused himself to the bar with a smile. He sat on a stool, looking up at the mirror to keep watch on Roo as a woman wearing a loose wrap over her bikini sat down in the chair he'd just left. Freddy must have seen her approaching.

She pushed her thin, mirrored sunglasses up into her hair. "Hi," she said.

Roo put the beer down. Smiled. He was about to tell her he needed his space, but then she set her phone down on the table between them. "Hi," he said. "I'm Roo."

"Natalia," she said. "Are you staying here on vacation, too? Or do you live here?"

"Hotel." The phone was only a year old, in a battered case with what looked like diamonds on the edge. An expensive accessory.

"Well, we picked a horrible time to go vacationing, didn't we?" she asked, and waved at the bartender. A glass of white wine appeared seconds later.

"Why?" Roo asked.

"The hurricane?" she said. "I know my parents said coming down in the summer was not smart. Heavy weather, east coast, Florida, the islands, all hellish. Megastorms. They just come and come and come. But, this one. They say it will be a category six. They've been saying, one day, it will come. All that heat in the atmosphere. It was just a matter of time."

Roo looked up from the phone. "Category six . . ." Zee had been focused on that.

"It's going to be a big, powerful storm," Natalia said. "My friends are all telling me I should fly home right away. But I thought, here in this solid building, I should see something like this. I haven't made up my mind, though. I have just a few days to do that, I guess."

"What's the name?" Roo asked.

"The hurricane?"

"Yes."

"Okath," she said.

"Okath." Roo glanced back down at her phone, lost in thought.

She sighed. "I think you're more interested in my phone than me. Is it the diamonds?"

A spell seemed to have dissolved, Roo realized. He was so caught up in his own little world. She was a tourist, here hoping to have some sort of fling before jetting back to whatever world it was she inhabited.

Maybe Roo could have used that. They could have used each other.

Never too late. "Natalia," Roo said. He pulled his sleeve up to show the scars on his arms. "The man by the bar is not just a friend, he's keeping me under custody. And watch. I'm not under arrest . . . but it's complicated."

The less he explained, the more she'd fill in.

Roo smiled. "Let's just say, I have other things on my mind besides a storm. And I'd really, really like to use your phone. But I need you to lean in a bit closer."

She did, a faint excited smile on the edges of her lips. Danger in paradise, Roo thought, as he tapped her phone around to face him.

"They won't let you have a phone?" she asked, eyes twinkling. "Am I participating in something illegal?"

"Most definitely," Roo said. "Now lean in closer so that man at the bar can't see me using your phone, and keep talking to me."

"Ooh."

After several drinks together, she trailed him back up to his room.

"This whole room is under surveillance," he told her at the door.

"I don't care."

"Freddie's not going to leave," Roo said, opening the door.

"He can watch," she said, leaning in to kiss him.

Roo laughed and pulled back slightly. Natalia looked in at the medical equipment. "What is all this?"

Roo pulled his shirt back. "I got shot," he said, showing her the recently healed shoulder.

"Recently?" She raised a hand, then thought better and lowered it.

"Yeah, a few days."

"It looks almost healed."

"Modern medicine. And with thanks to U.S. research. They know more about how to heal gunshot wounds than almost any other nation."

Natalia snorted. "How did it happen?"

"I don't want to think about that," Roo said. "I've been thinking about nothing else for too long. I need to escape."

"I can help," Natalia said.

Freddie slipped between them and shook his head. "Far enough," he said.

"Apparently," Roo said, "I'm allowed a little flirting, but my captors say no more."

Disappointed, she turned back down the corridor. Roo watched her keep walking then stop and look down. She looked back over her shoulder at him quizzically, and he bobbed his head and smiled.

"Thank you," he mouthed.

She shrugged a bare shoulder and kept walking.

Freddie followed him at early dawn down the stairway. "Breakfast?" the soldier asked, smiling.

Roo took the steps quickly. That was damn amazing. They'd

peeled open his legs, wrapped the bone in a scaffolding of bone substitute that would dissolve as his own grew back in, and sealed him back up. Now all he had was a slight limp and dull pain. "No, there's something I want to see."

He skipped down past the restaurant and bar and to the lower level of the hotel, which hadn't been altered in decades. He walked out onto the pier. "What time is it, Freddie?"

"Six fifty in the a.m."

Cutting it close.

A boy stood at the end of the pier flying a kite. The bright red, boxy thing was a few hundred feet up in the air already and the boy was playing out the line further and further. Good.

Roo walked past the boy to the trash can at the very end of the pier.

"Come, Freddie. Look at that ocean," Roo said enthusiastically.

Freddie eyed the blue-gray ocean mildly, while Roo casually reached into the trash can.

Instantly the soldier had a pistol in hand. "What's that?"

Roo slowly raised a harness into the air. Then started to shrug it on.

"Mr. Jones, what is that for?"

"Freddie, you can take a shot and stop me. But that is your only choice," Roo said. "And I have a feeling that if Aman Constantine finds out you shot me, you will have a very, very bad day. Also, don't scare the young boy."

Freddie looked at the wide-eyed boy with the kite staring at him, and slid the gun back away. "I'm a soldier," he said. "It's okay."

Roo finished snapping the harness and stepped over to the boy. "It's okay, son, I'll hold your kite. You go now."

The boy ran down the pier.

A plane skimmed over the green coast, engines a growing buzz. Freddie looked up at the kite. "*Ras* . . . you arranged all this with that woman's phone, yeah? You know how much trouble you causing me?"

Roo clipped the kite's carbon filament wire to the back of his harness. He held out a hand to Freddie. "Good-bye, Freddie."

Freddie ignored the hand. "The woman you looking for? She is in Barbados." He shrugged. "If trouble is coming, I might as well go all the way."

Then he shook Roo's hand. He frowned and looked down at the case-less phone Roo had slipped him. "Give that back to Natalia, please," Roo said. "Thank her for letting me use it to arrange all this."

The plane swept overhead and the nose caught the kite. Roo sat down and bent forward. The dock accelerated away from him in a rush of back-pounding, neck-stretching air. It felt like he'd been swept into a cyclone.

Freddie dwindled away on the pier as Roo rose higher and higher. Roseau's plastic and concrete buildings, brightly colored against the dark green of Dominica's hills, slowly shrank back away like a receding postcard from paradise.

21

Barbados, on the southern reach of the Caribbean's bowed curve, rarely suffered the destructive battering of hurricanes. Much like Grenada, St. Vincent, and Trinidad and Tobago, it lay south of the usual paths. But that had been changing over the last few decades as more hurricanes ventured farther south as well as farther north.

Okath swelled as it spun. Computer algorithms smart enough to outwit any average weather person predicted the curving arms of the superstorm would sweep through the southern Caribbean.

No one was safe.

The pilot of the plane that had just snatched him up, Angela Assim, pulled Roo into the plane herself and checked him over with a tiny first-aid kit while the plane flew itself on autopilot.

"Tomorrow they'll be shutting Grantley Adams Airport down," she told Roo when he told her he wanted to be dropped off in Barbados. "Preparing for the storm of the century. Hopefully what you need is there, because chances are, we ain't leaving the island tomorrow until the storm passes."

Once she'd checked his neck, she gave him a few painkillers for the soreness. "I haven't done a pick-up like that since training," she chuckled. "Wasn't sure if the nose would hold the wire."

"Comforting," Roo said, clambering through the interior of the small propeller plane to sit in the copilot's seat. Angela normally took skydivers up in it; there was room for a few people in back and a large door to let people jump out.

Angela's small company took adventure tourists up in the air over the islands for jumps. But she also worked with the Caribbean Intelligence Group, training young recruits just as happily as she did the adrenaline seekers, which is how Roo first met her.

"So what's in Barbados?" Angela asked. "I've heard some rumors that you have a vendetta against some industrialist. Thought you had put those kinds of days long behind you. And when you went quiet on all of us, I thought you'd retired to your boat."

She'd known Roo a long time. There was a lot of gray in her tightly kinked hair. But for Angela the sky always called, Roo knew. Always would.

"I retired. The world didn't," Roo said as they flew south over the ocean.

"Ah."

Angela gave him his silence until somewhere east of Grenada. "I have a parachute in the back," she told him.

"No," Roo said. "Land at Grantley Adams. They know I'm coming."

"I thought you were trying to get away," Angela said.

"Changing location to get closer to the action," Roo said. "The last time I charged in without support, I almost died. This time, I want the CIG at my back. Or at least, I want to help them."

They surrounded Angela's plane with police Land Rovers, flashing lights, Barbados Defense Forces: everything. Roo was hustled off in the back of an armored vehicle while police questioned Angela.

The local CIG head, Anton Rhodes, sat in the back of the utilitarian vehicle with Roo. "The last thing we need are headlines that say 'Rogue CARICOM secret agent arrested over connection to terrorist attack on Aves Island.' What were you thinking?"

The train of cars, lights flashing, flew down the highway past a rounded patch of green in a roundabout with a great statue of a bronze slave breaking free of his shackles, face lifting up toward the sky. "Do you love this island, Mr. Rhodes?" Roo asked.

"What?"

"Do you love these hills, these people, the beaches, heading down to Lawrence Gap to go party? Because if Beauchamp is on your island, all of that might be gone."

"You've been watching too much Hollywood," Rhodes said. But he looked thoughtful.

"Beauchamp wants to cull the world population," Roo said. "He thinks it's the responsible thing to do. Too many of us starving. With fewer of us, there will be more to go around. That's what he said to my face. I think he might be planning to test his plague on an island first."

"And you think he'd really commit murder on such a scale?"

"He lost family. Losing family will make you crazy."

Rhodes scratched his chin. "Family is everything."

Police escorted Roo deep into a bunker underneath a nondescript government office building. More CIG people trickled in. Phone calls were made, and hasty teleconferences went on in offices. Across the breadth of the Caribbean, it seemed, decisions were being made about Roo's future.

But, Roo knew, those decisions were about all their futures, not just his.

Rhodes returned to the conference room Roo had been locked in under guard. He carried a tray with a carafe of coffee and some donuts. A minor peace offering.

He poured a hot cup for himself and leaned back in one of the plush leather chairs. "Beauchamp arrived on a private jet. Hardly a reason to be suspicious of the man."

Rhodes half turned in his seat and waved at the wall. It glowed to life. Rhodes pulled a series of grainy images up onto it with a few gestures of his hand.

"Based on word from Aman Constantine we pulled surveillance of the airport," Rhodes said. "Here is Mr. Beauchamp, of course."

Roo nodded, his jaw clenching.

Rhodes continued. "It was his luggage that caught our interest."

On the wall, three large men slid a five-foot-wide case right from the cargo area of the plane into the back of a truck with a ramp. Four more large cases sat inside the plane.

"We don't know what is in those cases, but . . ." Rhodes waved at the air, and another picture slid into place. "We have surveillance from Aves. Same cases. So whatever is in those, they came from his lab. And they're undeclared. So that's illegal. Let's assume what you told Constantine, as wild as it sounds, is true: they have weaponized plague here on the island."

Roo leaned forward. He'd said nothing. He'd been expecting hassle. More SIS and CIA. But instead, Rhodes and the CIG were taking him very, very seriously.

Rhodes saw his expression. "Roo, I'm not sure what's going on here. I am listening to you because the last time you reported something this insane, no one listened. Then we all watched a nuclear bomb go off in the Arctic and you went dark for all these years. Now you come back out of nowhere, with a warning. And the old hands who worked with you back then: they telling me I should be taking you deadly serious. That's why I'm still here."

Roo relaxed. "Thank you," he said, a heavy weight he hadn't even realized he'd been carrying fading away.

"This man might not be able to attack the whole world. But if he tries to release some plague, and it is here in Barbados, then forget SIS and the CIA. Because it's our problem. We have to move against this man now, no matter how powerful he is. And trust me, he is very powerful. Many of us risk our careers. If we're wrong, it is over for us. You understand that?"

Roo nodded. "I understand. Look, Beauchamp tried to kill me the last time he saw me instead of turning me over to the police . . ."

"Yeah." Rhodes swiped the surveillance photos away and replaced them with a new wall-sized display of assembled photos prepared by some staffer somewhere.

"What's this?" Roo asked, looking at another lavish party photo.

"The man in the center is the Right Honorable Havish Lamity, the ambassador to America. The party is something that began only recently here on Barbados, though I understand there are others up and down the islands. This isn't a post-hurricane charity, but a Hurricane Ball."

Roo stood up and looked at the high-definition images. "I see a lot of jewelry and expensive tuxedos." And marble columns, ice sculptures, attendants with silver trays.

Rhodes put his coffee down and stood alongside Roo. "It's only been in the last decade that the hurricanes have gotten bad enough to start hitting as far south as Barbados. The Hurricane Ball is a new thing. They often get together before they all fly out to safe places, throw a magnificent party. For the Hurricane Ball, they stay put for the storm and enjoy it together."

"And Beauchamp is going to this Hurricane Ball?"

"The guest list is . . . exclusive," Rhodes said. "But we got a peek at it. What we want you to do, now, is go there."

Roo looked over. "You know what happened the last time I showed up to a party. He tried to kill me."

"Yes. Right now we are counting on it. We're tossing you in, Roo. A live grenade. Because we need something to happen so we can come down on this man like lead brick. Right now, all we know is that you claim he has this virus, but we have nothing concrete."

"You're hoping he'll kill me."

"Try," Rhodes said. "Or, to be honest, even succeed. Either way, we get what we need. We're going to mic you up, add some video, and turn you into our very own human ROV. You are going in to poke the bear, Mr. Jones."

"Good," Roo said. "How do I get in? The list is exclusive?"

Rhodes pulled a gold-leaf ticket out of the inner pocket of his jacket. "Call me your fairy godmother."

Roo examined the ticket. "Who's August Charleton?"

"The sponsor of this latest Hurricane Ball. A financier for one of Barbados's more interesting projects, the Verne Plus." A picture of a long artillery barrel replaced the glittering party scene. Roo looked at it for a while, and then realized his sense of scale was all wrong. There were tiny people down at the base of the barrel, which was suspended by cables inside of a long bridge-like structure. It was an easy quarter of a mile long.

"That's a big gun," Roo said.

"It's the resurrection of an old project. In the 1960s a Canadian-American research team used U.S. Navy guns to try to build a system to shoot small satellites into orbit. It was called Project HARP. Barbados was a great launch point, as it aimed east out over the Atlantic. They shut it down, and the inventor later tried to build a supergun for the Iraqis. Either the Israelis, the Americans, or Iranians assassinated him in 1990; none of them wanted a dictator with the ability to shell their countries from hundreds of miles away."

"And Charleton's building a successor?"

"They've built a twenty-inch-bore cannon. Longer. Project HARP shot a mini-satellite a hundred and twelve miles up. The Verne Plus puts five hundred pounds into orbit. For a fraction of the price of a rocket. Fairly clever. The government helped co-fund the plan; the idea was to make Barbados a center for space launch activity around the project. What didn't raise alarms at the time was that Charleton turned down the offer to use the old HARP facility near the airport and Barbados Defense Forces training grounds; he purchased tracts of land near Hackleton Cliff, and a lot of land downrange of it, to build the complex. Guess he and Beauchamp didn't want the BDF being close by."

"They plan to launch people?" Roo asked in amazement, looking at another picture of the barrel. It pointed up into the air at a forty-five-degree angle in this shot, explosive gases gushing out from the end.

"No, you'd end up meat-flavored toothpaste, so it's just satellites and equipment. Fuel," Rhodes said. "But it stands to make Charleton a very, very rich man."

"Do I get a gun?" Roo asked.

Rhodes snorted. "No. See, this is a party full of dignitaries and very—and I want to stress this—very, rich people. You go on, you get your response, and we go from there."

"Right. I'm human chum," Roo said.

"Exactly."

Rhodes swapped back to a photo of the exclusive partygoers. "We're going to have to dress you up. A tailor will be in tomorrow," Rhodes said.

"When's the ball?"

"Just before Okath's landfall. Two days. Time enough to get you tailored up, mic you up. Hopefully no one gets it into their head to try and stop this."

"Just two days," Roo said. "Been one after another."

"Heavy weather," Rhodes said.

22

The limousine whined along as Roo looked at the beaches passing by. Villas crowded the white sands, their foundation pillars raising them up off the ground so that storm surge could sweep under them. A whole generation of beachfront property had long since been battered away by hurricane-force weather. Insurance companies no longer insured houses that sat on ground level on a coast anywhere in the world.

But the mansion they pulled into the driveway of was built right on the land, like an inland house. But it hid behind protective walls. The outer perimeter of the property had fifteen-foot stone walls as thick as any ancient fort, with gates of steel so thick they could have worked in a canal.

In the heart of the hurricane fortifications, the marble

pillars of an overly art deco mansion were braced by angular statues of Titans holding fast, their grim faces lifted up toward the skies.

As they passed through the giant steel gates, Rhodes looked out at the cars lined up in front of them. "I think some of those are running on gas; they haven't been converted," he said.

They both stared at a Porsche 911's muffler for a moment.

"Hell of a statement," Roo said. "Literally have money to burn for fun."

"Many of these guests probably do," Rhodes said. "You have your ticket?"

It was the third time he'd asked. Roo didn't bother to respond. He unzipped a small bag at his feet and pulled out a pair of new work gloves he'd overnighted to the office Rhodes had kept him in.

"What are those?" Rhodes asked.

"Every well-dressed man needs a pair of gloves," Roo replied.

"Those are work gloves."

"They sometimes come in handy for just that," Roo said. He opened the door, not willing to wait for the car to make it all the way to the polished stone steps leading up to the entryway.

Rhodes grabbed his shoulder. "Be careful."

"I will."

Roo slid out and shut the door. It was raining, the hurricane beginning to make itself felt. But the tuxedo slicked the rain away with its hydrophobic fibers.

Security guards with portable scanners checked him over

and took the ticket. A computer verified its unique RFID signature. "If you did not make arrangements to have valet parking, and you need to return to your home, we have tornado-armored Humvees available to take you wherever you might need," one of the guards said. He pointed at one of the vehicles, parked outside by a clump of coconut trees. It was black and massive, covered in slabs of thick impact armor and with small slits for windows. "Would you like to reserve one for a return trip right now?"

"No," Roo said.

Inside the great ballroom Roo paused a moment. There were models of large rockets hanging from the ceiling, a sign of Charleton's influence on the party. But the rest of the decoration was hurricane-chic. The walls danced and flickered with images of windswept ocean east of Barbados. The cliffs on the east coast had dramatic footage: cameras up at the top showed massive waves thundering against the rock.

Step into the right spot, and tight tunnels of audio would fix on a person's location. The hum of the party dipped away. Roo found himself briefly standing in a spot where the thud of waves striking pounded his chest and the hiss of spray drifting in the aftermath filled his ears. Wind howled.

He stepped out and back into the snatches of random conversation.

Roo drifted into line at a small temporary bar. "Hi," said an intense man with silvered hair. "I'm Gregor Upton, I don't think I've met you before. What's your line of work?"

Roo shook his hand. "Prudence Jones. I'm mostly retired these days. I used to be in security. You?"

"Hurricane refits," Upton said. "I built the walls for this mansion. The owners viewed putting it up on pylons as gauche."

"View's better on pylons," Roo noted. "You'd get to see the beach."

"The stone walls are retractable." Upton waved the objection away. "When hurricane season is over they lower them so that the beach is viewable. Beats the hell out of hammering wood over your windows!"

As they waited their turn for drinks, he talked about his work growing more artificial reefs on islands up and down the Caribbean to help with storm surge and beach mitigation. "I also am spending a lot on a project to genetically engineer tougher foliage. There's some neat things you can do with seagrape trees, but I think the good money's on mangroves. We really need more mangroves to blunt hurricane damage. The more people we can put into hardened high-rise buildings, and restore reef and greenage around them, the less increased hurricane activity hurts us."

Roo took one of his cards and politely disengaged.

The tiny earpiece embedded deep in Roo's ear canal kicked on. "Roo, this is Rhodes. I'm riding shotgun."

Roo grunted.

A waifish woman with deep green eyes talked to him for a while about bauxite derivatives and hurricane insurance, and then Roo had to listen to an older government official talk about the Beijing Accord meetings, where he'd played some role in advocating for an infrastructure bank that invested in bike highway systems across the world.

The lights dimmed, cutting off the humble bragging. At a

set of steps around a chocolate fountain at the front of the room a bald-headed man raised a hand. Screens faded away, and the audio qualities of the room shifted as devices kicked in audio tunneling focuses to allow him to speak to everyone softly.

"Thank you so much for attending yet . . . another successful Hurricane Ball. One of many more to come, I'm sure, given the Atlantic's busy summer." People in the room chuckled. "I am your host for Okath, and I want to say, thank you for trusting me to this. As your host, I'm allowed just a few words, I promise I'll make this brief. I won't pull a Petrov on you."

More polite laughter, obviously an inside joke. Roo noticed some people glancing around, then joining the laughter. Those who didn't laugh would stand out.

A way to separate who was new to the ball, Roo thought.

"You all know we've come a long way since the government-dominated days of missions to orbit and beyond. Many know that I think it's important that we, as a species, find a way to live off our planet. Not just because our world now turns against us with storms and disaster, but because there are those among us filled with a desire for war. All it would take is *one* dangerous nation, *one* rogue state, to take us all down with them."

Charleton paused dramatically and looked at his audience.

"My life's work has been to create a very cheap way to put lots of what we need into orbit, and the Verne Plus gives us just that. It is an important leap for our species. And for us. Imagine, not hunkering down in a building like this, but watching these storms from orbit. Secure. Safe. Above it all."

Behind him a live satellite picture of the great swirl of Okath's arms appeared as a hologram in the air. As if everyone in the room were already above the atmosphere. In Charleton's vision of the future, they were all looking down at the inconvenience of the storm. Above plagues. Above it all.

Upton had moved back Roo's way, and nodded at him. "One vision of the future," he groused. "Never mind trying to fix what's on the ground. Just leave it all behind and run away."

Roo scanned the attentive audience for some sign of Beauchamp.

"After this remarkable storm passes," Charleton continued, "I invite any of you who wish to come and see a launch of the Verne Plus for yourselves. The location, on the east coast of the island where the Atlantic hits the shore, is stunning. However, to demonstrate the all-weather abilities of our system, we will actually be making a launch tonight, right in the middle of the storm. A weather instrument system that will remain suborbital and take measurements of both Okath and, at the other side of its trajectory, a new hurricane already developing off the horn of Africa. So please, enjoy our live feeds, or just head upstairs to the blast-proof windows and enjoy the storm!"

Video appeared on walls of the strikingly long barrel of the Verne Plus. Live hurricane feeds resumed on others. Some guests headed for the curved stairs up toward the top of the mansion.

There were antique wooden chairs and tables in nooks and quiet spots around the edge of the ballroom. Roo sat down at one with his empty glass, watching the hundred or so guests.

An attendant in tails appeared and held out a stiff piece of paper. "The menu, sir."

"Oh." Roo stood. "I'm not hungry, I didn't realize that's what the chairs were for."

"Of course," she said. Her long hair was expertly pinned, lacquered, and sculpted into a spiral shape. More hurricane references. "Can I refill your glass?"

"I think I'll just leave it and go upstairs to see the storm," Roo said.

"Very good, sir," she said, as if he'd just made a wise choice of some sort.

He meandered away, up the long sweep of stairs and through corridors. Small clumps of people sat on couches and chatted about things Roo couldn't hear due to invisible audio chips neutralizing their words outside the bubble of space they stood in.

There would be deal-making going on. Business. Fortunes making connections.

"Roo!" hissed Kit. She grabbed him by the arm and pulled him down the corridor.

She spun him into a bathroom, locked the door behind them both, and yanked a small pen from a purse. She clicked it and static swamped Roo's earpiece.

"Katrina Prideaux, formally Beauchamp," Roo snapped. The anger in him boiled over, threatening any attempt he had been planning of being even-tempered if he saw her. "It seems every time I meet you, I meet a whole new person."

"I can't believe you came here," she muttered, ignoring his anger. "You might have made things worse if he saw you. Do you know if he saw you?"

"You should have told me you were his *daughter*," Roo shouted.

"Hush. Life is packed with the misery of things we *should* have done." Kit searched through her purse for something. "I *should* have realized I'd be followed, instead I ended up getting your nephew killed. Almost got you killed. Couldn't talk you out of going right to the labs. I should have just left with the frog. It had the info I needed, but I stayed to help with your mess. What are you hoping to do here, something even more spectacular?"

Roo folded his arms. "The CIG is listening and watching everything, and I promised them I wouldn't do anything. But the short answer is: I'm here to kill your father. Somehow."

"You're not broadcasting," Kit said.

"What?" As soon as he said that out loud, he felt silly. The static. Of course.

She waved the pen in the air. "I'm using the same technology you had on the boat to jam any signals."

Roo reached for the pen, curious. Kit grabbed his wrist. "I need you to pay attention, Roo. You need to tell this to your people. Get your attention off revenge and onto the bigger issue."

"Which is?"

"The reason I helped you at the island. The reason I helped you storm that ship to get away. My father and his people are launching the engineered plague tonight, in the storm. They're going to use the Verne Plus."

"They're dumping it into Okath?" Zee's obsession with storms and wind patterns now made sense.

Kit nodded. "To spread it around the Caribbean and into

America. The moisture-rich storm environment will help the virus from getting dried out. A second launch directly into Africa also finishes it up."

"It's going to be hard to bomb them in the middle of a hurricane," Roo said.

"And a cruise missile capable of sterilizing the coastal area near the Verne Plus might well veer of course in those winds and kill Barbadians," Kit said. "Or worse, spread the virus across the island if it doesn't quite hit right. So you need to mobilize troops when your team comes to get you out of here. Now, please answer my first question: did my father see you?"

"I don't think so."

"Good, then he won't launch early." Kit looked relieved. She slid a capsule out from her purse and jabbed the end into Roo's forearm. It spit against his skin.

"Kit!"

"Sorry. It's just a sedative. I need a head start. I didn't think you would show up here. Not after what you'd been through."

Roo leaned against a sink, his vision failing. "You should have . . . told us . . ."

"I've been doing the best I can. I just now heard Charleton give the speech saying he was launching in the middle of the storm. That was when I realized what he was doing. I'm sorry, Roo." She grabbed his shoulders and helped him slide gently down to the polished marble tile floor. "There's just one last thing I need to tell you. The fever: did you notice what its victims had in common?"

Roo breathed deeply, trying to fight the drugs. "They . . ." He frowned.

"The immigrants in France. My husband, Hamid. They all had high melanin counts, Roo. They were brown-skinned."

"Zee didn't have *that* much melanin," Roo said. Zee had passed as white in Europe. In fact, it made him a useful agent for the CIG, even if Zee was as Caribbean as anyone else in the office.

"That may have given him the time he needed in Florida to contact you before he died," Kit said. "My father lied to you about the fever. I've been able to do some snooping of my own, Roo. The virus is targeted. I think it hunts specific genes related to skin color. He has been terrified of what he calls the clash of civilizations in Europe. He thinks we're living in the final days of the end of Western Civilization, and is determined to strike first."

"Kit . . ."

"He killed Hamid, Roo. I'm going after him. I have to stop him. For Hamid. For me. For everyone. You'll be out for fifteen minutes, Roo. That's all I need, a head start. Talk to your people."

Roo's eyes had been closed for a while, but now her words faded away as well.

He startled himself awake with a dry mouth and wiped drool off the side of a numb face with his sleeve. He unlocked the door, swaying for a second, then pushed it open. An annoyed man standing outside said, "Finally!"

"Rhodes?" Roo jogged down the hallway.

"Where the hell have you been?" Rhodes snapped. "You

went offline when you saw Katrina Prideaux. We have a few men inside as waiters, but they couldn't find you."

"I'm okay. Listen . . ." As he moved down the stairs over the party Roo summarized everything, talking silently into his sleeve, shoving past guests who made disgusted faces at his lack of manners as he moved toward the main doors.

Rhodes was quiet for a second. "A virus that targets . . ." He swore. "I'll mobilize. Barbadian police and soldiers will work with us. Caribbean Special Forces are in Trinidad; they won't be able to fly out."

Roo stopped at the door and looked at one of the screens. "You have forty minutes," he said.

"Forty?"

"The Verne Plus launch is counting down live in here. Forty minutes. I'm not sure what Katrina is planning, but she's fifteen minutes ahead of us."

He turned from the screen to leave. But not before he spotted Beauchamp's familiar face. The man was holding a flute of champagne and smiling . . . until he saw Roo.

The shock on his face gave Roo a thrill of satisfaction, but then Beauchamp began to move through the crowd at him.

Roo kept walking. The massive doors he'd come through earlier had been shut and barred, but a side door now allowed guests in and out through an airlock-like system of sliding steel doors.

He was struck by the wind the moment he stepped outside. His locks fluttered and flapped, and he had to brace his feet carefully and lean forward. The rain stung: needle sharp and painful.

"Oh thank God," a man in a suit with a woman thirty years his junior stumbling next to him shouted at Roo, hurrying past. "Here are the keys, make sure you get it in the garage *right* away! It's a vintage, original Tesla Roadster, I waited far too long to get here."

"I *told* you," the woman shouted. "I said to you not to delay, but you had to call . . ."

They were cut off by the sliding doors.

Roo looked down at his tuxedo, his mouth open to say something. Then he looked at the key fob, and at the Tesla sitting in the lashing rain.

Forty minutes.

He slid into the vehicle, set the mirror, and looked up to see Beauchamp step out of the doors. Roo almost got back out of the car. Right here, right now, Beauchamp was just fifty feet away.

But there was a Verne Plus launch to stop.

Roo hit the accelerator and peeled out of the drive, heading for the massive gates of the estate. Beauchamp shouted into a phone and one of the massive tornado-proof Humvees moved to the door to pick him up.

23

The Roadster kicked and skidded on the wet road. There was no one else out, it didn't matter that he spent the first few seconds sliding sideways over asphalt. Like any given electric car with a good motor, all the torque was available to the driver. No waiting for the gas to explode and slowly transmit its power down through an axle.

On a dry day it meant getting from zero to sixty at what used to be considered supercar levels of acceleration.

The wipers could barely keep up with the rain as Roo sped along the highway, hydroplaning through patches of wet road where the ocean spilled over the beach, up over retaining walls, and onto the road.

"Roo. What are you doing?" Rhodes asked.

"Going after her," Roo said.

He leaned forward to plug in the location of the Verne Plus into the large screen, tapping it out with his fingers. He missed seeing the dark object in the rain gaining on him in the mirror.

"Don't do that," Rhodes ordered. "Stay put. Let us get in there."

The armored Humvee struck the back of the Tesla, almost riding up onto the trunk. Roo instinctively floored the accelerator. The back of the car wiggled, struggled to keep to the road, and then broke free of the thick metal bars on the front of the monster behind him.

With so much water on the ground the tires slipped and spat, failing to find traction. But Roo managed to pull away from the constant lumbering of the Humvee.

Where was the highway going? As long as he followed the coast, he was going to struggle in the puddles the Humvee powered through.

Roo yanked the wheel right and headed inland.

"Do you hear me, Roo?" Rhodes asked. "Because I can still see you driving away. We put a tracker on you."

In the rearview mirror Roo watched the Humvee just barely make the turn, taking out a street sign as it hopped a curb to follow him.

"Okay, Beauchamp," Roo muttered. "Let's see what we can . . ." He abruptly shut up and hit the brakes. They stuttered, adjusting to the wet road. A large section of a galvanized steel roof bounced down the road at them, a lethal wobbly tumbleweed whipped before the storm winds, ripped off some unlucky person's house.

Roo slalomed left to dodge it, slamming a concrete retaining wall and scraping the side of the car. It whipped past, rattling and clanking, and struck the Humvee.

The armored car obliterated the roof and kept coming. A single sheet of galvanized steel caught in one of the window ports flapped about in the wind, until it too broke free and flew away.

"Shit," Roo said.

"Roo!" Rhodes shouted. "What the fuck is going over there?"

"Rhodes, you wanted a response from Beauchamp? I've got it. He's going to kill me, or I'm going to delay him from getting out to the Verne . . ."

"Damn it, Roo." Rhodes sounded halfhearted as he swore, though.

Glancing at the map to make sure the road wasn't a dead end, Roo veered right in a spray of water, the back end of the car finding purchase in some gravel along the road.

The car bottomed out as the road plunged down. Roo fought to keep speed and control. He smiled as he saw the Humvee miss the turn and try to come to a stop.

Another turn to throw Beauchamp off his tail.

Roo slowed down. The Roadster became more amenable to turning. The gusts of wind, now pushing seventy miles an hour, slapped the sides of the car. But it was sporty, low to the ground, and didn't flip.

He kept his hands on the wheel, compensating for the wind, wincing as debris struck the sides, loud as gunshots.

"You have people headed over there yet?" Roo asked Rhodes.

"Gearing up."

Roo took another turn to route himself back toward Barbados's east coast, where the island faced the Atlantic's fury with high cliffs. The Roadster followed the hills as they climbed up higher into the heart of the island, the wind growing more and more furious as he faced the true brunt of the growing storm.

And it was only getting started.

He didn't have a weapon. Maybe he should have led Beauchamp back toward Bridgetown, close to the CIG office. Because if he was unprepared for the man back at the labs, he was vastly less prepared for him now.

Or maybe he just needed to keep the man busy, now, instead of worrying about Kit. Or getting to the Verne complex.

Roo slowed and stopped. A tiny chattel house had blown across the road. Only twenty feet wide, it was a small, cottage-like wooden structure that had been sitting on a rock foundation near the road. The bright green and pink paint looked recently shellacked, so someone had done restoration work on it.

Remarkably, the whole thing remained intact, so Roo slowly crept toward it. It had been blown down the road into a protected spot by a berm.

He didn't want to hurt the house. They had survived since the days of slavery. Tiny, often made without nails so that they could be disassembled quickly and moved from one estate to another with its occupants, there were fewer and fewer of them each year due to the hurricanes. Hurricanes that hadn't been a major part of the island's past.

Despite the lack of nails, this one was so well made it had

lasted this long, and defied hurricane after hurricane. It had remained mobile up to the end.

Roo had the Roadster half off the road as he slipped past.

He didn't see the Humvee; he heard it over the howl of the wind. A distant grumbling sound that suddenly roared into full rage as Beauchamp threw the vehicle out of the dark.

Roo gunned the Roadster and heard traction control struggle with the slicked mud caked on his tires as he moved back onto the wet road.

He glanced in the mirror just in time to see the Humvee blast through the middle of the chattel house. Brightly painted planks of wood exploded, driven apart by the sharp angles of steel plating on the front of the Humvee. Roo gritted his teeth.

"Rhodes," Roo shouted. "I think I'm in trouble." The Roadster slid out as he struggled to accelerate away.

The Humvee sluiced through the water on the road, ignoring the wind, and powered into the Roadster's side. The world spun in a screeching whirlwind of shattered glass and scraping as the Roadster flipped up, then over. The impact knocked the wind out of Roo and left him dazed.

Upside down, still being pushing along the road, Roo fought the boiling mass of water being shoved into the sports car while trying to get out of his seat belt.

The Humvee braked hard. The Roadster scraped along the road ahead of it, still upside down, until it screeched to a stop.

"You seeing this, Rhodes?" Roo struggled to scramble out. "I told you I needed a gun, man."

There was no reply. Maybe the earpiece had been knocked out.

Roo staggered to his feet, barely able to handle the wind punching him around.

Beauchamp fumbled his way out of the Humvee with two of his familiar neo-Nazi bodyguards. Neither of them had guns. They'd all been at the party.

It would probably make little difference, Roo thought, shielding his eyes from the stinging rain. Three of them against just him, and Roo's head was throbbing hard enough that he could barely focus in the wind. It sounded and felt like they were all standing behind a jet engine right now.

The three men spread out around him, and Roo got ready.

One of the guards stepped in. But as he did so, Roo saw the remains of the chattel house moving. More pieces broke apart as the rest of the small house gave up.

Debris flew down the road at them. Roo crouched, shoving against the wind to get in front of the Humvee to shelter. The nearest neo-Nazi turned to see what Roo had run from just in time to have his head cut clean off by a sheet of galvanized roofing.

The body stood, leaning back against the wind for a moment as blood fountained up into a cloud of red mist that whipped off along with spray from the road.

His corpse tumbled to the ground.

The other guard scrambled to get back into the Humvee but was struck by a beam. Roo heard the crunch and saw him stumble in the wind. Then he slumped to the ground.

Beauchamp dove back into the Humvee.

"Get out here you coward," Roo shouted, running around the front of the vehicle. He pushed against the wind and crawled up onto the vehicle, grabbing the door handle and yanking it open.

A chunk of wood fluttered through the dark and struck him in the temple. Roo started to fall back, but a strong pair of hands yanked him in inward.

The door closed with a solid *thunk*, and Roo rolled into a space between the seats.

24

Roo cracked an eyelid and groaned. He tried to move his hand, but realized he couldn't. Bright lights overhead dazzled his vision. He squinted. He was inside a large, concrete-block building that looked like a warehouse. But with racks of capsules and equipment behind heavy-duty plastic shields to keep them airtight. Lots of cables in the ceiling.

The room had been built around the back end of a very, very large breech. The Verne cannon. It looked like a metal tunnel, headed for the sky, poking through the warehouse. Behind and along the barrel, pneumatic pistons the size of houses held it in place and presumably absorbed the shock of firing. The middle of the warehouse was a giant pit, with metal walkways leading up to the breech so that it could be loaded or reached by workers.

"Mr. Jones, welcome back to the land of the living. For now." Beauchamp leaned over him, blocking the light.

"Where am I?"

"The Verne Plus is twenty inches wide," Beauchamp said. "We don't load a shell in it, but something more like a cruise missile. We fire it out, and at the apex of its natural curve, it fires and heads for orbit. Only, we're not sending anything to orbit this time. We're putting an explosive aerosol in it. And, of course, you."

Roo struggled, but he'd been strapped in securely. He looked around the metal tube's interior. "You know I wasn't sent in alone," he said, looking back up.

"By the time any of your 'colleagues' get here, Roo, you'll have been fired off down the barrel. You'll be accelerated so fast every bone in your body will break. The blood will be drained out of your head in a split second. If you manage to survive that you might, if you're lucky, return to consciousness at the very top of the parabola. You'll get to experience the magic of weightlessness."

"You couldn't just put a bullet up in my head, no? You want me to suffer."

"I want you to see what I've done. After the apex of your parabola, you'll descend to the heart of a hurricane forming off the edge of Africa. The fairing will jettison, so you will be able to experience this if you are still alive. It's there that the payload will separate and disperse."

"The plague," Roo said.

Beauchamp looked pained. "I got the idea when I experienced what you are about to experience. I paid to go on a trip to space. And when I was there, in orbit, I spent an entire day doing nothing but staring out of a porthole down at our world."

Roo jerked his head back as Beauchamp leaned in closer.

"I could see it in all its beauty, Mr. Jones. The wisps of clouds hovering just above the great patchworked land below. I could see the impact we had made. Forests being cut into by the orderly geometry of development. I could see the runoff from great rivers spilling out into the oceans. I could see the dead spots. The constant queue of storms in the Atlantic. Dust storms. Floods. And at night . . . I could see humanity clustered on the surface like bacteria, our wasted energy blazing out to the universe."

"You should have stayed up there and out of everyone's business," Roo said.

"It gave me the perspective to see what needed to be done," Beauchamp said. "It will be the perfect storm. Like selectively cutting a forest so the fires don't destroy all the trees, this culling will cleanse continents. It will ease resource use, lower population. It will prevent the clash of civilizations. People will stay in their own natural countries, because there will be enough for all."

"You've got to be fucking kidding me. That's some racist bullshit." Roo kicked at his restraints, and pulled a muscle somewhere in his left thigh, the one still sore from the healing bone.

Rhodes, Roo thought, I really hope the location tracker you put on me is still working.

"Racist?" Beauchamp yelled. "You look at me and you think that, don't you? But don't you *dare* call me that. The men who kidnapped me, they were racists. Racist against Westerners. They tortured us. Raped my wife. No, you are the racist, Jones, throwing that card out the moment you hear something you don't like."

"What, the first person who says it dealt it? That shit hasn't been true since kindergarten," Roo said.

"No. The things I believe are *facts*. I hate no single person. But no one will face the fact that world is overburdened. Failing."

"Bullshit. A person in the third world uses a tenth the material and resources of someone like you, Beauchamp. If you're serious about what you believe, you're targeting the wrong group."

Beauchamp snarled. He grabbed the fairing to shut Roo in. "Do you have any last words, Mr. Jones?"

Roo thought about it. One always knew people like this walked around. He'd encountered epithets, people who stared at him a little too long. Everyone had seen old video of people goose-stepping in black and white.

But staring at a crazy-assed dude like Beauchamp left the mind a bit scattered with a cross section of just simple rage, and not a little bit of bewilderment.

What the hell did you say to a Hitler 2.0 wannabe?

"Fuck. You," Roo said calmly.

"Good-bye, Prudence Jones," Beauchamp said.

"It's Roo, motherfucker!" The inside of the capsule faded to dark with a bang and then the sound of latches locking him in.

When he was a kid, in a cinder-block home with a distant relative, he'd seen a show about a magician who could escape from any restraints.

The trick was dislocating the thumb.

With the capsule closed, there wasn't going to be too much time before launch. Roo felt himself being moved around. Heard muffled voices outside the capsule as Beauchamp gave orders.

Roo pulled on his right hand. Yanked against the rope restraints until he felt skin beginning to scrape off against the rope as he strained with everything he could manage.

The capsule trundled about some more, headed for the walkways over the pit so it could be loaded into the barrel of the Verne cannon.

Roo arched his back and yanked until he felt tendons stretch. The pain made his eyes water, but he didn't let up. Not until the faint popping sensation of the thumb forced him to scream.

He pulled his hand free.

Now for the other.

Roo began to pull, and looked up in surprise as the capsule opened. He hadn't heard the fairing being unfastened. Too much focus, too much pain. Kit leaned in, her blond hair dangling down. "Roo? Are you okay?"

He stared at her, nodded, then raised his right hand, the thumb dangling uselessly. "Knife?" he hissed. The hurricane was in the background. Always. Like the sound of a large jet airliner landing overhead, but on constant repeat.

She was already cutting his other arm free, close enough to him that she didn't have to yell. "I see you've met my father again. A pleasant man, yes? Do you still want to have that drink on the shore together you promised me back in Dominica?"

"Now more than ever," Roo said, pulling his feet out.

She helped him out of the capsule. It was perched on a flat trolley just under the massive open door of the barrel's breech, looking for all the world like the closed vault of a bank door . . . for giants. Katrina grabbed his thumb as he stepped forward and yanked back on it as he moved away from her.

It popped again. This time the yank of pain was followed by the aching absence of constantly strained tendons and muscle stretched out past their limits.

Roo took a deep breath. "Thanks." There was a worker in overalls slumped near the motorized trolley. He'd been the one tasked with loading it up. "Your work?"

From the outside, the capsule Roo had been in looked like a large cruise missile. But one just barely large enough to fit Roo inside while lying down. Some of the lines revealed its mini space shuttle abilities, like the fact that it had gray heat tiles on the underbelly. That would allow it to withstand reentry into the atmosphere when it returned from delivering a small satellite to orbit.

A window shattered somewhere in the distance.

"He'll wake up in ten to fifteen," Katrina said. "I prefer quiet right now. Hurry, the cameras are down in this half of the loading zone. I didn't jam the ones looking at the barrel itself, but someone will still be sent out to take a look." She had a large duffel bag with her. She grabbed four fist-sized packs of adhesive explosives and a remote detonator. "So here's our dilemma. There's a capsule already loaded inside the Verne. You were going to be number two on the launch agenda tonight."

Roo looked up. Water was dripping along the barrel, seeping in from between where thick rubber baffles kept the weather out.

"My explosives won't crack the barrel. The breech is mechanized, we can't open it from here. But there's a control room." Kit handed him a small submachine gun from the duffel bag. "We blow it up, we stand a chance of stopping the launch. It'll be dangerous, though. Like, stealing a helicopter off a boat dangerous."

"Do you have any grenades?"

Kit handed him two. "All I have, plus the explosives in the bag."

"If we can hold the control room until backup arrives . . ." Roo muttered.

"How far out are they?"

"Minutes?" Roo wasn't sure how long it had taken to shove him in the capsule and tie him down. "But we can't wait."

"I agree," Kit said firmly.

Roo looked at her. "Your father might be in there. Are you going to be able to . . ."

"We talked about this already. He contributed to my genetic material," Kit said, her jaw set. She slung the bag over a shoulder and held up a submachine gun of her own. "He stopped being my father a long, long time ago. I'm here to stop him. He killed my husband."

"Okay." They crossed the warehouse, stepping through pools of water accumulating on the floor and dripping down into the concrete trench by the breech.

They opened the door to the outside and the wind ripped it away off its hinges. Roo put his hand out and looked back at her. "Hundred miles an hour?"

"And building."

Enough to blow them away standing upright. The wind thundered loud enough to overwhelm his eardrums and drive deep into a space behind his sinuses. A hundred yards away the control center, a concrete bunker with no windows, was lit up in spotlights. The mud between the two buildings was a no-man's land of squall, flying mud, and wind.

"Get low!" Roo shouted. Kit nodded.

On hands and knees they pushed forward across the mud between the loading bay and the control center, the wind tearing and ripping at every piece of clothing. It felt like a thousand hands yanking and shoving them around.

The rain needled into Roo's skin.

He started to shiver. The wind chill, even though it was summer in the tropics, was stripping the warmth out of the air.

They were right outside the door of the bunker.

"Hey! You. Stop!" The faint voice of a guard reached them.

The man struggled up against the wind at them from around the corner of the bunker. He had a pistol aimed at them, but the hurricane winds battered his hand.

Roo stopped. He turned back to face the man. "Don't shoot," Roo shouted at Kit.

"What?"

"We're too close to the bunker, they might hear it."

Then Roo stood up. The guard had been keeping his distance, not wanting to get jumped.

But they were in the middle of a hurricane.

"Hey."

Roo jumped into the air and spread his arms and legs. The wind caught him, eagerly throwing his body through the air a few feet over the ground. Roo slammed into the man's chest in midair and knocked his weapon loose. They tumbled and bounced into the mud, grappling at each other.

Then Roo got his forearms wrapped around the man's neck. He could see a small swastika just under his right ear.

With his legs clenched around the stomach, his back pressed deep into the mud, Roo slowly choked him to death as the wind battered him with aerosolized mud.

He staggered back to Kit, waiting at the door to the bunker. She held up three fingers. Then two. One.

Roo kicked in through the door. It was like smacking a wall. The wind was holding it closed shut. Kit waited for him to get it slightly open, then jammed the barrel of her gun into it to lever it open wide enough for Roo to enter, submachine gun up tight to his chin. "Get down! Down!"

Bullets kicked the concrete around him as people fired.

Roo sprayed the room in the direction of the fire, then zeroed in on the first shooter. He went down in a spray of blood.

Another neo-Nazi had dropped for cover right as Roo entered. Now he stood up with a gun. Kit, sweeping in from behind, shot him in the temple.

"Anyone else want to try that?" Roo asked. The other three men standing in the room dropped their guns and raised their hands. "I'm Prudence Jones of the Caribbean Intelligence Group, this is Katrina Prideaux of the French Secret Service. No one is to fire the Verne Plus, understand."

"Everyone, facedown, hands behind your backs," Kit ordered.

One of the technicians near the wall of computer screens raised a hand tentatively. "Mister Beauchamp saw you on an external monitor," she said.

Roo pointed his gun at them. "And?"

"He started the launch countdown. Already. Is that a problem?"

"Yes," Kit said, walking over to her. "Abort. Now."

The technician shook her head. "There are two keys. I'm Annabelle, the head of operations, so I have one." She held up a key on a necklace. "Beauchamp took the other one, at gunpoint. You need both to stop the countdown."

"How long do we have?"

"Six minutes."

"Where is he?"

Annabelle pointed at one of the monitors. "You'd better hurry."

In the misted static of the wind, Beauchamp staggered

along the walls of the warehouse wrapped around the Verne cannon.

"He's headed for the parking lot."

Roo reached into his pocket and pulled out the gecko-feet gloves. "He's going for the Humvee. I'll go after him," he said to Kit.

"I should go," she said. "I'm capable of doing what needs to be done, Roo. I can do it."

"I know you can. I don't doubt it. But these gloves are my hand size," he said, holding them up and wiggling them. "And the wind has picked up enough so that anyone out there is going to need all the help they can get."

"Be careful."

"Keep Beauchamp's pet Nazis on the ground," Roo told her. "I'll be back with the other launch key."

"We'll watch the cameras," Kit promised.

The inside of the control bunker was quiet, warm, and still. An oasis of light and calm.

Roo opened the door and stepped back into the maelstrom.

25

Roo crabbed his way through the mud after Beauchamp. It only took a few seconds to realize he wasn't going to catch the man before he reached the parked cars. Several of the lighter compacts had slid across the mud and stacked up against the back of the warehouse, cracking the wall. But the Humvee remained in place, rocking back and forth.

Beauchamp looked back, and Roo saw the triumph on the man's face. It faded when Beauchamp turned around: a tank broke through the mud, churning debris up with its tracks as it roared toward them.

For a moment, Beauchamp twisted back and forth, not sure whether to still try and run for the Humvee or turn back on Roo. The tank covered the distance as they both stood and watched, smacking into the vehicle and shoving it aside as it skidded to a stop.

The tank's main barrel dropped and spun, aiming at the warehouse. The cavalry had arrived.

Roo stood up and pointed at Beauchamp. "Him!"

Two Barbados Defense Force soldiers popped nervously out of a hatch. They aimed rifles at Beauchamp, who immediately spun and ran for the far side of the warehouse. Bullets kicked up mud, but he turned the corner unharmed.

The soldiers looked at Roo, puzzled, but Roo was already running after Beauchamp. In just seconds he covered the length of the warehouse and found his target climbing the scaffold steps on the outside of the Verne cannon's barrel.

"Beauchamp!" Where the fuck was he going?

Roo made it to the metal stairs, thankful for the gecko gloves. They attached to the railing, helping him hold on gratefully as the wind tried to fling him away.

The barrel pointed up into the air, aiming off the coast of Barbados and over the dramatic cliffs. Roo shielded his eyes and looked up to see Beauchamp moving up the massive barrel. The wind whipped hard at his suit, and the man struggled to inch along, holding onto the rigid metal stays that ran from the barrel up to the scaffolding around it.

"Beauchamp!" Roo shouted.

He didn't hear Roo. Not in this constant thundering howl of wind. The last time he'd been buffeted this bad Roo had been dangling at the end of a line hanging off Angela's plane, watching the harbor in Roseau recede from under his feet.

Roo grabbed the barrel with his gloves and began scurrying up to catch Beauchamp. It was awkward, and occasionally eddies of gusts within the overall thundering roar would shove at him from the side and force him to lay flat while he regained his grip.

But with much grunting and grimacing, he caught up to Beauchamp.

Beauchamp, sensing something was wrong, turned back and saw Roo following him. He screamed something, but Roo couldn't hear him above the wind. Roo reached back for his recently acquired pistol and aimed it at Beauchamp.

"Give it over!" Roo shouted.

Beauchamp held out his hand. "*You* drop it. Or I *will* drop this." He opened his fist and the silver launch key whipped about in the wind.

Roo dropped the pistol. The wind swallowed it. He looked down at the ground far below him. A sixty-foot fall. But into mud.

Beauchamp laughed. "I'm going to throw this away, and it's going to fly away with the storm. Then I'm going to watch the launch from the barrel itself. Even if you kill me, you can't stop the change coming."

There was only way to get the key back to the control room, Roo thought. He wasn't sure if the mud would cushion him enough. Or where the hurricane would blow him as he fell . . .

"The world will see!" Beauchamp shouted above the storm. "It will see how much better things will be when we have more . . ."

Roo's biceps screamed as he bounded forward on arms and

legs in a crouch. Beauchamp reflexively tried to block Roo instead of dropping the key, as Roo had hoped, and Roo grabbed it. He held it close to his chest.

His gloves latched onto Beauchamp's hands, but his whole body dangled over the air. "More what?" Roo asked Beauchamp, pulling himself almost face to face. "More for just you?"

Roo's fingers slipped, even despite the gecko hold, and Beauchamp tugged and tore at the gloves. Roo let go with one hand, the one he'd grabbed the keys with.

Beauchamp's face lit up with triumph. "I know those soldiers have come for me. That's why I ran up here. I'm done, but my work will live forever. I will leave a legacy . . ." Roo's hand slipped further, and Beauchamp unfastened the glove. "But you, Mr. Jones, are dead."

Roo slipped free and fell.

He clutched the key tight to his chest as he was spun around, buffeted and tumbled by the incredible wind. He had no control, no awareness of where up or down was.

Until he struck the mud on his back.

Roo lay there, staring up at the maelstrom around him, the mud surrounding him. But he had the launch key gripped tight to his chest.

When Kit stumbled over to him, he just held up the key. He would have smiled, but it hurt too much.

26

The eye of the hurricane was a moment of calm. At the center, the winds ceased. The clouds faded away and the sun struck the island.

Everywhere one looked: a veil of clouds.

Barbadian soldiers dragged Roo out of the mud and into an armored personnel carrier where a CIG Special Forces medic started looking him over.

"One hundred and twenty broken bones, including the jaw, so don't try to speak," he muttered. "Man, you left a five-inch-deep impression back in that mud. You lucky to be alive."

Rhodes clambered into the back of the APV. "We have fifteen minutes before the eye wall hits, and we're all lucky the storm veered to hit us," he said. "Let's get him to safety."

The moment of calm in the middle of a hurricane, Roo

thought. He'd known some people who left their homes, thinking the storm was over. Or just curious to see what the world looked like outside in the temporary calm.

They'd often get caught as the hurricane resumed, the winds changing direction.

"I want to come," Kit said.

Rhodes looked at Roo, who nodded. And despite the painkillers the medic pumped into him, regretted the movement.

She crouched next to him. "We had just a minute to go, Roo. When I saw you fall, I thought it was over."

He squeezed her hand. Waved her closer to whisper, "Your father?"

"We found his body," she said. "After he ran up the barrel to get away from you all, after you got the key, he just stood up there until a gust took him. In the end, too much of a coward to face us. His body's down on the cliff. Someone will recover it later."

Roo nodded. Winced again. He still wanted to tell her something else. Something that occurred to him while lying on his back in the mud. It felt like he'd had an eternity to mull things over there. "We still . . ." He was going to add, ". . . have work to do." But he had to pause.

"Don't talk right now," she cut him off. "Whatever it is, it can wait. I'll need to go lie low, if Rhodes will let me. When you recover, we'll talk."

She looked at Rhodes. "Least I can do," he said.

Roo took a deep breath and turned his head back to look at the ceiling of the APV as it trundled to life in the eerie calmness around them.

27

A light drizzle from a summer rainstorm pattered against the side of the *Spitfire* as Roo sat at anchor. The white sands of Bridgetown beaches gleamed despite the gray skies. The work of reconstruction was going on across the water. Heavy equipment was still moving cars that had been thrown into inconvenient places, like walls and onto bridges. Several boats still lay scattered around town. But life bustled. Music blared from a park. People were out buying food, buses running on schedule again.

"Hey," a voice called from the side.

Roo hopped out to the starboard scoop and looked over. Kit stood on the front of the dinghy, holding up a case of Red Stripe and a bag of groceries. "Permission to come aboard?"

"Always," Roo said, and helped her up after tying off the painter to the dinghy.

Roo fried some plantains while the rice cooker steamed away. They sat in the cockpit and watched the sun ponderously settle toward the blue line on the horizon as boats sailed by.

"I hoped you'd come by," Roo said, when he finished his beer and threw the remains of the rice overboard for the fish.

"When Rhodes told me you'd snuck out of the hospital and gone to Aves, I thought you'd left Barbados for good."

Roo smiled. "I promised you a drink," he said.

"It's not really a drink if I deliver it, though, is it?"

"Then I'll have to owe you another." He laughed.

"Is that a promise?"

He nodded.

Kit looked over at the cockpit seat nearby. "So what's all that?"

Roo pointed at the plastic backpack-like object. "That's a rebreather for diving. Wet suit. And next to it, a speargun. You've seen one of those before."

Kit's smile faded. "You're not going fishing. What's really going on?"

"I said I was going to hunt down the people who killed my nephew. And Beauchamp is dead." The motley assortment of Eastern European neo-Nazis he'd collected to be his bodyguards and do his dirty work had scattered to the winds. "But there is a small loose end."

"What is that?"

Roo pointed to the three-hundred-foot mega-yacht in the harbor. "While Rhodes and his people are finishing their investigations, Charleton, the creator of the Verne Plus, was asked to stay on the island while things were cleaned up. He's right over there."

"You think he's involved?" Kit asked.

"Well, he denies understanding what Beauchamp was up to. Says he just needed the money and partnership," Roo said. "I'm dubious. I need someone to sit on deck and watch the boat while I go over. And if I don't come back, to let Rhodes know what happened. At the very least, I'd like to have a discussion with Charleton."

"That's why you came back with your boat?"

"Yes."

"And after that?"

Roo opened another beer and pointed at the sun. "You ever wonder where the sun goes after it sets?"

Kit looked out over the ocean. "Far, far away . . ."

"There's always room on the *Spitfire* for you," Roo said. "Even if all you want is an extra room in the other hull. I know you had someone you loved killed by your father, I know you need to grieve. On many fronts. I can't say I'll be comfortable to be around because I have my own cloud to get out from under. But, sometimes it's easier with a friend."

She raised an eyebrow and smiled. "It is."

28

A ghost in a black wet suit, Roo removed an oversized, black window that he'd cut open and slipped into the master suite of the mega-yacht.

When Charleton came in Roo stepped out and blocked the door. "Make a sound, I'll shoot you in the chest with this speargun. You won't be able to scream for sure after that. Understand?"

The man jumped, startled. "Who are you?"

"That was an amazing speech you gave at the Hurricane Ball," Roo said. "Destiny, the species, so on. And then that madman tried to use your space facility to launch a deadly plague."

"I've already said, I had no idea. I've been struggling with investment in the program. Beauchamp promised, and delivered, help I needed."

Roo nodded seriously. Then looked around the mega-yacht. "Struggling with investment."

"Look . . ." Charleton started. "What's your name?"

"Prudence Jones."

Charleton nodded. "Yes. Okay . . ."

Roo interrupted. "I deal in information. Security. You know, after every disaster some conspiracy theorist always says that someone made Wall Street trades based on how it would have affected things. Think of it like, insider trading, but for terrorist attacks and disasters. Of course, it's always some racist asshole claiming it was some minority who knew about it, and it's part of some conspiracy of this or that. But as a freelance spy I always have to take this sort of thing seriously and follow up on it.

"Now, in your case, Charleton, you buried it pretty deeply behind false corporations, but you turn out to have made heavy investments in companies that would have benefited from our mutual friend's plan to kill a chunk of the human race."

Charleton sat down at a tiny desk and sighed. "Beauchamp was a zealot of the worst order. In the strictest sense of the word. And here's the thing, there are lots of zealots out there. Doesn't matter whether it's Beauchamp, or someone else, it's going to happen. Some idiot in a garage somewhere will build a virus that looks for a certain kind of DNA."

"If anyone pulls that trigger, it's going to unleash a worldwide epidemic of groups all releasing bioweapons to kill each other," Roo said. "It's Pandora's Box. Worse than nukes."

"But someone's going to do it first," Charleton repeated.

"People like Beauchamp have been dreaming about a weapon like this since Mengele in World War Two."

"So you thought: why not know who it is? Why not profit off the information?" Roo asked. And saw Charleton smile slightly in agreement. He was reaching for something under the desk, hoping Roo didn't notice.

Roo tracked the movement.

"Now you understand why I think it's *imperative* that humanity not remain only on the surface of Earth," Charleton said mildly.

"You know, my grandmother was very religious," Roo said. "Always said, love of money was the root of much evil. And Charleton, you love money very, very much. I see that you're reaching for something; I wouldn't, if I were you."

"Well . . ." Charleton said. And, very unwisely, pulled the gun out from under his desk.

ACKNOWLEDGMENTS

I owe a debt to the many readers of *Arctic Rising*, the book prior to this one. Many of you wrote me letters asking to see more Prudence Jones. I'd been hoping that it would make sense to make *Hurricane Fever* a book with Roo's point of view, so it was a real treat to get that encouragement. Thanks also to those who forward me news clippings or climate change stories that they think I may be interested in. It's all grist for the mill.

I couldn't have written this without the patience and support of my family, so thanks go to my wife, Emily, as always, as well as my twin daughters, Calli and Thalia, who often have to show up at my elbow and let me know it's time to knock off work for the day.

This book had two editors, a first for me. Many cynics

today wonder whether editors are still in there getting their hands dirty. Trust me, this book would have been far more hobbled were it not for the help of Paul Stevens at Tor Books and Michael Rowley at Del Rey UK.

I also have to thank Sarah Goslee for help with an early read of the book. Any of the science that I got right is thanks to her. All mistakes are my own. I will note I decided in draft to exclude some of the details about a race-targeted virus and how the mechanics of it would work. The idea of some future Mengele reading the book and taking notes squicked me out.

One of the stranger side notes of the history of alternate space access is the HARP gun project, an attempt to actually straight-up shoot small projectiles into outer space. They didn't quite make it before the project was canceled, alas. Somewhere there's an alternate history where Barbados is a major space launch facility, and I decided to revive that possibility.

I have to thank a few people who took the time to help me visit the remains of the HARP gun project, which was an amazing day of research:

My thanks to Karen Lord (another champion of Roo), her friend Fatima Patel, and Robert Sandiford for helping me visit the HARP gun grounds. My thanks also to the Barbadian Defense Forces for allowing me access to this unique piece of Barbadian and alternate space access history. Being escorted out to see the ruins of the giant guns set up to launch micro-satellites was truly useful in helping get the last section of the novel set up.

I also would like to thank the organizers of AnimeKon Expo in Barbados (particularly Omar Kennedy and Mel

Young). As a kid growing up just next door in Grenada, I would never have guessed I'd be back down just forty or so miles from where I was born to celebrate science fiction, games, cosplay, and movies, as well as meet so many cool readers who are both islanders and lovers of science fiction. Being a guest at this unique event allowed me to research the HARP gun and decide that Roo had to get involved with it for this book. If you are interested in science fiction, pop culture, comics, and the Caribbean, you should make the time to visit Barbados for it.

Lastly, thank you to everyone at bookstores who promoted *Arctic Rising* and readers who passed the word around, thus allowing *Hurricane Fever* to become real. This wouldn't have happened without your support.

young). As a kid growing up just next door in Grenada, I would never have guessed I'd be back down just forty or so miles from where I was born to participate in science fiction games, cosplay, and movies, as well as meet so many cool readers who are both Bajans and lovers of science fiction. Being a guest at this unique event allowed me to research the HARP gun and decide that Zoo had to get involved with it for this book. If you are interested in science fiction, pop culture, comics and the Caribbean, you should make the time to visit Barbados for it.

Lastly, thank you to everyone at bookstores who promoted *Arctic Rising* and readers who passed the word around, thus allowing *Hurricane Fever* to become real. This wouldn't have happened without your support.

Enjoyed *Hurricane Fever*?

Read on for a sneak peek from

ARCTIC RISING

Also by

Tobias S. Buckell

Available now from Del Rey

1

Centuries ago, the fifty-mile-wide mouth of the Lancaster Sound imprisoned ships in its icy bite. But today, the choppy polar waters between Baffin Island to the south of the sound, and Devon Island on the north, twinkled in the perpetual sunlight of the Arctic's summer months, and tons of merchant traffic constantly sailed through the once impossible-to-pass Northwest Passage over the top of Canada.

A thousand feet over the frigid, but no longer freezing and ice-choked waters, the seventy-five-meter-long United Nations Polar Guard airship *Plover* hung in a slow-moving air current. The turboprop engines growled to life as the fat, cigar-shaped vehicle adjusted course, then fell silent.

Inside the cabin of the airship, Anika Duncan checked her readings, then leaned over the matte-screened displays in the cockpit to look out the front windows.

The airship's cabin had once held twelve passengers, but was now retrofitted with a bunk, a small kitchen area, supply closets, and a cramped navigation station. Tourists had once sat in the cabin underneath the giant gasbag as the airship glided over New York's tallest buildings. After that tour of duty, the United Nations Polar Guard purchased it well used and very cheap.

Airships didn't use much fuel. They could put observers into the air to monitor ship traffic for days at a time, wafting from position to position with air currents.

It saved money. And Anika knew the UNPG was always struggling with a lean budget. It showed on her paycheck, too.

"Which ship should we take a closer look at, Tom?" Anika asked.

She'd unzipped her bright red cold-sea survival suit and rolled it down to her waist, as it was too hot for her to wear fully zipped up as regulations required. She had her frizzy hair pulled back in a bouncy ponytail: a week without relaxant meant it had a mind of its own right now. She'd consider letting it turn to dreads if she could, but the UNPG didn't approve. And yet, she thought to herself, they expected her to sit up in the air for a week without a real shower.

Someone once told her to just shave it. But she *liked* her hair. Why hide it? As long as it was tied up, regs said she could have longer hair.

Now Thomas Hutton, her copilot, was all about the regs and then some. He had his blond hair millimeter short. Shorter than required. But even *he* wore his survival suit halfsies.

It was one of those balancing acts: if they kept it cold enough in the airship's cabin to wear the suits zipped up, using the tiny, cramped toilet was torture.

Particularly, Tom said, for the guys.

"Tom?" she prompted.

"Yeah, I'm looking, I'm looking." He walked back from the nav station, the top half of his suit floppily smacking along behind him as he peered down through the windows along the way.

Four ships were funneling their way into the Lancaster Sound from the east, where Greenland lurked beneath the curve of the horizon. The ships looked like bath toys from up at this height. Three of the ships had large wing-shaped parafoils hanging in the sky overhead. The parafoils, connected to the ships by cables, reached up to where the strong winds were blowing to drag the ships through the water.

"I want to take a closer look at that oil burner," Tom finally announced.

"You are getting predictable," Anika said as he slid into the copilot's seat. Though one of the things she liked about Tom was his easy predictability. Her own life had been chaotic enough before coming so far north. It was a different pace up here. A different chapter of her life. And she liked it. "It *is* supposed to be a random check?"

He pointed at the black plume of smoke trailing from the stacks of the fourth ship in the distance. "That one sticks out like a sore thumb. Hard to say no to."

Anika tapped the scratched and well-worn touch screens around her. She pulled up video from one of the telephoto-lens cameras mounted on the prow of the cabin and zoomed in on the fourth ship.

Thirty meters long with a bulbous-prowed hull, flaking rust, and colored industrial gray, the ship was pushing fifteen knots in its rush to pass through the sound.

"They seem to be in a hurry."

Tom glanced over. "Fifteen knots? She hits a berg at that speed she'll Titanic herself quickly enough."

The Arctic still had an island of ice floating around the actual Pole. It was kept alive by a fusion of conservationists, tourism, and the creation of a semi-country and series of ports that sprang up called Thule. They'd used refrigerator cables down off platforms to keep the ice congealed around themselves despite the warmed-up modern Arctic, a trick learned from old polar oil riggers who'd done that to create temporary ice islands back at the turn of the century.

It was an old trick that didn't really work anywhere else but near the Pole now. But even the carefully artificial polar ice island that was Thule still calved chunks, some of which would get as far south as Lancaster.

Hit one at the speed this ship was going, they'd sink easily enough.

"Shall we get closer to him and sniff him over?" Anika asked. "Remind him to slow down."

Tom grinned. "Yeah, their credentials should come through shortly. The scatter camera's up. Let's see if this ship's radioactive."

The neutron scatter camera, mounted on a gimbaled platform right next to the telephoto cameras, hunted for radioactive signatures. Port authorities had been using them to hunt for potential terrorist bombs for decades. But what they found, over time, was a secondary use for the scatter cameras: catching nuclear waste dumpers.

At the turn of the century, after the tsunami that washed over East Asia, UN monitors found themselves contacted by East African countries about industrial pollutants washing up on the beaches. People had been falling sick after approaching large, well-insulated drums washed up from deep in the ocean. People had also been showing statistically high rates of cancer near coastlines throughout countries where standing navies and coast guards just didn't exist.

Toxic waste, including spent nuclear fuel, was clearly getting dumped off non-monitored coasts by commercial shipping.

The gig started when a shady company got the lowest bid for safely storing fuel or industrial waste. Ostensibly, they were transporting it out of country to another location.

In reality, once offshore of some struggling African country with no navy, they'd dump it.

Even so-called "first world" countries weren't immune. A statistical study of waste-transporting merchant ships thirty years ago showed a higher number of merchant ships "sinking" in the deeper Mediterranean.

Charter an old leaker, stuff it with barrels full of whatever the host country and its businesses didn't want. Take the big payout, head out to sea, and then experience difficulties. Instant massive profit.

The African and Mediterranean dumping had

faded with the EU and East African naval buildups and public outrage. More dumping was going on off Arabic coasts these days. The post oil-boom nations were too busy trying to destroy each other for what little black gold was left to have the capability to worry about what was going on off their coastlines.

But now the Arctic was also seeing dumping. With the whole Northwest Passage open and free of ice, merchant ships could cross from Russia to Greenland, on through Canadian polar ports, and then to Alaska. Which also meant they crossed over some very deep Arctic water.

As nuclear power boomed across Eurasia and the Americas, with smaller corporations offering small pebble-bed nuclear reactors to energy-hungry towns and small cities demanding an alternative to oils needed in the plastics industries, the waste had to go somewhere.

Somewhere was more often than not . . . out here where Anika patrolled.

Hence the old, repurposed UNPG spotter airships with scatter cameras. Anika and her fellow pilots hung above the Northwest Passage helping monitor ship traffic that came from the world over. But mainly, they were hunting for ships with radioactive signatures.

The program had proven effective enough. Word had gotten out, thanks in part to a major UNPG advertising campaign online. For the past seven months Anika's job had become rather routine.

Maybe even a little boring.

Which is why, for a moment, she didn't notice the sound of the scatter camera alarm going off.

2

Anika gunned the turboprop engines to shove the airship down toward the choppy ocean.

"Do you have an ID on the ship?" she asked. The ship could be nuclear powered, she guessed. There were plenty of bulk carriers that were. But this one felt way too small for that.

Tom had a tablet in his lap and was paging through documentation.

"The transponder onboard claims it's the *Kosatka,* registered out of Liberia. Papers are in order. She cleared herself in Nord Harbor." He looked across at her. "She's already been cleared by Greenland Polar Guard. We shouldn't even be paying attention to her. If we hadn't left the camera on, we would have just pinged the transponder and let them through."

They'd dropped a couple hundred feet, and the *Plover* picked up speed in the still air as the four engines strained away.

"Is there anything about radioactive cargo when she cleared Greenland?"

Tom shook his head. "She's clean on here. Do you still want to get in closer?"

That was Tom, following the letter of the law. The rules said the ship was cleared, that someone had checked it over in Greenland. They didn't need to run a second check.

"Someone in Greenland could have slipped up," Anika said. Or, she thought silently, been bribed. She picked up the VHF radio transmitter and held it to the side of her mouth. This was weird enough to warrant a closer look, either way. "*Kosatka, Kosatka, Kosatka,* this is UNPG 4975, *Plover,* over."

Nothing but a faint crackle came from the channel.

Tom waved his tablet. "Says here it's a private research vessel operating out of Arkhangel'sk."

"So they are registered in Liberia for convenience," Anika said. "But operating out of Russia. And they're studying what?"

"It doesn't say."

"Search around online, see if you can find anything."

"Already on it."

Anika piloted them down through the black plume of smoke in the air behind the Russian vessel. They were catching up to it.

Once abreast, she would run the scatter camera again. This would get them better data for Baffin Island. This way whoever was doing this couldn't then claim the camera flagged a false reading. Even if the ship dumped its waste, Anika could prove it had been carrying something obviously radioactive.

Then the gunships would get involved. And boarding parties.

But that wouldn't be her problem. Which was why Anika liked flying. Back in the Sahara, after she'd put Lagos well behind her, she'd flown as a spotter for the miles of DESERTEC solar stations out in the middle of nowhere. High over the baking sand, she'd run patrols looking for trouble.

Like a god looking down from the clouds, she'd directed guards out to the perimeter to make sure Berber tribesmen weren't really disguised terrorists looking to blow up the solar mirrors that ran most of North Africa and Europe.

Anika throttled back as she matched speed with the *Kosatka* and glanced portside, down at the ship. It was a few hundred feet away. She could see the silhouettes of figures behind the glass panes of the cockpit windows looking over the ship's decks. The gasbag of the *Plover* had blocked the sun out for *Kosatka*. Surely the bridge crew had noticed her by now.

They had. Two men opened a rusty door on the side of the bridge and looked at her, shading their eyes as they did so.

They ran back inside.

"Well, they're paying attention now," she laughed.

Kosatka was a beater. Rust showed everywhere, and where it didn't, it had been sanded away and covered in gray primer. Patches of the stuff blotched the entire ship.

"*Kosatka, Kosatka, Kosatka,* this is UNPG *Plover* off your starboard side, over."

"Case of beer says they're dumping," Tom said, standing up and looking over her to the ship.

"What kind of beer are we talking about?" Anika asked as she fired up the scatter camera again. She backed the readings up to a chip and slipped them into a pocket on her shoulder. Old habits. Hard copy trumped all. Half the equipment on the airship broke down, and she didn't want to lose the data. Dumpers deserved nothing more than to rot in jail, she figured. And she'd be really annoyed if some slipup of hers let one of them slip through. "If it is that cheap 'lite' beer you had at your barbecue last month, I don't want to win a bet with you."

Tom looked wounded. "Jenny picked that out, not me. I was stuck in the air with you all that week, remember?"

"I remember." Anika looked over at the radio. Still static.

"What kind of good Nigerian beer should I bet, then?" Tom asked, sitting back down and looking up his results for the search on the ship.

"Guinness will do."

"Guinness?"

"Number one in the mother country," Anika said. "Someone told me they sell more of it back home than in Ireland." She tapped the picture of her and her father sitting on a blanket on Lekki Beach just outside Lagos. Each was wearing a crisp white shirt, holding a pint. Big smiles. Hot sun. Cool ocean.

"No shit?"

"None at all." Anika grabbed the mic. "Let's see if we can raise them and get them to heave to, okay? Next step: we call in the nearest cutter and get this over with. The camera still thinks they are hot."

Before she could call again, a heavy Russian voice crackled over the radio. "Yes, yes, hello. You are United Nations Polar Guard. Correct?"

Anika sighed. "The crew doesn't know how to respond to us on the radio properly." She keyed the mic. "*Kosatka,* switch to channel forty-five, repeat, four-five. Over."

She waited for confirmation, but none came. She was considering switching to channel forty-five when Tom tapped her shoulder. "What's that?" He sounded as if knew, though, but just couldn't believe what he was seeing and wanted confirmation.

Anika glanced over. The two men had pulled a small crate out onto the metal deck around the bridge. Anika squinted at the contents, but spotted the distinctive and familiar long tube of a shoulder-held rocket-propelled grenade launcher.

No time to react, no time to think. She yanked on the joystick and gunned the turboprop engines to maximum. The massive, lighter-than-air machine banked hard to the left as she flew just fifty feet over the old ship's superstructure.

Crossing to the other side of the ship would force those men to move the RPG over, Anika thought. That'd give her a minute. And it would get them further away as the airship struggled to accelerate toward its top speed of seventy miles an hour.

This was bad, Anika thought. Probably worse than Nairobi.

Definitely worse than Nairobi.

"Is that what I think it is?" Tom shouted at her over the roar of the engines.

"RPG." Anika yanked her survival suit up over her shoulders and zipped it up.

"Jesus Christ," Tom said. "Jesus Christ."

Anika snapped her fingers to get him to look at her instead of back at the ship. "Hey. Stay calm. Zip up your survival suit. And grab the controls."

He fumbled at his suit with one hand and held the joystick loosely with the other. She left him to hold their course and raced back down the cabin.

She kicked a large plastic chest open with one booted foot and pulled out an old Diemaco C11 assault rifle packed inside. She slapped a clip in it, shouldered it, and stood up in front of the rear window.

Some small part of her wanted to join Tom's mantra of "Jesus Christ," over and over again, but she knew that was the sort of useless shit that got you killed. You needed to take action.

She flicked the safety off.

They'd pulled clear of the ship by several hundred feet. The two men had moved to this side of the bridge, and one of them got the RPG launcher up onto his shoulder and was aiming at the *Plover*.

Anika's heart raced as she yanked the rear window down. She could hardly focus as she aimed and fired a burst from the Diemaco, hoping she was in time. The ear-bursting chatter shocked her. It drowned out the engines.

A flare of light burst on the *Kosatka*'s bridge as the RPG launched and flew right at her. Anika scrunched low and winced. This was it.

The entire airbag over the cabin shivered, but didn't explode.

"Did they hit us?" Tom shouted back at her.

"I think it punched through the bag but didn't explode. It just kept going. Check the bag's pressure."

"We're losing gas and lift," Tom yelled.

Anika propped the Diemaco up on the windowsill and tried to get a better shot at the men on the ship, forcing them to take cover in the bridge with their launcher. Waste-dumping *bastards*. An RPG? This was the Northwest Passage. They were just north of Canada, not in some war zone.

The *Plover* slipped slowly out of the sky as the *Kosatka* churned on past.

Up front, Tom got on the radio. Over her quick bursts of fire, Anika could hear him calling for assistance, his voice suddenly sounding pilot-calm as he followed a routine. "Nanisivik Base, Nanisivik Base, Base this is *Plover*, we've been hit by an RPG. We're under fire. Repeat, under fire. We need assistance by *anything* in the area."

Anika kept the men pinned inside the bridge with her rifle. But now another man with a launcher appeared down on a lower deck. Anika swiveled to shoot at him, but he fired first.

She kept firing just ahead of that flash of fire, trying to intercept the insanely fast blur of the rocket leaping at her airship.

The rocket struck the bag and this one exploded as it hit a structural spar inside. Melting fabric rained down around the cabin. Alarms whooped from up front in the cockpit. "We're going down!" Tom screamed.

Anika could feel it: her stomach lifted toward her chest. The *Plover* dropped out of the last fifty feet of air in a dignified, fluttering spiral that gave Anika enough time to make sure her survival suit was zipped and to make sure that she had braced herself against the corner of the cabin.

Outside, the waves became choppier and more defined with each split second as they rose to meet the airship.

The *Plover* smacked into the Arctic Ocean with an explosion of spray and flaming debris as the burning gasbag overhead collapsed and draped itself over them with a fluttering sigh.

3

The world darkened. Electronics sparked and fizzed, then blew out for good. Painfully cold water slapped Anika's face as it poured through the shattered windows, shocking her.

The Arctic might be ice free, but it was still damn cold.

"Tom? Can you hear me?" Ruined equipment and a buckled ceiling blocked her way forward. "Tom?"

"Anika? I can get out, are you okay?"

"I can get out through a window. Get clear of the debris, I'll swim around to you. Okay?"

He paused for a moment. "Yeah. See you on the other side."

He sounded relieved.

The cabin's natural displacement had kept the wreckage floating somewhat, but she knew it was starting to settle and would soon get to sinking. Anika didn't have much time.

She swam clumsily along to the back window and took a deep breath. There was helium in the gasbag, that was why the first rocket had gone clean through without igniting a massive explosion.

But she didn't want to take a big gulp of helium while swimming through the remains of the gasbag and end up passed out, facedown in the cold water.

She ducked briefly underwater and swam free of the cabin.

But there was nowhere to surface. The heavy fabric of the gasbag sat on the water.

Lungs bursting already, Anika kept moving along, looking for light.

There.

She burst free and up out of the water. The wind stung her face, but she'd never been so glad to see the gray clouds overhead.

Shivering, almost convulsing despite the survival suit, she pulled herself on top of the floating debris and looked around.

"Tom!"

She pulled herself up over a large spar attached to a pocket of fabric, still filled with helium and listlessly floating just above the surface, hoping to spot Tom and orient herself.

Instead, she found herself staring at the bow of the *Kosatka*. It had turned around and was now bearing down on the remains of the *Plover*. A massive bow wave piled up in front of the *Kosatka*, rippling through the debris of the fallen airship and scattering it even further.

Water surged through the mess, soaking Anika.

The ship shoved its way through like an old icebreaker, leaving a mess of even smaller pieces of airship behind it. The mounds of cloth, broken spars, and helium and air pockets underneath that kept the mangled wreck still afloat, slapped up against the side of the *Kosatka,* screeching against the old, barnacled hull.

Anika watched its bubbled and rust-pitted bulk sweep past her, a giant moving wall of metal. After it pushed its way through the worst of the debris, the engines coughed back to life, thrumming so powerfully her chest ached. They'd coasted through with them off to protect the propellers.

The churning water threw Anika around, doused her, and then just as abruptly, the water calmed a bit, broken by the ship's passing. Anika floated in the quiet, listening to the fizz of disturbed air bubbling around her.

It was so damn cold, it was almost all she could think about.

After a moment she fumbled around inside her suit and pulled out the EPIRB. It was the size of a small flare in the palm of her gloved hand. She broke the seal on it and then put it back inside a zippered pocket.

The tiny radio beacon inside the device activated, and it began to pip audibly to let her know the distress signal was going out. She lay back, still shivering, and yanked the suit's inflation strings.

The survival suit filled with air and bobbed on the surface.

Anika yanked the hood as tight around her face as possible, pulled her legs up to her chest as best she could, then wrapped her arms around her chest and waited for rescue.

So damn cold.

4

A ferry skidded on hydrofoils over the dark ocean, floating almost magically on the air above the waves. When it slowed, the foils sank deeper into the sea, unable to hold it up. The ferry's hull slowly settled down into the water, until it looked just like any other ship.

High above the ferry a parafoil hung in the wind. The taut cables beneath it vibrated and sang as the kite-sail began to dance a figure-eight pattern overhead, allowing the ferry to slow down enough to meander through the debris.

Anika tried to sit up, forgetting for a second where she was. The movement sank her, and cold water washed over her face and dribbled down the sides of her cheeks. It even got inside the suit a bit, down her neck and onto her shoulders.

As the ferry picked its way through the debris of *Plover,* Anika waved weakly at it. "Over here!"

Someone on the deck spotted her and the ferry changed course.

An orange life preserver hit the water a few feet away. Anika clumsily paddled over to it, then pulled it on underneath her arms.

Three burly men in plaid shirts and blue coveralls hauled her out of the water and over the railing, grunting as they helped her onto the deck.

The contrast of sudden heat from the ferry cabin and the cold water she'd been pulled out of started her shivering again, her teeth pressed against each other so hard they felt like they would shatter. Her muscles spasmed, like she was having a seizure.

One of the men threw a first aid kit on the dirty metal floor in front of her.

"Come on, we gotta get this off you," said another man behind her, yanking at the strings she'd pulled so tight.

They stripped the survival suit off her, and then someone grabbed a pair of scissors and cut her wet uniform away. Someone else wrapped a dry thermal blanket around her.

The warm air between her skin and the survival suit disappeared, and that sent her into another round of deep, bone-shaking shivering.

"Tom," she told them, teeth chattering. "Tom." She wasn't sure if they could understand, and she kept repeating it as best she could.

"We're looking for him," someone said into her ear as they rubbed her arms.

A thermometer beeped, and Anika felt pressure against her ear release. "The shivering's okay," the voice behind her said. "Means you're alive. Your temp's a bit low, but you're fine. Keep shivering and moving and rubbing your arms."

Anika took an offered cup of warm water.

"Sip it," they told her. "No gulping."

She almost dropped the cup, but with focus and determination, she managed to bring it shakily up to her lips and sip. She hunched in place on the floor, listening to the thermal blanket crinkle and crunch every time she shifted.

"Got him!" someone shouted.

A few minutes later they dragged Tom in, dripping water, and the whole routine repeated itself. Only Tom didn't look so good. His uniform was sopping wet; the survival suit hadn't gotten zipped quite properly.

His lips were blue, Anika saw. Tom was almost translucent, a pale man almost tailor-built for living in this polar world. But it didn't matter to the cold water.

A redheaded man with a long beard held up a satphone as they wrapped Tom in a thermal blanket. "UNPG's five minutes out by helicopter. Jen? They want you to drop the parafoil."

A short, wind-burned woman in her late fifties with a ruddy face and straw blond hair walked out into the cabin. "Five minutes? Shit. Hey! Everyone on deck, we're pulling in the sail!"

The redhead remained bent over Tom, checking his temperature. When he sat back and glanced at Anika he didn't have to say anything. It was in the posture. Anika saw. Tom was in bad shape.

A minute later a large amount of parachute-like material dropped to the flat back deck where the crew of the ferry grabbed it and rolled it up.

As the parafoil was being packed away, she could hear the *thwap* of rotor blades approaching.

Two UNPG search-and-rescue men dropped out of the sky on ropes and hit the deck. They conferred with the redhead, shouting over the noise of the hovering helicopter.

Then, consensus reached, they hauled Tom out on deck, fastened him to a basket, and all disappeared back up in the air.

"They're low on fuel. They said they've been in the air since your mayday call, all the way from Nanisivik. They'll send another helicopter for you," the redhead said, appearing in the door.

Anika leaned back against the steel bulkhead behind her. "I understand. Does anyone have a satphone that they can lend me?"

Jen, who Anika took to be the ferry's captain, had a thick, plastic-covered phone with a whip antenna: all functional and weatherized. The logo GAIA and a smaller TELECOMMUNICATIONS was stamped into the side in raised letters with a globe in the background. Anika slowly punched the numbers in to dial Nanisivik Base.

"Claude here," replied a smooth, but slightly tired-sounding Québécois voice on the other side.

"Commander, it's Anika Duncan," she said through jaws still clenched from the cold.

"Anika! A second chopper's about fifteen minutes out from you," Commander Michel Claude said quickly. "Are you okay? They said you were okay. They said Tom needed to be flown back right away."

"Yes, yes, I'm doing fine," Anika reassured him. "They were right to leave me if they were low on fuel." She didn't want to be responsible for her rescuers getting themselves in danger as well due to something as simple as running out of fuel.

She could hear Michel let out a deep breath. "We have two cutters headed out at top speed for the area. We've put out an alert for the *Kosatka*. Five airplanes, two airships, and the Canadian Navy and U.S. have been updated. We're looking over a recent satellite scan of the area. We *will* find and catch up to these assholes."

"Thank you, sir. If you hear anything more about Tom, please call this number back."

She handed the satphone back over, and Jen exchanged it for some faded blue jeans, a garish neon yellow t-shirt, and a thick, beige Carhartt jacket. "You're about five eleven?" Jen asked.

Anika nodded. "Five ten . . ."

"Those'll fit you well enough." She shook her head. "You're damn lucky we were out here."

Anika pulled them on, loving the feel of warm cloth against her skin. They'd almost died. Then almost been rammed. Then frozen. She felt numb, not just physically, but mentally.

And exhausted.

But she had enough energy now to remember to ask for her uniform. She unzipped the shoulder pocket and found the backup from the scatter camera. She slipped it into her new jeans.

The ferry was on its way to Thule's floating assemblage of old tankers, barges, and laced-together ice islands at the Pole. There they'd offload goods in the hold and workers for Gaia, Inc., a multinational company with interests in carbon mitigation. For now, though, they'd remain in place until help could get to Anika.

Fifteen minutes later she was out in the whipping cold of the rotor wash of another helicopter, into the rescue basket, and then being winched up.

As one of the chopper crew busied himself getting an IV in her arm, Anika stared out at the gray sea and the bright evening sky to the west of them.

That's where the *Kosatka* was, somewhere out there over the curve of the horizon.

Another chapter of her life had just slammed shut, Anika realized, as anger gelled inside of her. A chapter of routine, calm, and knowing what each day would hold. A peaceful chapter. A good chapter.

But that was over.

5

Tom's wife, Jenny, leapt up from a padded bench near a nurse's station at the Nanisivik Hospital and grabbed Anika in a fierce hug. Her small hands gripped the back of Anika's jacket. "Oh my God," she said. "They said you were okay. I kept thinking, if Tom's spent the same amount of time in the water as you, maybe they weren't telling me everything."

Anika squeezed her back. Having Jenny as a friend was like having a hyperactive, overly eager-to-please, little white sister. But it was okay. Jenny and Tom were the closest things Anika had to family out here in the Polar Circle. Anika was slow to make friends, a casualty of the last ten years spent hiring her services out as a pilot. She kept to herself and kept others at a distance, as she was going to leave anyone she met in a few months when she hopped off to a different job. And maybe a part of the fact that being distant came so naturally to her was due to the violent early years before she earned her first chances to pilot. Back when she'd always had to carry a gun. "I think his suit got water in it. I got off easier."

"I'm so glad you're okay."

They hugged again. Anika got a mouthful of Jenny's blond curls. Then she pulled back and looked Jenny in the eye. "And Tom?"

"He's peeing into a jug right now, made me leave the room," she said.

"He's awake? He's okay?" Anika felt the hundred pounds of anxiousness that had been clinging to her drop away.

Relief prickled at her.

Jenny nodded. "He's really tired. But he's talking." Her translucent green eyes teared, and she wiped at them with a sleeve. "I'm sorry."

Anika shook her head. "Sorry? You have nothing to apologize for."

Jenny rubbed her upper arms nervously, her sweater sleeves flopping about. "I don't understand how you can be so calm. Anika: they shot you down."

"Calm?" Anika thought about it. She wasn't calm. She was still running on adrenaline and shock, that's all. None of this had penetrated that outer wall, a pilot's levelheaded ability to run through a checklist while something was going wrong.

Anika had been through some tight spots. She knew the shakes came later. She wasn't sure what was going to happen once she wrapped her head around everything that had just occurred.

Jenny knocked on the door. "Are you done in there?"

"Yeah," a familiar voice said. A husky, scratchy, and frail-sounding Tom.

"Okay, we're coming in then," Jenny said cheerfully.

Anika followed her, wrinkling her nose again at the smell of hospitals. She didn't like them. She associated them with dying relatives. There was nothing worse as a child than being forced to go visit and make small talk to family members whom she only occasionally saw. They were always hurting, tired, and scared in hospitals, and that put her off.

But this was Tom, and she felt angry at herself for those childish memories.

He looked pale. And tired. He was wrapped in warming blankets, with a slightly bent container of urine hanging off the side of a bed rail.

"I guess I owe you a case of beer," he said when he saw Anika step around the curtain with Jenny.

Anika smiled. "I'll let it go. Just this once."

He reached a hand out, and she took it, shook it firmly, and then he pulled back into the blankets, shivering. "Christ, it's like I can't ever get warm anymore."

"Worse than Polar Bear Camp . . ." Anika agreed.

They both nodded. Every new UNPG pilot who arrived on base got initiated by being taken to "camp." In reality, it was a large icy lake near some dramatic foothills not too far from Nanisivik.

You had to jump into the ice-cold water and swim a single lap. If you refused, they'd toss you in.

But afterward they'd gone to the hot tubs along a wooden platform near the road to the lake and drank.

That had ended well, Anika thought. This hadn't.

Tom looked up at her, apparently coming to the same conclusion. His smile had faded. "They fucking shot us out of the fucking sky, Anika." There was wounded outrage written across his face now.

Anika felt the same thing. "I know. I don't . . ." Actually, she wasn't sure what she wanted to say next. She hunted around for words. "I can't figure it out. They have to know they're being hunted. Where can they go?"

"Guess we'll find out soon enough," Tom muttered.

Half an hour later, Anika stood outside the hospital, blinking up at the bright Arctic night. They'd had it darkened inside.

From outside, the hospital looked like the world's largest Quonset hut. A giant aircraft hanger. Arctic architecture chic, according to some Montreal designer who'd stamped his mark on what seemed like every public building out here. The hospital itself was basically a smaller building inside the giant hanger, which let them keep small gardens and trees in the lobby year round.

The buildings in the deep Sahara Anika had lived in when she'd worked for the DESERTEC project used the same principle: create a large space of protected air in a dome, then build a small piece of the world you'd come from inside of it.

They were like space stations, she thought, but sitting on the pieces of Earth's land that were too alien for anyone to survive in.

Her Toyota ran out of power three miles up the gravel road from base housing. She walked the rest of the way, jacket pulled tight, hugging herself, her breath billowing out into the air and then being yanked away by the wind. She'd go back for the car in the morning, push it the last flat miles, and hook it up to the charger.

Inside her square prefab, one of the hundreds all splayed out across the Arctic gravel in spiral patterns, she turned the heat up even further and shucked off the stranger's clothes.

She considered a bath. The appeal of soaking in warm water until she'd chased every last chill from her bones was strong. But she was tired enough that she feared she would fall asleep in the tub.

Instead she took a shower so hot it felt like it would burn the top layer of her skin away.

Then she crawled into the thick sheets and comforter under the gaudy poster of an airship advertising an old Nollywood movie.

For once, the beams of light from around the corners of the shades didn't bother her. She fell asleep the moment her head hit the pillows.

And what felt like seconds later, she sat up.

The house phone rang again, and she rolled over and picked up the old headset.

"Nika!" said the scratchy voice. "Is that you?"

She hadn't even gotten in a fuzzy hello. Her father sounded scared, hopeful, nervous, and angry, all at the same time.

"Father . . ." She blinked against the light streaming in around the darkening blinds. Hearing his voice, even if transported from so far away, made her feel better.

"I cannot believe you did not call me. Here we are, hearing this news that says an airship was blown out of the sky near Baffin Island, and you have not even called us to let us know you are okay, or even sent us a message? I called your phone over and over and over again. Then your aunt says to me that she has another number for you and that's how I finally reached you. I almost died from the worry."

Anika braced herself against the headboard from the onslaught of clipped, angry words from her father as he lectured her. "I fell asleep," she said, rubbing at her eyes. "And yes, it was me they shot at."

"I . . . what did you say?" Her father lost his train of thought.

"They shot me down. Me and the other pilot."

A long silence dripped from the other side of the phone. Then finally her father collected himself. No more yelling now. "Are you okay, Anika?"

Anika slumped forward around the phone. "I don't know. I haven't thought about it all yet. I am just . . . still thinking over what happened. And trying to figure out why."

"But you're not hurt?"

"No." Suddenly she now wanted to hear him drone on about her cousins, and who was pregnant, and what was coming into season in the markets. She wanted to hear about the air conditioner that kept breaking down in the window of his Lagos apartment and hear him complain about the heat. All those mundane details of life back home, that she usually wanted him to skip on past, now sounded like delicious nuggets of familiarity and normalcy.

"I thought you flew normal patrols," her father said. "I don't understand. I thought you had taken on a *less* dangerous job. This isn't the Sahara."

The phone beeped. Anika looked at the incoming

call. Commander Michel Claude, the phone blinked.
"I thought so, too. But I have to go," Anika said.

"You should call your mother," he said quickly. Anika sat, letting the words roll past. "You are close enough to *visit* her. Whatever our pasts, she will have heard the news story. She will want to know her daughter is safe."

Anika pursed her lips. "It was good to hear your voice. But my commander is calling. I have to go."

"Well, be careful, Anika," her father said. "And think about it."

"I will," Anika promised. Then she switched to the incoming call. She took a deep breath. "Commander?"

Michel sounded tired, his voice scratchy from lack of sleep. "Anika . . . I'm very sorry about this. . . ."

Anika's stomach lurched. This couldn't be good. "Commander?"

"I know you were just with him, but Tom passed. I'm so very sorry."

Anika closed her eyes and bent over on the side of her bed. "I was *just* there. He seemed okay to me. He made jokes."

"I saw him as well, Anika. But it happened."

She gripped the phone and heard a piece of plastic in the case crack. There was no going back to bed. No time for curling up and waiting to process what had happened. "We need to hunt down these assholes who did this to us, Commander. They need to pay for what they did. I want to come in and *do* something; I don't think I can sit here by myself."

Michel paused for a moment. "You sure about that? You up for flying out to Resolute?"

Anika sat up. "What's in Resolute?"

"They've found the *Kosatka*, trying to hide in the harbor with other ships. The U.S. Navy has a patrol boat there, and the local police have the crew in custody. Can you fly our Investigations Unit guys out there to participate in the interrogation? They might use you to ID any of the guys. If you can."

"Of course I'll do it." She stood up.

"There's a light jet being fueled up right now," Michel said. "They'll be waiting for you."

The Arctic Cap has all but melted, oil has run low and Anika Duncan, former mercenary turned United Nations Polar Guard pilot, patrols the region to protect against pollution and smuggling.

In a daring plan to terraform the planet, the Gaia Corporation develops a revolutionary new technology, but when they lose control, our best potential solution to global warming may become the deadliest weapon ever known.

As a lethal game of international politics and espionage begins, it will be up to Anika to decide the fate of the Earth.

Part techno-thriller, part eco-thriller, ARCTIC RISING is a fantastic dystopian science fiction adventure that will appeal to fans of everyone from Michael Crichton to James Bond.